T0354773

East Slope Justice

East Slope Justice

Ron Boggs

EAST SLOPE JUSTICE

iUniverse books may be ordered through booksellers or by contacting:

iUniverse
1663 Liberty Drive
Bloomington, IN 47403
www.iuniverse.com
1-800-Authors (1-800-288-4677)

Because of the dynamic nature of the Internet, any web addresses or links contained in this book may have changed since publication and may no longer be valid. The views expressed in this work are solely those of the author and do not necessarily reflect the views of the publisher, and the publisher hereby disclaims any responsibility for them.

Any people depicted in stock imagery provided by Getty Images are models, and such images are being used for illustrative purposes only. Certain stock imagery © Getty Images.

ISBN: 978-1-5320-4418-2 (sc)
ISBN: 978-1-5320-4417-5 (e)

Library of Congress Control Number: 2018902538

Print information available on the last page.

iUniverse rev. date: 04/28/2018

Prelude

For most folks the events of eighteen months ago are long gone and forgotten, but not for Axel Cooper, the Sheriff of Rankin County, Montana.

In mid-October Axel had been recruited to be the local liaison to a federal law-enforcement task force. The goal was a high-altitude ranch – Crestfallen – owned by the Ryan family, rulers of the so-called Irish Kingdom, a remote corner of the county populated by several related families that considered themselves a self-governing community. A seasonal ranch sheltered a run-away federal fugitive, as well as a methamphetamine lab. Axel's assignment was to guide the task force on a nighttime trek over Ajax Pass in the Harlan Range of the Rockies. However, his every move had been second-guessed by Jack Hilton, a U.S. Marshal out of Denver – a man with a checkered past looking to regain his stature by whatever means possible.

For Axel, Crestfallen – the event – was a watershed, more meaningful than his exodus from Illinois, his retirement from the Coast Guard, or the sudden death of his first wife.

At Crestfallen Axel shot and killed two men – an undercover FBI agent and a grandson of the Kingdom's ailing monarch. In an attempted escape, the two had charged Axel's creek-bed position. One of them fired on Axel from short range. With the duo closing in, Axel shot in self-defense.

Only afterwards did Hilton reveal that one of the dead men was an FBI agent. Hilton immediately attacked Axel to deflect responsibility and disguise his prior dealings with the Kingdom.

Axel wrestled with fact that he had extinguished two lives amid Hilton's self-serving accusations and the Ryan clan's attempts to kill him.

Axel's exoneration took the efforts of a U.S. Senator, the governor and the assistant commissioner of the Montana Highway Patrol. The local newspaper, The Rankin County Courier, fairly portrayed the events of Crestfallen and its aftermath, but, as with all such public events, there are some who still question the facts and conclusions and posit alternative interpretations.

The burden of Crestfallen is still part of the fabric of Sheriff Axel Cooper as he now faces a contested re-election.

Chapter 1.

It is illegal to hunt elk in the Yellowstone National Park, even in the backcountry away from the throngs of robust hikers, traffic jams, naïve campers and, in the winter, the snowmobile dragsters. But the grizzled rancher was not really hunting. He was on horseback driving the small herd of elk through the sparse, lodgepole pine forest, then down into a snow-patched coulee and out of the Park. No fences to cross, but the going was rough through the patchy, crusted snow on the steep terrain. He steadily wrangled them downhill around the snow mounds and boulders, and down through clusters of aspens near the creek with its brittle ice covering. Then he pushed the herd into the pastures of the nearby ranch. With his rifle cradled across the pommel of the saddle, he rolled with the steady gate of his sure-footed sorrel. The rifle was for protection from bears. The elk were his reluctant partners in his illicit endeavor.

It was only mid-afternoon, but the rose-colored promise of an early March sunset was already scribed low across the slate-gray sky. And the temperature was already dropping. The rancher had a mental picture of himself as a classic cowboy of the late 1800's on his weary horse ambling down out of the mountains and pushing a small herd of cattle. He thought to himself, *"Find the leader and keep on him. Don't let none of them cows get too far to the flank. Stay behind 'em, pushing. Press them to move on down the draw, through the trees, across the creek. Keep 'em pocketed, and on the move. No rush, we've got all night."*

There were no witnesses at eight thousand feet in the Harlan Range, north of the Park. The nearest road, other than overgrown timber trails, was a snow-packed two-track that dead-ended at the ranch – his ranch.

The hay and salt lick that the rancher had prepared would keep the elk in the low rolling foothills for a couple of days, long enough for the rancher to register a complaint with the Park and for Park management to send out several junior rangers to push the elk back into the Park. For the rangers it would be just another winter day in the service of their country.

Chapter 2.

Not much moved in the early morning in Grant, Montana, especially during a mid-March cold snap. Frigid temperatures were accompanied by an ongoing snowfall that had already delivered a foot. The town, nestled into the east slope of the Harlan Range, was quiet. Through the mist of falling snow, a strand of amber streetlights on Broadway glowed like a set of parallel airport runway edge-lights on a foggy night.

Riley Wellington straddled the massive snowmobile at the all-night gas station-convenience store just north of town. As he waited, he considered that while Grant was only twenty-seven miles from the northeast corner of Yellowstone National Park as the crow flies, it was sixty-five miles on The Flyover, a narrow, winding road etched into sheer granite slopes. It needed thirteen switchbacks to go up, over and down the eleven thousand foot pass. It was closed to automobiles from the middle of October through Memorial Day. *But not to snowmobiles.*

He cradled his insulated helmet and surveyed the silent, monochrome diorama of the small town. He wanted to get moving. People were after him.

Two days ago Wellington failed to appear for his federal trial for stock fraud. He knew that the pre-trial deposition of his co-opted partner would eliminate any doubt that the pair had effectively stolen over five million dollars from their unwitting clients. But that theft was minor compared to what he had done yesterday.

First there was Cody Ritter, his business partner, and then there was the truck wreck. Wellington knew in his heart that it really did not matter what he did. *I'll never see the inside of a jail, no way. They'll come looking, but they won't find me. Should they get close, I'm ready to shoot it out. And if they get me, they get me. But they're not going to – simple enough.*

Wellington and Cody Ritter had closed the office six weeks ago when the feds made their first inquiry. But Cody, ever the precise engineer, had shared with the investigators every detail and transaction of their scheme in exchange for the promise of a modest sentence.

Wellington figured it would be at least three days before anyone found Ritter's body.

Ritter had lived alone, so the first person inside his apartment would probably be the weekly cleaning lady. She'd find him sprawled on the kitchen floor – just where he fell after Wellington hit him with the butt of his heavy pistol. Wellington was startled at how little effort it took. One step to the side and one behind Ritter gave Wellington a clear shot and with a quick swoosh – a powerful chop between the second and third cervical vertebrae – and Ritter quietly collapsed. The blow had not even broken the skin.

And then, there was yesterday's Ice Box Canyon accident. There was a witness and somebody might have gotten hurt. It could be an immediate problem.

After killing Ritter, Wellington had headed south out of Billings towards Grant. Ten miles north of town the two-lane canyon road twisted and turned with the Vermillion River. On a steep incline he swung out to overtake a slow-moving old pickup. It suddenly sped up, as though offended at being passed. Only when the two trucks were side-by-side did Wellington see the sharp turn ahead and the blue nose of the semi-tractor trailer turning towards him. He shot a piercing glare at the driver of the old pickup. The driver looked back in astonishment and slowed down, but not quickly enough for Wellington to slide over in front. The semi barreled downhill on the snow packed road. Wellington reckoned that his immediate options were to sideswipe the old pickup off the road into the river, stop altogether or pray that the semi would cling to the far right near the canyon wall. He momentarily considered that there was a fourth, but unacceptable, option – a head-on collision.

Wellington said out loud, "I gotta go." He flashed his headlights at the semi and floored the accelerator of his Silverado. With the vehicles a hundred yards apart and closing at a combined rate of over hundred miles an hour, the semi gracefully moved to the right. It plowed into the snow berm on the shoulder rocketing a snow plume straight up in the air. Then its right front tire dipped into a drainage ditch and pitched the truck away from the road and into the canyon's near-vertical rock wall. The grating metal-on-rock screech hung in the air as the semi caromed off the wall with a display of airborne snow and sparks. Then the truck violently swung over onto its left side. In his rear-view mirror Wellington saw the truck skid down the road on its side and the towering cloud of snow in its wake. He had thought of stopping to call for help, but surrendered to a primitive instinct –*immediate escape.*

* * *

The mountains would provide his shelter and protection; the sooner he got there, the better. Wellington had arranged to swap his Silverado for the snowmobile in town. Today he would take it around the winter barricade and then up The Flyover into the mountain wilderness. He would stay for five weeks – time enough for the authorities to curtail their search. At the beginning of May he would hike out of the mountains into Princeton, a town just north of the Park, and find a cached old pickup – part of the swap – and disappear amongst the Park's early adventurers.

The girl, Carrie Baxter – a new addition – would have to do the same. She was a fresh-faced twenty-two year old, the daughter of a local rancher and a recent college dropout. Wellington figured that she could not be taller than five-foot-two or weigh much more than a hundred pounds. She was keen to go into the mountains, even though Wellington had not told her where they were going or why.

He leaned forward to peer around the gasoline pump farthest from the front door of the glass-walled Montana Petro station. The girl had gone to pay for the gasoline, but she was taking too long. *Come on, let's go.*

Damn, it's cold. The massive snowmobile had been out all night. In the five minutes since they pulled out of driveway at Tyler White's house the engine's temperature gauge had yet to move.

White was a local mechanic, friend of Carrie's, who had swapped Wellington's Silverado for the modified, heavy-duty snowmobile and an old pickup. Wellington knew that in the deal he gave more than he got – but on second thought he realized that it mattered little, since he was on the run with a stack of cash.

Wellington put on his helmet and flipped the face shield down to block the swirling wind and the drifting crystalline snow. *What's taking her so long? Drop the money on the counter. We don't need the fucking change.* He stayed behind the pump out of the attendant's sightline. At six-foot-four, two-seventy-five, in a pair of carbon black bib overalls, he would be easy to remember – not what he wanted. *All she had to do was pay for the damned gas. And she's fucking that up.*

He scooted forward again, and secured his helmet strap. He said out loud, "Let's go!"

As though waiting until his patience was almost gone, Carrie Baxter burst through the door. She waved a carton of cigarettes. *Cigarettes?* He had only given her ten dollars to pay for the gas. *Christ, she must have stolen them.* His next thought was a recurrent one since he'd agreed to take her along – *this girl is going to get me into trouble.* He repeated it out loud to himself. Then he revved the engine and lurched forward, fishtailing across the lot towards Broadway. Over the engine whine and through his insulated helmet he heard her yell. He cut the throttle and turned back towards her.

Her breath froze in short, quickly disappearing white puffs. In a bulky snowsuit and large insulated boots she was running fast – leaving a fluffy snow-cloud behind her.

An old man came out of the station in his shirtsleeves. He slapped the stock of a short, lever-action rifle against the doorframe and took aim. Then he lowered the rifle slowly. Wellington wondered if he had changed his mind or some invisible force had taken hold of the barrel and turned it away.

Carrie Baxter ran towards the snowmobile yelling at Wellington, "Go, go, go! He's coming." She dove onto the machine and slid her free arm around his waist as Wellington gunned the engine.

Just as the treads took hold, Wellington heard the rifle's crack. The shot ricocheted off the snow-covered concrete pavement, grazed the back of Carrie's left calf and struck the snowmobile's air filter with a metallic *thunk*. She screamed in pain. The cigarettes went flying. She threw herself forward against Wellington and grabbed his Ruger 357 Magnum pistol holstered on the snowmobile's frame – the bear gun. She pushed herself off the machine, flopped into the snow and pulled off her bulky mittens. She held the Ruger with both hands and aimed at the old man.

Wellington screamed into his face shield, "No, Carrie, no!"

The old man silently stared at the pistol and then eased behind the doorframe.

Her first shot shattered both panels of the station's front glass wall, spraying shards in all directions. The pile of firewood stacked outside the front door was pummeled with slabs of falling glass that exploded on impact. The second shot blew out the glass door. Her last shot struck the old man in the upper thigh and threw him off balance. He grabbed the doorframe with one hand, steadied himself and fired with the other. His shot struck a gas pump with a metallic clang. He dropped the rifle on the doorsill and slowly fell backwards into the station.

The sound of the shots reverberated in the still air, paralyzing Wellington.

Carrie dropped the pistol, picked herself up, grabbed her mittens, took two steps and threw herself onto the bulky saddle of the snow machine.

Wellington could not see the old man. *Oh shit, is he dead?*

"I need that gun", Wellington told himself. He took off his mittens, slung his leg over the wide saddle and carefully retrieved the pistol. He blew off the snow. As he looked up towards the station, he saw that the old man had crawled to the door, retrieved his rifle and now sat leaning against the doorframe. The old man looked up at Wellington and cocked the rifle, chambering a new round.

Wellington kept the pistol behind him, walked backwards towards his machine and climbed on in front of Carrie. He was ready to drive away when the old man raised the rifle and yelled, "You son of a bitch."

Wellington looked at the pistol in his right hand and turned back towards the rifleman as though to say something. Instead he brought up the pistol and rested the barrel on his left arm and, without intense aiming, fired two successive shots. The old man fell inside the building. Wellington thought he heard the clatter of the rifle hitting the floor.

Wellington holstered the pistol. He dismounted, knelt down and examined Carrie's wound. He pulled apart the material of her snowsuit to reveal a shallow, bloody slash across her calf muscle. Blood ran down the back of her leg and boot and had already begun to pool in the snow. He stood and turned to look at the station. The scene had not changed, save for the blood at the front entrance.

He muttered, more to himself than to Carrie, "We're out of here," and re-mounted the snowmobile in front of her.

He turned his head back towards her and said, "Christ, why'd that old guy come after you? Why'd you shoot him?"

"He shot at me first. Hell, look at what you did?"

Again, more to himself than to Carrie, he mumbled, "Yeah, dumb and dumber. We're not staying here, that's for sure."

He depressed the thumb throttle. The snowmobile leaped ahead. Carrie tried unsuccessfully to get her arms all the way around Wellington and lock her hands together. They rocketed six blocks down Broadway south into town under the glowing streetlamps. Suddenly, a front-runner hit a large chunk of ice and momentarily threw them off balance. The quick jolt caused Carrie to yelp in pain. Wellington slowed down. "He got you good, huh?"

She didn't answer. Wellington depressed the accelerator further and they sped all the faster down Broadway towards The Flyover.

Chapter 3.

Axel Cooper, the Sheriff of Rankin County, learned early on that rural law enforcement was more of a lifestyle than an occupation. He was never off-duty and often put in sixty-hour weeks. To Axel's surprise his commitment and schedule meshed well with his wife's. Anne Lynwood-Cooper was a medical doctor and, more importantly, the lead practitioner and executive director of the Rankin County Clinic, an affiliate of Billings General Hospital. Her schedule was as unpredictable and strenuous as his.

As busy professionals they cherished their modest home in Grant as a sanctuary from their public obligations and scrutiny. But their privacy in the small town was minimal and fragmented.

An early morning call could be for either of them. Or both. Today's pre-dawn call from Rankin County's Combined Emergency Dispatch – CED, pronounced as *said* – was not unusual.

They were both sound asleep. Axel was face down, with his head on her pillow. His right leg straddled hers as she slept soundly on her back. His arm rested on her stomach, contributing to the image of a spider that had rappelled from the ceiling and softly descended upon her. The cordless, boxy CED receiver was on the other side of the bed. His first concern was to get out of bed without waking her. In a single athletic move he pushed himself up, spun around, swept the CED receiver off the nightstand and tiptoed into the bathroom, softly closing the door behind him.

The dispatcher promptly reported that there was a shooting at the MP station. Spike Reynolds had been hit and was bleeding badly. While the call was nominally for Axel, it would also send Anne into action. The local EMTs had been alerted and were on their way. Axel stated that he'd be at the MP station in fifteen minutes and he would tell his wife that Spike was soon to be on his way to the clinic.

Anne had rolled away from the phone's buzzing and pulled all the covers around her. She appeared to have resumed her motionless, deep sleep. He stood next to the bed and enjoyed her peaceful, child-like smile. For the thousandth time, he reminded himself that Anne was the single best feature of his life. He hated to wake her. But he knew she would want him to – Spike deserved the best medical professional the Rankin County Clinic had to offer. And that was Anne.

Anne Lynwood was a local all-star, a Grant high school valedictorian who went on to the university in Missoula, med-school in Seattle and a residency in Denver. She returned to Grant as a board-certified emergency room physician dedicated to bringing quality medical care to rural Montana.

Anne was a tall woman. At five-ten she was only three inches shorter than Axel. At home she usually wore her auburn hair in a ponytail, but at the clinic it was twisted into a neat, professional-looking bun. Anne was statuesque – thin, but shapely, a feature she usually tried to hide at the clinic by wearing bulky smocks.

Axel and Anne had been married just under a year – and on a daily basis Axel marveled that he could be so happy – again. Ten years ago he had courted and married Avey, a spritely high school teacher and the daughter of rancher from Glendive. During the first year of their marriage Avey was diagnosed with pancreatic cancer, and she died at home within six months. He promptly sold the house in town and moved back in with his brother Arlyn at his ranch eight miles out of town. In recovery Axel worked some eighty-hour weeks and spent many long, quiet evenings on Arlyn's porch watching the last rays of the sun play with the foothills of the east slope of the Harlan Range.

Axel gently shook Anne's shoulder and whispered, "Honey, shooting at the MP. Spike's been shot. You've gotta get up. The EMTs are on their way."

She blinked her eyes and looked up at him. "Ax, what'd you say? Or was I dreaming?"

"The MP. Spike's been shot and the EMTs are on their way. I don't know anything else."

She sprang out of bed, pushed past Axel and said on her way to the closet, "My God. Spike! I've known him for thirty years. Boy, I hope it's not serious."

Axel threw on a pair of faded Wrangler jeans and a plaid flannel shirt. As he was lacing-up his White field boots, Anne asked him if the MP had been held up.

"Don't know. We'll both know a lot more in fifteen minutes," he answered.

Once he was fully dressed Axel called his undersheriff only to learn that both of his on-duty, night shift deputies were on the road and more than a half hour away. He could get to the MP station sooner than either of them.

Axel sought out Anne in the spare bedroom where she was getting dressed. He quickly stepped behind her and caressed her waist in a one-armed hug. With his other hand he swept her hair away from her face. Before she stopped flitting her eyelashes he kissed her softly on the cheek and twirled her out of his arms. As he headed towards the bedroom door, he sang out, "I'm off, Babe, see you at the clinic. Here we go."

"Eat something, Honey. You'll fall over if you don't. Be careful."

"Love ya."

As he strode through the sparsely furnished house, he grabbed two bananas off the kitchen counter. At the back door, he slipped on his well-worn, ochre Carhart jacket, donned his light gray, wide-brimmed hat – his personal badge of office – and was out the door into the blowing March snow.

It was about an hour earlier than Axel usually went to work and he was struck by how cold and dark it was – mid-March with no signs of spring. Indeed, winter was still operating at full strength. As he tucked his head into the crook of his arm to cut the bite of the frigid, swirling wind, he thought that back in Illinois the daffodils could already be in bloom.

It was on a whim that he arrived in Montana – a respite after his Coast Guard service to spend time with his older brother. Arlyn taught him how to fly fish, introduced him to the strong, independent people of Montana and the beauty and unforgiving hostility of its wilderness. Axel now understood the unreliable weather, the long winters and tight-lipped ranchers.

His county vehicle, a white SUV, was parked in their driveway with its nose pointed to the street for a quick getaway. Anne's Ford pickup enjoyed the comforts of their attached, heated garage. In deference to his late-sleeping neighbors Axel did not activate the SUV's siren system, but he did turn on the overhead light bar. He ate one of the bananas in three bites before he got to the corner on Broadway. There he caught a glimpse of the EMTs' van as it turned off Broadway heading west on State 34 towards the clinic. There was no other traffic.

At the MP station Axel was unpleasantly surprised to see three City of Grant police vehicles. They were parked with their light-bars blasting bolts of blue and red in all directions. A uniformed policeman sat in one of the vehicles, while two others walked the station's perimeter with flashlights scanning the snow-covered ground. The entire lot down to the street had been cordoned off with yellow plastic, crime-scene tape. Axel figured that the city's Chief of Police, Leslie Marsh, must be in the building.

Axel parked and noted the time and temperature on the building's digital display – 6:04 AM, fifteen degrees. As he slammed the vehicle's door, he said out loud, "Well, what in the hell's going on here?" With both hands he secured his hat against the wind. In an instant he was ready for the weather and for Chief Leslie Marsh. *This is my territory – not his!*

Axel ducked under the plastic tape and walked towards to the building. He tried to be slow and methodical in order to remember the scene. For the sake of the investigation he needed to suppress his anger at the presence of Marsh and his police force. Axel glanced at the gasoline pumps and surveyed the driveway. Snowmobile tracks ran from one end of the lot to the other. Near the exit to Broadway splotches of blood melted the snow. He said to himself, "Blood. How'd that happen?"

Outside the front door the snow had been trampled and had absorbed a lot of blood. The glass door and front windows were blown out and glass splinters, slabs, and shards littered the floor. A few were coated with blood. Blood splotches near the door already showed signs of crystalizing and sparkled in the blue-gray glow of the overhead fluorescent tubes. A thick swath of deep crimson ran from the door to the cashier's counter. Axel stepped up to the building's entrance. Marsh stood in the corner farthest from the door. He was smoking a cigarette. At the threshold, Axel nodded to the chief and scanned the room. Without looking back at Marsh he said in a somber, flat note of acknowledgement, "Chief."

The new station-convenience store was decidedly not within the city limits and, therefore, not within Marsh's jurisdiction. Early last year MP sought to build its new station within the city proper. The city council had ignored the advice of their legal counsel and refused to issue a building permit on the grounds that they already had enough gas stations – MP would take business away from the locally owned stations.

"Morning, Sheriff," responded Marsh, who had obviously learned of the incident before Axel and had taken command of the scene – command that wasn't his.

Axel asked, "So, how bad was Spike hurt?"

As though Axel wasn't even in the room, Marsh stared out a side window at one of his illuminated patrol vehicles. He said, "Spike was hit once in the leg and once in the upper arm. Lost a lot of blood." He turned away from the window and scanned the room, looking at the blood smears. "But he was squawking 'bout a damned girl that shot him over some cigarettes. He said she'd jumped over the counter and snatched a carton. That'd be a snatchin' snatch." Marsh turned back to the window with a self-satisfied grin.

Two weeks earlier Marsh had filed a petition to run on the April ballot against Axel for Rankin County Sheriff. Marsh had promptly initiated a slanderous whisper campaign claiming that Axel was an incompetent outsider. Marsh voiced an opinion about Axel's every move – from scheduling late night patrols on State Road 176, the winding extension of Broadway that followed the Vermillion River through Ice Box Canyon en route to Billings, to the domestic abuse arrests that were and were not made.

Axel Cooper was neither incompetent nor an outsider. He had lived in Montana for thirteen years. He had worked in Montana law enforcement for all of them – he was completing his second, four-year term as county sheriff and before that had been a Montana state trooper for five years. Prior to that he was in the U.S. Coast Guard chasing down Florida smugglers and drug runners. Recently, the governor had appointed him to the oversight board of the Montana Highway Patrol. He was a bona fide veteran of the Montana law enforcement community.

In his heart Axel *was* the Sheriff of Rankin County and the *only* man for the job. Marsh was out to steal his identity and that simply was not going to happen. It might be an elected position, but as far as Axel was concerned, it was going to be his for as long as he wanted. Certainly, Marsh was not going to take it from him. Axel reckoned that however this incident turned out and regardless of Marsh's interference, it would not be another *Crestfallen.*

Leslie Marsh was a short, thin man with deep crevices in his weatherworn, elongated face that attested to his years as a the Montana cattleman. He had a receding chin, a razor-thin mouth and a beak of a nose. He was a heavy smoker and had the gaunt, drawn-out look of a man who rarely slept. Behind his back his patrolmen called him Dent, short for rodent. Marsh had been Grant's chief for two chaotic years, and Axel wasn't the only one in town who hoped he would soon fade from the law enforcement scene.

Axel was at least five inches taller than Marsh. He had managed to retain most of his youthful strength and fitness. He wore his light brown hair short – shorter than Anne thought he should – and was usually clean-shaven. He weighed about two hundred and ten pounds, the same as he had when he left the Montana Highway Patrol, and only ten pounds more than when he left the Coast Guard. He figured that he could easily weigh forty pounds more than Marsh. Axel's size, posture and military bearing gave him – what they called in the Coast Guard – a command presence.

At this moment he wanted to pick Marsh up and throw him out the open door. And he knew he could do it.

Axel held the common but rarely spoken opinion that Marsh's appointment by the Grant city council was a simple move by his extended family to secure yet another spot on the public payroll for one of their own. The retiring chief quietly resigned the day after Marsh's appointment, terminating the proposed sixty-day transition period. The old chief wanted nothing to do with Marsh.

In Rankin County vying for elected political office was, while nonpartisan, competitive and occasionally a sloppy, mud-wrestling match. In addition to the verbal punch and counterpunch there were dirty tricks. Many unresolved property crimes involved political rivals. The County Board candidate who complained that the incumbents did not maintain a bridge – one that was subsequently washed out in a spring flood – found his tractor sitting in the middle of a creek. The rancher who campaigned for a restructuring of the irrigation water allocation system managed by the Water Rights Commission was suddenly accused of sexually harassing a woman he had never met. A justice of the peace known to be hard on Grant's drunk drivers had his car stolen and left at the Costco in Billings.

Now, the two men stood across from at each other in the shattered, aluminum-framed structure of glazed concrete block. Every adult in Rankin County had an opinion about MP. Along with the weather, the latest auction price for feeder steers, the strength of the tourist season, and the mid-summer motorcycle rally, the MP gas station was on the list of common topics in saloons and coffee shops. Axel shared the townsfolk's disdain for MP – a nameless, faceless corporation. It had inserted itself where it wasn't wanted. MP and its mercantile counterparts had already squeezed the locals to the point that every fourth storefront on Broadway was vacant.

Axel pulled out his cell phone and punched the contact button for the Billings office of the Montana Forensics Crime Lab. The lab was a branch of the Montana Highway Patrol and, except for the resident scientists, was staffed by state troopers, rotated in from the field on a regular basis. Cooper tried to avoid bringing outside law enforcement agents into his jurisdiction, but Rankin County, like fifty-two of the fifty-six Montana counties, did not have the resources to do any high-tech evidence analysis.

The call was routine and proceeded as though both participants had scripts until the Billings trooper said, "Previously reported," in a flat mechanical voice.

"What? Previously reported?"

"Yes sir, seven minutes ago. Chief Marsh of Grant called it in. Trooper Chap McCarthy is already on his way."

"Fine." Axel cut off the call. He raised his eyes to stare at Marsh, who was still standing near the heat vent in the far corner. One thought burned in Axel's head. *This crime is my responsibility as Rankin County Sheriff, not yours.*

Axel stared at Marsh across the room. Carefully avoiding the blood on the floor, Axel tiptoed to the self-service coffee counter to the left of the front entrance. He held up a paper cup in Marsh's direction, silently asking if he wanted coffee. Marsh shook his head.

While the building had lost half of its glass walls, exposing it to the wind-driven snowfall, the fluorescent glow and pop music continued unabated. The song was "The Dance" by Garth Brooks. Axel knew the song and self-consciously smiled at its improbable presence at this crime scene. The phrase Garth was singing was "Yes, my life is better left to chance. I could have missed the pain, but I'd have had to miss the dance." After a flash of reflection on the appropriateness of the song to the moment, Axel shook his head to refocus on the business at hand.

Axel carefully walked back to the shattered doorframe, turned and surveyed the floor tile by tile. He sipped his coffee and stroked his unshaven chin thinking about how to deal with Marsh. Then he took off his wide brimmed hat and ran his fingers through his grizzled hair.

He had made it to the MP station in nineteen minutes after he picked up the call from the CED dispatcher. The dispatcher said she had called the EMTs. But, for one reason or other, she didn't mention that she had already called Chief Leslie Marsh.

Chapter 4.

Arlyn Cooper, Axel's brother, owned eight hundred acres east of Grant – no cattle, but a worn out ranch house, a new multi-car garage, a thousand feet of frontage on McNally Creek, a good septic field and a reliable well. He lived alone and was pleased with that. No need for any roommates, live-ins or wives. Arlyn was only three years older than Axel, but most folks would guess they were five or ten years apart.

Arlyn was a fly-fisherman who supported his modest lifestyle as an independent electrician and, occasionally, as a guide. He was well regarded as the county's best backcountry fisherman. He knew the branches and tributaries of the Vermillion and Ginger Rivers like the creases in his palm. As for his home creek, he knew every ripple, sunken log, undercut bank and back-eddy.

Arlyn's first thought as he awoke was that his nose was cold. The fire was down. In the middle of the night he had scooted his bed closer to the cast-iron stove and away from the single-pane windows to get warmer. Putting up the storm windows had not come to the top of his to-do list. And he was not about to pay somebody else to do it. So the windows lay, numbered in their proper order, on the attic floor above the garage. He only thought about them at times like this.

He swung his feet out of the blankets and onto the floor. He accepted the cold and stretched out his hand to touch the antique potbelly. It was colder than his hand. He opened the door of the stove and saw a few bright, crimson specks among the ashes from the midnight refueling. *Damned aspen burns like paper.*

Arlyn stood up, walked around the motorcycle frame next to the table and let the dog out. Standing in his socks and undershorts in the open doorway, he inhaled deeply and the moisture in his nose crystalized.

He mumbled, *"Holy shit,"* as he leaned out to read the thermometer on the outside porch wall – fifteen above. He stood on the windblown, snow-free porch and wrapped his arms around himself while the dog did his business. Horizon to horizon was a black ceiling studded with distinct stars, each no bigger than a pinprick on a black canvas. Overnight drifting snow had laid a blanket over his front yard, covering a fallen cottonwood and rusty implements. The tools and equipment came with the place when he bought it, and he figured they just might be useful if he ever took up ranching.

He snatched an armload of split aspen from the stack on the porch and with his elbow, flipped the screen door open. The dog shuffled between his legs to get in front of Arlyn into the relative warmth of the house.

It was going to be a long day. He planned to wire a new garage at Phil Simpson's place, out in the far southwest corner of Grant – back into the foothills of the West Harlan Range and do some fishing in a nearby spring creek. He wouldn't be home until late afternoon. He banked some logs in the stove to last a while.

Arlyn dressed and laughed to himself. He had installed propane heat in the garage where he stored his truck, fishing gear and electrical supplies, but all he had in the house was the potbellied stove. *Yeah, Zak had better stay in the garage today.* After a quick breakfast of cold cereal he was ready for the day. He could get coffee in Grant on the way.

In the garage he gathered his toolbox, a coil of heavy twelve-gauge wire and cartons of junction boxes, wall switches, plastic wire connectors and a submersible pump. He arranged them in the back of his ten-year old Chevy pickup truck. He then went to the far wall where several fly-fishing rods and reels were neatly displayed on a peg-board.

The far southwest corner of the city had several spring creeks that came out of the ground and ran ice-free all year. Arlyn figured that with an afternoon warm-up and some cloud cover there could be a hatch of midges on Wolfshot Creek that ran through Simpson's ranch – a reward after five hours of stringing new wire, installing a new water pump, and wiring a new panel and an array of outlets and switches. He assembled and loaded his fishing fanny-pack carefully and threw it in the front seat of the truck. Two half-assembled rods were already in the wooden rack that ran across the truck's back window, where many Montanans displayed their hunting rifles.

As Arlyn turned to go, Zak sat on his haunches and panted expectantly. Arlyn looked down at the three year old Labrador. He turned away and climbed into the truck, but then on second thought, held the door open. He nodded and the dog gleefully jumped in, clambering over Arlyn's lap with his wet feet to the passenger seat where he sat on top of Arlyn's fanny pack. The old pickup fired right up, and Arlyn and Zak left the ranch on McNally Creek and headed west on Route 34 towards Grant.

The snowfall started two miles from his house and was heavy by the time he got to Grant. Arlyn stopped for coffee and gas at the near west side Cenex station, past the new clinic. The gas station operator, a friend and fellow fly fisherman, asked Arlyn if he knew anything about the shooting at the MP station north of town. Arlyn said no and asked if anybody was hurt.

The attendant answered, "Yeah, a guy just came through. He said he saw the medics wheeling somebody out. I heard the sirens and saw the EMTs turn into the clinic."

"Looks like Axel's got some sheriffing to do."

"Reckon so."

Headed west again, Arlyn began thinking about how his younger brother had arrived in Montana. Axel's high school years were tough; he was suspended more than ten times, usually for fighting – it seemed to Arlyn that Axel always started the fights – whatever the professed provocation. He just liked to fight, even though he lost two out of three encounters. And the schoolwork just wasn't interesting. Joining the U.S. Coast Guard got him out of the Chicago suburbs and away from his disappointed parents, while most of his friends went off to college. Arlyn did not want to be the *townie* – the loser left behind while others expanded their horizons. Staying home meant living at home, getting a low paying job or, worse yet, getting a better paying position in the Coopers' third-generation insurance agency. Axel wasn't ready to work in an office all day, working for Dad, being nice to customers on the telephone and answering their stupid questions. And Mom and Dad couldn't follow him into the Cape

May, New Jersey boot camp and be any further disappointed in their younger son.

The Coast Guard was good for Axel. The early months of training gave him constant supervision, from the shine on his shoes to his verbal interactions with other rookies. He scored a record time for the fifty-foot rope climb, a feat that caught the attention of the training company commander and earned him his first choice of more advance training. He chose salt-water shore patrol – an entrance into law enforcement. After several early promotions he ran his own six-man, forty-seven-foot drug-chaser out of Key West. He was twenty-six.

From Arlyn's perspective it looked like his younger brother had found a career that suited him perfectly. However, at the end of his third hitch, Axel resigned. At the time he said that he had seen enough blue water and there wasn't much opportunity for further advancement. He came back to Illinois. A week at home convinced him that he needed something else. He had been out of the Coast Guard exactly one month when he showed up unannounced on the front porch of Arlyn's Montana ranch.

Over the following months Arlyn and Axel made the tour of the local bars and went hiking, fishing and elk hunting. Then one October day after of splitting firewood for five hours, Axel told Arlyn that he had was going to sit for the exam to become a Montana Highway Patrolman. With a credit for his Coast Guard service he scored over a hundred percent.

Chapter 5.

Inside the battered building Axel turned to Marsh, who had unzipped his parka to display his pearl handled revolver and its hand-tooled leather holster. Marsh wore a pale blue shirt with a brass star on his chest, navy blue trousers, polished black boots, and a broad-brimmed hat embellished with gold braid and a cluster of four five-pointed stars.

He looked at Axel's phone and said, "Yeah, I called it in. I figured the sooner the better."

Axel shook his head to clear his thoughts of the absurd, almost comical, spectacle that Marsh presented and thought – *This case is mine and I'll handle it. Let's get this conversation over with.* Out loud he said, "What else do we know?" He had to consciously avoid completing the question with the word *asshole.*

Marsh's initial response was a smooth, extended exhale of cigarette smoke that Axel took as an expression of police chief's intent to savor the moment. Marsh then moved over to the counter, leaned on his elbows, rubbed his pointed chin and took a deep draw on his cigarette.

Axel wanted to get the conversation going and said, "Looks like he bled quite a bit. This all Spike's blood?"

"Yeah. Hers is outside. Spike stayed down after the big guy's second shot. Grazed him in the arm. Spike thinks he mighta hit one of them."

"Wait a minute. Big guy? How many were there?"

Marsh flicked his boot towards a small rifle that lay on the floor underneath a display rack. "That's Spike's. There were two – the girl and a guy. They're on a snowmobile. That's what the miner told me."

"The miner?"

Marsh pulled a piece of paper out of his shirt pocket and turned towards Axel. He continued talking while looking down at the note. "Augie Metcalf. Middle thirties. Lives down in Everhart. He stopped for coffee on his way up to Cisco," referring to the well-paying palladium mine thirty miles west of Grant in Tower County. "He saw the windows blown out and came in about five-thirty and found Spike on the floor bleeding pretty good." Marsh pointed to a spot on the blood-smeared area by the side of the ice cream freezer.

"He say anything else?"

"Well, yeah, I guess. Spike told him they took off on a snowmobile. A young woman and a big, big guy, going south on Broadway. Both wore bulky snowmobile suits with bibs, helmets, face shields and big collars. He drove. Her outfit was yellow. His was black."

"Anything more on the guy?"

"Well, just that he was a big, big guy. Black coveralls. Black helmet. Face shield. Big black machine. Spike shot into the snow and the bullet bounced up and hit her in the leg. She ran to the snowmobile, got a big pistol and shot at Spike. And hit him in the leg. She left the big revolver in the snow. Guy comes back to get the gun, Spike shows himself with his rifle in-hand and the big guy takes a couple of shots. Hits Spike in the arm. Spike dove back into the station, but says he didn't really get a good look at the guy. Stared at the pistol. Large revolver."

Axel flicked his head and considered the phrase *a big, big guy* – that was also the description of the driver of the white Silverado that caused Saturday's semi-trailer accident in Ice Box Canyon. *This can't be a coincidence. This case is even more important than it was a minute ago.*

Marsh kept talking, "Metcalf called 911. Kid had a web belt and made a tourniquet out of it. Arm had almost stopped bleeding. But, I really hardly spoke to Spike. The EMTs got here just before I did."

Just as well, thought Axel. "Where's Metcalf?"

"Told him to go to work. He had a seven o'clock shift.

"You got a phone number and address?" Then as though on autopilot Axel said, "Course you did, you told him we didn't need him anymore. What – two minutes ago? You couldn't have held him for me. No?"

"Hey, buddy, I'm just trying to give you a leg-up here."

Axel's personal cell phone rang before he could respond. *Just as well, I'd probably say something to Marsh I'd regret later.* The ringtone was a special one he had set up for calls from his wife. It sounded like horses neighing. The call would be important.

He turned away from Marsh and spoke softly, "Hey, Babe."

"Got Spike."

Axel looked up at Marsh who didn't appear to be interested in monitoring the call.

She continued, "Gunshot broke his femur. Arm's going to be OK. Surface wound, butterfly bandages. But with that leg, he's got to go to Billings pronto. Got a life-flight coming down. He's bled a lot, but the artery is intact. He's on two fast-drip IVs with morphine and antibiotics. Got him in a compression-traction brace that should suppress bleeding and work to keep the heavy thigh muscle from contracting and tearing him up any worse."

"Is he going to make it?"

"Yeah, if Billings gets at him soon enough. Gotta keep his pressure up. Lotta fluids. He's a tough guy. Talking away. You'd think he came in for a flu shot."

Axel marveled at how Anne could describe an injury and treatment in words that anyone could understand. And yet she could turn on her technical medical vocabulary when necessary to communicate with other medical professionals.

Axel momentarily looked up at Marsh and then said to Anne, "Can I talk to him before he flies? When do you think the 'copter will be down?"

"The sooner the better. Probably twenty, thirty minutes."

"Marsh is here with three coppers and a couple of patrol cars. I'll have to swap them out with my guys, and the state forensics is coming down. We gotta find the shooters. The driver could be the hit-and-run guy from the other night."

"What, the truck crash? Marsh there? MP's not in town, everybody knows that."

"Later, Babe, later. I'll be over as soon as I can." Axel signed off, tucked the cell phone in a front pocket of his jeans, and looked up at Marsh, certainly a different sort of challenge than the crime scene in front of him.

Marsh stared at the floor about three feet in front of Axel and said, "Dispatch called us first 'cause Spike thought the bad guys turned south into town. Our patrol car was at the airport and didn't get down to Broadway fast enough. Saw nothing. Still patrolling south Broadway."

Axel mentally framed yet another pronouncement for Marsh, something like, *"This is not your problem. It is mine, and you can go back to your desk and shuffle traffic tickets. And while you're there, why don't you try to figure out how to control your pack of hormonal bullies, especially that young guy who drew his weapon on an Iowa tourist who didn't pull over fast enough. Please leave now."* But he didn't say anything, other than, "Right. Nobody's seen them since?"

"Nope."

Montana had used their Homeland Security federal funding to coordinate emergency response teams and now had ten unified, all-services dispatch systems throughout the state. The local dispatch unit was under the control of a relative of Marsh's. Cooper didn't quite know the relationship, except that it was through Marsh's mother's side of the family.

Axel had things to do and he'd had enough of Marsh. He shook his head and said, "Right. I'll take it from here. You're done here."

Marsh threw his cigarette on the floor and stepped on it as though it were an offending grasshopper. Incredulous, Axel stared at the cigarette butt and said, "Chief, we got ourselves a crime scene here. You know we can't be messing with it like that."

"Hey, don't get smart with me, boy. I'm just here helping you out."

"Really," Axel said flatly.

Marsh walked past Axel towards the door. He stopped, put his hands on his hips, and stared out at the pumps. He snarled over his shoulder, "Hey, fella, you mess with me and you're gonna wish you hadn't. I'm on to you and your brand. You can't imagine how many ways I'm gonna mess with you." He paused, turned to face Axel and then, looking straight into Axel's eyes, said, "You're gonna be surprised, I *am* going to solve this crime and win this election. This is *our* Montana, and we run it *our* way. And ya know, ya can't marry in. You got to be born here. Mighty fine looking wife you got, Sheriff. Montana girl, but she's not running. You, the stranger, are gonna' get beat."

With a bit of exaggeration Axel turned his head and focused on the small video camera in the upper rear corner. Then he turned to focus on an identical camera in the other corner – each pointing a fish-eye lens at the two men. The cameras had pulsating red monitor lights confirming that they had just recorded Marsh's threats. Axel then swung his gaze to the video recording unit behind the counter.

Marsh spun around and flipped side-to-side to see the cameras and the recorder. He then ducked his head as though to avoid the cameras and scurried towards the shattered door. At the doorframe he scanned the outdoor scene and barked at his men, "Saddle up. Leave the crime-scene tape." He did not look back at Axel. He marched straight to an empty police SUV, climbed in and drove off with all wheels spinning in the fresh snow.

Pleased to see the back of Marsh, Axel played with the words *a big, big guy.* They rang in his ears. It couldn't be a coincidence. The Ice Box Canyon accident and this shootout had to be the same guy. *There were two bad actors on that snowmobile. They are somewhere in Rankin County, and they're going to be mine.*

Chapter 6.

Carrie Baxter didn't answer Riley Wellington's question about how seriously she was hurt, other than to emit a low, guttural growl. She groaned continuously as Wellington sped south, straight down Broadway. The deep snow muffled the whine of the engine and the slap of the treads, making her groans and growls stand out. At the last street of Grant's central grid, Wellington slowed down and turned left and then a second left into a dark, narrow alley bordered on both sides by small garages and snow-covered vehicles. He pulled over to one side and jumped off the machine. Between the houses and garages he caught a glimpse of a patrol car going north on Broadway. He was jarred by the fact that had he stayed on Broadway the two would have met head-on. *Holy shit.*

Carrie flopped forward, resting her helmeted head on the wide seat.

He pulled out a penlight and again knelt down in the snow to examine her bloody leg. He tore away more of the blood-soaked, downy insulation of her suit. Blood steadily oozed down her leg. While most of it seemed to flow into her boot, a steady trickle slid down the outside. *Carrie Baxter's trip into the mountains was over.*

Wellington took out a small roll of duct tape from his emergency kit and tore off a two-foot piece. He wound the tape around Carrie's small calf, pulling it as tightly as he could.

She yelped into the padded seat, "God, that hurts." She turned her head towards him. "Oh fuck, it hurts."

"Gotta do it."

She straightened up, flipped up her face shield, turned to look him in the face and said, with her jaw clenched tightly, "I gotta get this fixed. I don't want to die."

"Right. Where's the hospital?"

She pointed down the alley and said, "New clinic. Take the road west towards St. Vrain."

Wellington washed his bloody hands in the snow, put on his mittens and cautiously drove three blocks to the end of the alley and crept slowly back onto Broadway. *No traffic.* At the blue sign with the big white H he turned in front of an oncoming pickup and zipped down the town's main east-west street. He slowed and stopped a half-block from the clinic. *Close enough.*

He flipped up his face shield and said, "You can make it from here."

"What the fuck? Take me up to the friggin' door. Holy fuck, Riley, I just got shot. You can't just leave me here. Can't ya stay? I gotta get back to school."

Wellington stared straight ahead and said, "You gonna go up there and I gotta get lost."

He'd heard enough from this girl. She simply had no idea of the trouble they were in. He twisted around to face her, flipped up her shield and looked straight into her eyes from a foot away. Speaking slowly while turning his head back and forth, as though lecturing a young child, he said, "No, I can't go with you. You're on your own." He paused and then in a softer voice said, "I'm outta here. What do you think this is all about? I'm gone, disappearing, and this shoot-out of ours sure screwed things up. That guy back there could be dead and you need a doctor."

He flipped down his face shield and punched the accelerator. They took off down the street. He stared straight ahead, hoping that Carrie would fall off. She didn't, so he raised his left elbow and solidly hit her in the shoulder. The blow knocked her off the snowmobile and into her injured leg. She lay in the street and screamed at Wellington.

Wellington didn't turn around.

Carrie rolled over and got up on all fours and then slowly stood with almost all her weight on her good left leg. After securing her balance she shuffled through the snow towards the clinic, leaving a trail of crimson beads in the snow.

Wellington stared straight ahead. He didn't want to see her pathetic trek to the clinic. He fortified himself with the thought that he had done the right thing. At a hundred yards down the street, he flicked his head to the side and saw the back of her yellow helmet bobbing as she slowly tottered forward. She did not look back.

In a whisper that only he could hear, he said, "Luck." He revved the engine and turned back to Broadway.

Chapter 7.

With Marsh and his men gone, Axel moved back behind the counter and considered how he should start his search – two people on a snowmobile trying to escape. He would need all the help he could get. *But first I gotta talk to Spike.*

Axel called his undersheriff, Ollie Macy, this week's night-shift supervisor. The night shift normally ended at eight, overlapping half an hour with the day crew. Axel needed Ollie to take command of this crime scene and to work with the state's forensic guy. Ollie was studying for a forensics certification from the Montana Law Enforcement Academy. He wouldn't object to working overtime.

To Axel's inquiry Ollie replied, "Right, boss. I can be at the MP in three minutes. Spike OK?"

"Spike's flying to Billings. Broken leg. And hit in the arm. Leg could be bad."

"Wow!"

"Word is that our shooters went south through town, but you never know. Do we have a deputy in the office?"

"Yeah, Jennie Potts came in early. She's filling out forms on last week's drug bust."

"Have her take a snowmobile up to the barricade on The Flyover. They just might still be around. But she shouldn't chase 'em. *Armed and dangerous, do not pursue.* Got it? Have her call me on my cell when she gets there. Guess one of you'll have to lock up the office, unless Ange shows up early."

"Right. Call you on your cell?"

"Yes. Not CED. See you soon. I'm heading to the clinic as soon as you get here. Need to talk to Spike before he flies. Over."

Two minutes later Anne called. "Ax, I think we've got one of your shooters."

"What? You've got the girl who shot Spike?"

"Oh, yeah," she said confidently. "A girl about twenty or so just dragged herself up the drive. Collapsed in front of the entrance."

"Yellow snow suit? She's been shot?"

"Yep. A bullet grazed her leg. She'll be OK. Vicky's sewing her up right now."

"I'll be damned. Don't let her go."

"For sure. She's staying here, all right. Thrilled to be here. She was lying on her stomach trying to tell everybody what happened, like it was the most exciting thing in her life."

"I'm coming over now. I need to talk to Spike. And I'll send over a deputy to watch her."

"Well, she's not going anywhere soon."

"Understood, but she's a criminal suspect now."

"Got it. Spike's copter's 'bout twenty minutes out. You better get here quick if you want to talk to him. We've got him stabilized, and the arm's good, but I've never seen a worse leg fracture. We'll be wheeling him out before touchdown. I gotta go, but ask for me when you get here. Later."

Axel went back to imagining how the shootings occurred. If the girl stole the cigarettes, she could have walked in with a gun. But all she took was a carton of cigarettes? And why would Spike shoot somebody over a carton of cigarettes? One way or another, Spike was at the door with the rifle, got shot twice, fell back into the store and dropped the rifle. Axel said out loud in solitude of the windswept shell of the station, "Just doesn't make sense, unless you throw in a lot of bad decisions. Followed up by more bad decisions. This girl had better talk."

The station's signboard flipped to seven o'clock. Axel called the office in hopes that Ange would be there, and she was. She caught Ollie and Jenny on their way out. Ange Clausen was the department's long-time administrator, a Montana high school basketball legend and mother of the high school's two current top scorers. She was a Grant celebrity in her own right and prided herself on keeping up with all the pending cases of the entire office. Indeed, through her local networks she had helped Axel crack a number of investigations.

Axel figured that if the big snowmobile was going south on Broadway, it might be headed for The Flyover, Princeton and all the way to the Yellowstone National Park. Axel asked Ange to contact law enforcement in Princeton, a small cluster of locally owned restaurants and motels at the other end of The Flyover and just outside the Park. He also asked her to contact the Park officials.

Axel told Ange that Marsh arrived at the MP before him and said, "He must've gotten a call from the CED dispatcher before I did. Somebody's trying to give him a boost. So let's not use the Rankin County Dispatcher and CED on this. Can't trust 'em. Keep all our communications on our cell phones or the old Motorola radios. We've still got those, right? I've got mine in the truck."

"You bet, boss."

Axel peered around the corner of the building vainly searching for Ollie.

He continued his conversation with Ange, "Hey, did you finish the Butch Parker transcript? He's the guy who saw the truck accident."

"Sure, I e-mailed the transcript to the MSP in Billings yesterday. Only two pages. All he said was that a big white Silverado came up fast behind him, swung out on his left to pass him as they were climbing the hill. Driver was a big guy. Then the semi came around the corner. Silverado-man never touched his brakes. You know the semi driver died last night? From Denver, mid-thirties, wife with a coupla kids."

"No, oh my God, that's too bad. Just imagine coming around that corner in the Canyon and seeing two pickups coming at you. Got to choose between a canyon wall and the river. Christ, he didn't ever have much of a chance. S'pose the folks at Billings General did all they could for him. Sad, you say he's got a family?

"What I heard from the MSP was that he was thirty-five and had a wife and two kids in Loveland. Ran a weekly route for a meat packer out of Fort Collins. Did most of his driving in the early morning hours to avoid traffic and make deliveries before the stores opened up to the public. S'pose that Bud at the IGA knew him."

"Trooper said that it slid for over a hundred yards. This guy's death steps up the charges against our mystery driver. What do you think, vehicular homicide? Print out the transcript, would ya? Put it in the middle of my desk. I'll be in later, but first, I gotta talk to Spike before he flies to Billings. How about this, the girl dragged herself to the clinic a coupla minutes ago. Ollie should be here any minute. Has Potts left?"

"Yep, she's gone. Took a snowmobile."

Axel saw Ollie pull up next to the yellow tape on the Broadway-side of the MP station. "Here comes Ollie, gotta go. Spread the word – no CED on this one. Marsh is acting up."

The girl had been at the clinic less than an hour. And it was wasn't even eight o'clock yet, but Axel figured that Ange Clausen, with her innumerable, well-developed, but never-revealed Grant resources, might already have heard about the girl's arrival at the clinic and would know who she was. So he asked, "Hey, I gotta go, but do you know the girl, one of the shooters? Know her name?"

"Carrie Baxter," Ange said without hesitation or inflection.

"Holy mackerel." Two years ago Carrie Baxter had captained the Grant high school girls' soccer team to state Class 2A championship and earned herself a scholarship to Bozeman – Montana State University. She was the daughter of Don and Meredith Baxter – solid citizens, ranchers north of town – deep family roots.

"Christ, that's a bummer. Damn."

"You bet."

Chapter 8.

After dropping off Carrie Baxter, Wellington was amazed at his sense of relief. It wasn't so much that she was going to get the medical attention she needed, but that she was *gone*. She was somebody else's problem and he was on his own, just like he originally planned. But he couldn't get it out of his mind that he had agreed to take her along in the first place. He hadn't cached enough food for two. She was a tough outdoor girl, but the harsh conditions at the shed would have tested her to the breaking point. And God, it was cold and would be colder above the tree line. She undoubtedly would have wanted to leave in April, maybe even late March. And they inevitably would have split up and she would have told his story to any and all who were willing to listen. *Yes, she'll do that now, but she had very little to tell.*

His immediate problem, though, was that he was late. He had planned to be out of town before sunrise. Cars were now appearing on the streets of Grant. The sun peeked over the east bench of the Vermillion River and instantly pierced the veil of blowing snow.

Rather than go straight back to Broadway on the main road, Wellington went south on a side street. He zigzagged through the oldest part of town. As he barreled down Bryce Avenue, he suddenly realized he'd driven past Tyler White's house, where he'd spent last night. Wellington found Tyler amusing. He was so simple. *He did his business, took the deal I offered straight up and never asked one question.* Tyler had tuned up the five-year-old, high horsepower snowmobile, reconfigured the front-runners

44

and installed a hydraulic suspension for the rough, off-trail mountain conditions. Tyler had also arranged the escape truck that was already waiting in Princeton. And for this Tyler received the title on the Silverado. *Not a bad deal for Tyler White. But I can't believe he never asked me what I was planning. Or why.*

Tyler's neighborhood was Milltown, an area of small frame homes, set on river-rock foundations. Tyler had told Wellington that the hundred-year old houses were built fast and cheap to attract workers to the coalmine and sawmill. They were still cheap and often in disrepair. Some city blocks had small but well-kept homes with courageous saplings guarding the front yard, while the next block looked like a low rent trailer park, the side yards crammed with bicycles, barbeques, swing sets and motorcycles, and, on the curb, boat trailers and rusted-out old pickups. All this under a collapsed tent of new snow. *Not for me.*

The intersection of Bryce Avenue and South Street was a four-way stop. Wellington blew through the stop sign, as he had all the others, and swung left around the corner onto South to get back to Broadway. Full speed. A small car was quickly approaching the intersection. Wellington had seen it before he started his turn. To avoid the car he slid wide to his right, carving a large arc in the new snow. The heavy machine didn't sideslip, but halfway through the turn his headlights panned across a snow-covered pickup truck. Slowly but steadily, it was pulling out of an alley. While the windshield had been cleared of snow, the driver's-side window was pure white. From fifty feet away Wellington couldn't see the driver and figured that the driver couldn't see him.

Wellington braked hard and jerked the handlebars of the mammoth machine to the left away from the truck, but into the path of the oncoming car. The car veered towards the alley. The truck kept crawling out of the alley towards Wellington as though it was a slow-motion missile locked-on the snowmobile. Then, as though the truck driver finally caught sight of Wellington, he swung away from the snowmobile – directly into the car's path. Wellington jigged further to his left to avoid the now inevitable collision of the car and truck. Safely past the vehicles, he turned his head to see their choreographed embrace. The prolonged, muffled sound reminded him of a dump truck dropping boulders on dry ground. He never thought of stopping. He was escaping, nothing else.

Wellington took a deep breath, slid back on the saddle, ducked below the windscreen and accelerated east towards Broadway. *This, too, is not my problem.*

He got to the corner of South and Broadway before the drivers behind him were even out of their vehicles, and then he turned south towards the mountains. As he left Grant behind, he couldn't help wondering about the desperate lives that were lived in a small town like this.

But then, who am I to call anybody desperate?

He pushed down hard on the thumb throttle and the machine leaped forward, through the unplowed snow. The gauges showed that the engine was in good order. It had finally warmed up, both gas tanks were full, and the amp meter was vertical, *whatever that meant.* A newly installed, small digital read-out displayed an air temperature of eight degrees and a range of one hundred and eighty miles. Underneath his heavy helmet and visor Wellington smiled and said, "Good for twenty-two," the distance he'd calculated to his hideaway. *And here's the barricade.*

There were fresh tire tracks in the new snow. Two vehicles had driven up to the barrier and looped back to town. *Somebody's looking for me.* Wellington steered around the barricade, revved the engine and bucked the machine up and over the snow piled at the side of the road. Beyond the barricade the road was, as Wellington expected, unplowed and when he accelerated the loose snow sprayed up from the runners over the cowling and hit him in the chest.

Chapter 9.

It was a typically quiet Monday in March at the Yellowstone National Park's north-area administration office. Jim Fielder, the long-serving area supervisor, had spent two hours with the Park's construction manager reviewing the plans for new tourist cabins behind Roosevelt Lodge – sixteen two-bedroom, all-weather cabins with underground utility lines and a common septic system. The remaining questions were where to put the septic field and how big a parking lot to build for the small facility. They had adjourned their discussions with an agreement to meet tomorrow on the snow–covered site behind the lodge to stake out some alternatives for the Park superintendent's approval.

The green desk phone rang, two quick shrills, an external call. Fielder answered.

Chief Leslie Marsh started right in. "Jim, I got those elk down the hill yesterday. More than last time. Ten head. Down to the bottom of the coulee on my ranch. Should be there a couple more days."

"Goddamnit, Marsh, you can't be calling me here. Remember, you call the superintendent, my boss. This call never happened." Jim Fielder slammed the phone down before Marsh could respond. Then Fielder stared at the phone and said out loud, "Christ, that call's recorded somewhere. How dumb *is* this guy?"

Marsh softly set his office phone back in its cradle. He quickly shook his head and dialed the Park's general administration number. A male voice answered on the first ring. Marsh asked to speak to the superintendent, George Kenner. The response, in a slow, syrupy voice, was, "Now, that would be me."

Marsh quickly replied in a loud voice, "Well I am damned glad *somebody* answers your phone. I'm calling to tell you to get your sickly elk off of my land. Now! Just like last time, they come down the coulee. About ten of 'em."

Kenner was not disturbed by Marsh's verbal attack, and in a soft, professional voice, asked for Marsh's full name, ranch location and phone number. Marsh said he was the Police Chief of Grant, Montana, just over The Flyover through the Harlan Range, and he could be reached through the office most days.

"Now I remember you and I'm mighty respectful of your public service," Kenner replied. "Chief, I can promise you we will call you back with a resolution of this problem by noon tomorrow."

Marsh jerked his head to the side as though he'd been hit with a shovel and replied, "Fuckin' federal government. Somebody damned well better get back to me *today* or I'm goin' start shooting."

Kenner sat back in his desk chair, smiled and replied with a strong south Georgia accent that he saved for such special occasions, "Well, Mister Marsh, I'm sure you're a fine gentleman and run a well-ordered law enforcement enterprise up Montana-way, and considering the distance 'tween you and me, I can't be stopping you from doing just 'bout anything you set yourself to. Isn't that right?"

Marsh pulled the phone away from his ear and said in a threatening near-whisper, "You know as well as I do that elk carry brucellosis and my cattle are very susceptible. Some of these elk look pretty snotty. You trying to kill off my herd? Get your damned, sniveling elk off my ranch before I start shooting."

Kenner responded in a mild, well-controlled manner, "Now, Mr. Marsh, you've gone and said that twice. What I *can* tell you right now is that it's a federal offense to shoot at Park animals unless there's a threat of immediate severe personal injury. That's the law – immediate severe personal injury. And then he added, "Like maybe there's a cougar goin' chew yo ass. What you're fixin' to do is what I'd call ...". He paused and then softly whispered the word *poachin*. After a moment of silence, he continued, "Yeah, poachin, hope you heard that right. Even if it is on your land and in season, which I am sure it ain't, being the middle of March. Those wandering elk, ya know, they carry the American flag with 'em wherever they go. Just like our embassy in France is on sovereign U.S. of A. soil, those elk are like little embassies right there on your ranch. Hell, I'm new here, but they tell me last year a Wyoming rancher, who pled guilty, mind you, thinking maybe he could curry favor with the judge, he got hisself two years of federal time for shooting a grizzly at two hundred yards. And federal time, ya know, is full time. He'll be locked up for 'xactly seven hundred and thirty days. Probably miss a coupla calving cycles, wouldn't you say?"

Marsh scooted his chair forward, propped his elbows on the desk and started to formulate a response. He turned and looked out the window at the blowing snow and said, "Thank you, Mr.

Kenner, I think we're done here. You just have one of your folks get back to me," and hung up the phone.

George Kenner immediately called Jim Fielder and said, "Hey Jim, seems we've got some of our elk down on Chief Leslie Marsh's ranch up your way again. Marsh wants 'em over the hill back into the Park. Says they look pretty *snotty*. Brucellosis. Wanting us to move 'em out of there pronto."

Fielder replied, "Hmmm, Really?", waiting for his new boss to suggest a resolution to this problem.

After a long silent pause, Kenner continued, "I'm looking at the map. Marsh's place is over in the northwest corner, north of Westgate," referring to the town of West Yellowstone. No one else called the Park's western entrance Westgate.

Fielder responded, "Yeah, not the first time. Coupla ranches off that corner. Elk wander around a lot."

"Guess so. How do y'all want to handle this? What did we do last time? What do you think?"

"Hell, we usually just sort of round 'em up and then push 'em up the other side of the hill. That's what we did in January for Marsh. There's no fence or nothing. We give them a coupla day's feed in the Park. Not nature's way, but it's nothing in the long term. Depends on how many there are."

"Marsh said ten. I reckon we'd better get on it. No?" Kenner paused, then asked, "You know Marsh?"

"Sure, he's hard to avoid. He's at least the third generation on that ranch. Christ, he could push 'em back himself with two horsemen and a dog."

"Don't they just come back when the food's gone?"

"Never know. This is Marsh's third time this winter. And he had us up there four, five times last year. Elk like that southern exposure on that sidewall just out of the pines. More wind, more sun – snow thins out early."

"Guess we'd better send somebody."

"I'll send a coupla interns out this afternoon. Last time we pushed 'em a mile back into the Park. We shoulda gone five, I guess. Even that's no guarantee. But maybe we can head this thing off for next year." Fielder smiled.

"How's that?"

Fielder took a big breath and replied, "Well. We buy some of his acreage, leastwise up that sunny draw, if that's where they're going?"

"What, we *buy* land? The Park Service buys land? I've never done that. I've got no authority to do anything like that. Certainly not in my budget: You ever buy any property before?"

"Well, sure. We've done it four or five times since I've been here. Usually close to an entrance road, out east towards Cody. Lots of traffic. The money comes out of Washington. They've got an annual allocation for expanding animal habitat. We write up a request and send it in. Sometimes they send out folks to examine the land, other times they just send a check."

"Well, do ya think this guy's got a case? Is this something we want to do?"

"No skin off our nose. The money's there. If we don't take it somebody else will. The Secretary makes a point of spending the entire allocation every year. So's it gets replenished next year, you know – use it or lose it."

"Yeah, ya gotta love federal budgets."

Park Superintendent George Kenner looked at his watch. "Well it's two-thirty here, four-thirty in Washington, guess I'll call the boss and learn about this wildlife habitat fund."

Chapter 10.

The clinic was a one year-old, two-story brick and glass building just off Route 34, the town's main east-west road. It had canted, butterfly rooflines flying off left and right and a wide, tented entranceway running out to the parking lot with a neo-Georgian cupola over the far end. Axel had once suggested to Anne that the structure looked like an origami crane about to either squat or take off. She let him know that such commentary, however clever and appropriate, was not appreciated. Anne's perspective was that the clinic, whatever it looked like, was a substantial enhancement to Rankin County's healthcare system and provided her with meaningful employment and a good salary. Axel stopped commenting on the unusual design of the building.

He parked, removed his gun belt and stored it in a lock-box on the floor in front of the passenger seat. As he was about to slide out of the vehicle, the old Motorola unit rang. *Curious.* He picked it up and settled back into the seat.

"What's up, Ange?"

"Thought you'd want to know, we just got a call from the FBI, Billings."

"Yeah, Billy Templar?"

"No, it was some different guy, Clark Thorsten. He's looking for a fellow on the run. Didn't show last week for his trial in Billings. He's featured in their Internet report today. I pulled it up off their website. Nothing out of the ordinary."

"So, why'd he call?"

"Well, he's thinking that maybe his guy's in Rankin County."

"Was he spotted down here? What's his description?"

"Big guy, about six foot four or five, two-fifty. May have a beard."

"Big guy, huh, could be our other shooter, no?"

"Yeah. Could be."

"Who gave him the tip?"

Ange paused and said, "Thorsten said it was Chief Leslie Marsh."

Axel blurted, "Son of a gun. How'd Marsh know the FBI wanted him?"

"Thorsten said nothing about that, just that Marsh called in to see if they were looking for any really big guys. He said Marsh told him he'd had already called the Highway Patrol and the U.S. Marshals office. And they both referred him to the FBI."

"I'll be damned."

The windows on the SUV were fogging up. "I tell ya, Marsh is getting under my skin. What? He's trying to do our job?"

Ange said nothing.

After a pause, Axel continued, "Well, I guess we'll just have to find this bad guy before Marsh does. This *big*, bad guy, whoever he is, could be a three-time loser – a federal trial no-show, the hit and run driver in the Canyon, and one of the MP shooters. This boy have a name?"

"Riley Wellington." Then she spelled it out. "Thorsten was chatty. He gave me Wellington's whole story. Thirty-four. Lived in Billings over seven years. Stockbroker, accused of running penny stock scams – gold, platinum, copper mines down in Colorado, Arizona. Took about a coupla million bucks out of clients' IRAs and retirement plans. Thorsten said his case was pretty solid. Wellington's partner turned on him. And Thorsten was more than a little irritated that the Montana's U.S. Attorney offered Wellington a plea agreement with only a three-year sentence, minimum security. He called it a spanking. But Wellington wasn't interested. Wanted a full trial."

"And then he runs. Say, could you call Thorsten back and have him send down a picture, and a profile sheet on Wellington? And anything else that ties him to Rankin County. I gotta talk to Spike and Carrie Baxter before I call him back. Could be an hour. I want to make sure we're talking about the same guy. Maybe you could send a picture to my cell, and then I could show it to Baxter. I've got to go. Copter's coming for Spike. Call Ollie on the Motorola and tell him about this new twist. I think I'm going to have a few more questions for Carrie Baxter. Send somebody over here to the clinic. We gotta keep a watch on her, twenty-four-seven 'til we can put her in jail. I'm going to arrest her in her hospital bed. Right after I talk to Spike."

"Right, boss."

As Axel walked up to the clinic, the outer double doors opened automatically. As did the second set further down the entry corridor. He surveyed the new, sterile, but already familiar, intake room.

His thoughts were dominated by the fact that Marsh was actively working this case. And getting traction. *This is a Rankin County case. What could Marsh know that I don't?*

Before he got to the reception desk his cell phone rang. It was Jennie Potts. She started right in, "Boss, I'm at the barricade. We've got some old auto tire tracks that loop around in front of the barrier and it looks like a snowmobile just went around it. Wide tracks, deep sharp edges. With this new snow and wind they couldn't be more than an hour old. Wide, heavy machine."

"And then straight up the road?"

"Yep. After it got around the barrier. Right down the middle for as far as I can see."

"Gotta be our guy." Then, thinking out loud, he continued, "This guy might be the Silverado driver from the Ice Box Canyon crash." Then realizing that he was sharing his thoughts, he spurted, "But, hey, none of that is public, OK?"

"Right."

"Tell you what, follow the tracks as far as the Crystal Lake Road, a coupla hundred yards past the Ginger River Bridge. The question is 'did he take the turn up to Crystal Lake or just keep going.' If you see him, don't pursue. No hot pursuit. We'll have to round up a gang to bring him in. There's no cell service up there, so come back to the barricade and call me, cell phone again. No CED. Plan on staying there a while. Turn away anybody wanting to go around the barrier. Anybody. They can call me for permission. Clear? Then you call me, right?"

"Right, boss."

He pocketed his phone and walked further into the high ceilinged room and nodded to the intake clerk sitting at the reception desk off to his left. A small sign on her desk said 'No Cell Phones, Please.' He grimaced in a false apology, looked down, removed his broad-brimmed hat and unconsciously slapped it against his jeans to get the fresh snow off. The noise brought out Jackie, the triage nurse, whom Axel had known for years. She said Anne was with a patient, but that Spike was in the back on a gurney ready for his life-flight helicopter. Axel asked Jackie what time Carrie Baxter had come in. The answer was 6:23.

Francis Xavier "Spike" Reynolds was a local living legend. A teenage runaway from the hills of northern Pennsylvania, he initially worked in the local coalmine. He fought with the Marines in Korea and came back to Grant determined never to work underground again. After the war he ran local distribution for the mine until it closed, and then, as a well-known, usually responsible, sober war hero, he was appointed police chief and served until he retired after fifteen years. Then he bought a small ranch west of town and ran some cattle until oil prospectors offered him more for the land than he could earn in ten years of rigorous ranching. The prospectors – who had been so sure that they'd find oil – drilled three dry holes. Spike enjoyed telling of his response when they offered to sell it back to him for the same high price at which they bought it.

He had kept the ranch house, but when his wife died, he started spending most of his time cruising the streets of Grant – often underdressed for the weather, carrying a tall paper cup from the local coffee shop in front of him like an acolyte carrying a golden chalice to the altar. He'd held a library card for fifty years and could often be seen around town carrying a stack of books on his hip or in an over-stuffed backpack, like a kid walking home from high school. And for reasons unknown, he had a personal discount at the hardware store.

His wife had been a member of the McCarthy clan from the copper mines of Butte and had Montana family roots that stretched back over a century. Their children, siblings, grandchildren, nieces and nephews were scattered around the state. It seemed to Axel that every week one or more Reynolds or McCarthy was mentioned in *The Billings Gazette*.

Spike started working at the MP when it opened last fall. Most folks figured he did it just to have something to do. Couldn't sleep well at night, he claimed, so why not get paid for staying awake.

Axel had always appreciated Spike as a man that lived life his own way. He was a tough old geezer who had lived hard and in spite of his small stature and age was given a wide berth by the young town punks.

Even before he opened the door to the clinic's patient-transport room Axel heard Spike bellowing. He wanted coffee. And the nurse said repeatedly, "No sir, you're almost on your way."

Axel nodded to the nurse and silently stepped in front of the gurney where Spike could see him. Spike was lying on his back, propped up by two pillows.

"Ax, what? You working here too? Delivering coffee? If that's true, then get me some." Axel shook his head and Spike continued, "Your wife slapped me with this leg balloon and ...". He nodded towards an IV bag hanging from a post and continued, "I've got bottles of God-knows-what pouring into my arms. Hell, I'm so strung up I can't even scratch my butt. Now I gotta go to Billings and I s'pose you're here to interrogate me as to how in the hell I got here."

"Looks like they're taking care of you."

Pointing to his splint, Spike continued, "Christ, look at this thing. Like three beach balls sewn together. Man, she must've spent half an hour lining up these balloons, all the while they got me in some screw-wise torture rack to pull my leg out of its socket. And she put ten stitches in my arm. How could you live with that woman?"

"Very well, thank you. I hear your leg's in bad shape."

"Hell, a damned girl shot me. And then her big buddy shot me again. Think they're Bonnie and Clyde. And all for a carton of cigarettes."

Axel heard the helicopter. He judged it about five miles off. In the Coast Guard he could predict the touchdown of an approaching helicopter to the minute. He figured that this one was still at least five or six minutes from touchdown.

"So tell me, you're working the graveyard shift at MP, and what? The girl comes in to buy cigarettes? And runs out without paying?"

"That's screwed up. She came in to pay for gas. Small woman. Young. Yellow outfit. She's riding bitch on a big black snowmobile driven by a huge fella' in a black snowsuit. Really early. She gives me a ten spot for the gas and I make change and bid her adieu."

"She just left?"

"Well, she turned to go and I went back to stocking the candy rack, 'bout ten feet from the counter. You been there, right?"

"Oh, yeah. Just came from there. So, tell me about the shooting."

"Well, first I saw her in that big convex mirror making her exit. She was just about at the door and then she spins around and turned back. Threw herself over the counter, grabbed a carton and took off running like a scalded dog. I was pissed. Knew I couldn't catch her. So, I grabbed the Winchester. Was gonna fire a warning shot. I wasn't out to kill her or nothing. I didn't aim but at the ground, the snow." He looked up at Axel, cleared his throat and continued, "I'm not killing anybody over a carton of cigarettes. I just wanted her to know she couldn't pull that kind of crap around here. I could see she wasn't a druggy or nothing. Regular kid, I s'pose. Guess I bounced one into her leg. But she couldna been hit too bad. She jumped on and then off that machine with a big-ass pistol and threw herself into the snow like it was time for live-fire at the range. I could tell she'd handled a big pistol before. Two hands. Steady."

The helicopter was now less than five hundred yards out. A second nurse, a young man, came in to handle the gurney. The lead nurse said, "Spike, looks like you're going to take a trip."

"Tell me about the guy." Axel took a step back from the gurney, rolling the brim of his hat in his hands.

"Cold. I shouldn'a talked so long."

"Spike, the guy?"

Spike looked up at the ceiling and said, "Fucking giant. He straddled that snow machine. Had both feet on the ground, like he's riding a little bicycle. Elbows stuck out like wings. Head over the windscreen. He was easy a foot taller than the girl. He had a black outfit. Black helmet. They got their gas way out at number six, furthest pump out there. Away from the station. S'pose I should have figured something was going on. Most folks like to use the pump closest to the door. Girl dropped the pistol in the snow and he came back to pick it up. I snatched the rifle and he shoots twice. One of them grazed my arm and then I pushed off the doorframe back into the station. Had enough of that shit. Coupla minutes later a kid came in and probably saved my life. Damned leg was bleeding like a garden hose."

The roar of the helicopter increased, and the doublewide doors started to vibrate. The life-flight helicopter blasted the new snow between the doors as it descended.

The lead nurse approached Spike and Axel. She nodded to Axel. Spike's interview was over. She pulled out his pillows, tucked a quilted aluminum blanket around him, pulled a hood over his head and strapped him down.

The helicopter landed softly in a towering whirlwind of snow and lowered its engine speed, but the rotors kept twirling. Two men in white uniforms hustled out. Bending over, they ran straight for the room's open doors and Spike's gurney. The men spun it around and pushed it towards the helicopter. In two minutes Spike was airborne.

Chapter 11.

Wellington's destination was Ruud's Lookout, a broad granite shelf. The edge of the shelf offered a spectacular view of the entire Ginger River drainage. A sturdy machine shed and a twenty-foot diameter hole in the rock wall were all that remained of the hard-rock mining operation that had abandoned the site in the late nineties.

Getting up to Ruud's from the trail that ran along the river required a thousand foot, hand-over-hand climb up a steep, rock-strewn wall punctuated by an occasional dwarf pine. The miners had built a longer, but much more accessible route, one that could handle pack mules and high-clearance, four-by-four ore trucks. The five-mile road was carved into the almost vertical, granite wall, but required backtracking – one would have to hike miles beyond the Lookout towards the Park and then turn back to climb up the dead-end miners' road. Few fair-weather hikers were willing to expend the extra energy, and no one hiked either route in winter. But, Wellington had a third route up to Ruud's.

The fresh snow on The Flyover was deep, but not as deep as he expected. He accelerated and learned that by going faster, he could glide over the jarring ruts. The machine's high-pitched whine drowned out all other sounds. He was on his way and feeling better with every minute.

He failed to notice a raft of dark clouds that came up behind him until it arrived and quickly pelted him with thick, wet snow. Now he could see only fifty feet ahead, so he slowed to make sure he saw the Ginger River Bridge and the Crystal Lake turnoff.

At the lake he dismounted his machine and slow-marched, knees high, through the deep, heavy snow into a grove of trees and sat on a bare boulder under the protective umbrella of a large blue spruce. He was out of the pelting snowfall just as if he had gone indoors.

He pulled off his mittens, then stretched and wiggled his fingers. From an inner pocket he retrieved a foil wrapped sandwich and from another, a small bottle of coffee. The spicy meatloaf sandwich that Tyler White had made for him was still warm. The coffee had held its heat and let off a wisp of vapor as he poured it into the metal cup. After a short rest he was again ready for the mountains.

Back in the snow squall, he cleared the accumulated snow off the machine and sped down the familiar, well-marked Crystal-Ginger River Trail. This was the easiest part of the journey. Wellington relaxed and cruised down the wide, level trail.

The turnoff came up quickly – off to the left and then up a steep grade on the side of Mt. Elliott. Wellington depressed the accelerator and watched the tachometer run up as the sled labored on the incline. Fifty-five hundred was good. Tyler White had counseled him not to exceed six thousand rpms, even though the meter's redline was at eight. The trail moved to the south as he gained altitude, up to Sergeant's Corner, where it split. The Corner was on the crest of a lateral ridgeline. To the left the trail dipped into a shallow wash and then assaulted Mt. Elliott with innumerable, steep switchbacks before it joined a Forest Service trail that went up to the top. To the right, his route, the narrow trail dropped quickly and went across a wide bowl and into a thin pine forest. Once out of the trees the trail narrowed and climbed to Ruud's Lookout. He figured that he could be lighting the wood stove in less than an hour.

Chapter 12.

Axel turned to Vicky and said, "One down, one to go. Where's Ms. Carrie Baxter?"

"She's still in the recovery bay, down the hall from the elevator, last partition on the left. She just got outta the OR a while ago. We used a local anesthetic and a little twilight gas, so she might still be a bit groggy. Dr. Lynwood prescribed a painkiller, C – three, the 'complaint containment cocktail'. It'll do 'bout everything but give her zombie dreams."

"I'll have to remember that. Can I talk to Ms. Baxter now?"

"Yeah, but she'll be slow."

"Aren't we all?"

At first Axel thought he had the wrong cubicle. The person in the bed had her eyes closed and lay motionless on her back. She was small and looked to Axel like a high school freshman boy who hoped to grow to five-foot-four, one hundred and twenty pounds before graduation. A bandaged left leg was elevated by a heal-harness on a small pulley system. An IV bag with a line that ran to her right arm hung from a stainless steel rod attached to the bed. In the fluorescent light she was gray, a winter pallor, offset by the blond ringlets that masked one eye. Her cheeks were chalky white and her lips, dry and cracked.

Axel quietly sat in the corner, careful not to scrape the legs of the chair. Her clothes were bundled in two large plastic bags stacked in the far corner. One pant leg of her yellow snowsuit stuck out.

It was torn and bloodstained. She squirmed and her foot twisted in its harness. One eye opened a crease. She tucked her chin into her chest and looked at Axel.

"Carrie?"

"Yeah," she answered in a whisper.

"You OK?"

"Yeah, guess so."

"I'm Sheriff Cooper. Need to talk to you. Now."

"Yeah."

"Did you call your folks?"

She nodded and softly said, "Yeah, just before they sewed me up. Somebody, a doctor, gave me her cell phone. Talked to my dad. He's coming in."

"Good. I'd like you to tell me what happened this morning. At the MP." Then he rattled off her Miranda rights and asked if she understood what he said.

She said she did, pulled her hair off of her face and then pushed her head back into the thin pillow, staring at the ceiling.

"Pretty expensive cigarettes, huh?"

"'Fraid so."

"Spike Reynolds, the guy you shot, is on his way to Billings General."

"Hope he's OK."

"Me too. He's a tough old bird. His leg was broken pretty bad. Pretty bad. I don't suppose I need to tell you, but you're in a heap of trouble."

On the side table Axel saw a thin wallet next to a wristwatch and a simple gold chain. "OK if I look at your stuff?"

She slowly turned her head to see what he was talking about, and said, "Sure." She rolled her head back and closed her eyes.

He gently removed one item at a time and spread them out on the side table, twenty-eight dollars in bills, some change, a Montana State University I.D. card with a photo that made her look even younger, a Montana driver's license, an insurance coverage card, and a credit union participation card. *Nothing unusual here.* He unfolded a $57.95 paycheck from the MSU library system and then examined her driver's license – Carrie Ann Baxter, Grant, Montana, just turned twenty-two.

She licked her lips, opened her eyes, stared at the ceiling and said, "Yeah, I can't believe it. Stupid, stupid, stupid. Tried to lift some smokes and the guy ran after me, like I'd robbed a bank. Hit me in the leg." She scooted up in the bed so she could rub her elevated leg with her free hand. "Can I get some water?"

"See what I can find." Axel got up and went out through the crack in the white curtains. Shortly, he returned and said, "Coming soon."

He wasn't going to push her. She wasn't going anywhere. A local couple's little girl who did a very stupid, dangerous thing.

"I should not have shot back."

"That's good for starters. So, tell me what happened."

"Sure. We wanted to get out of town early. I wanted to go with him, up in the mountains. At first it was like he didn't want to take me, but I really wanted to go. 'Bout flunking out of school. I wanted to get away. Sorta' like Grizzly Adams, making it on our own.

"He filled the snowmobile's gas tank and I went to pay cash. It was like Riley didn't want to be seen. For some reason he had to get out of town. Running from someone. That old guy was a jerk. I don't know if it was the end of his shift, it was too early in the morning, I'm a girl or just what. Didn't say a thing. Acted like he was pissed off at something. Anyway, the meter said eight and a quarter. I gave him a ten-dollar bill. He threw the change at me and went back to stacking shelves, something back in the corner. Rubbed me the wrong way."

"So, you took the carton and ran."

"Yep. That's about it. Don't even smoke."

"How did you know Wellington?"

"Wellington? Who's Wellington?"

"Riley, the fella' you were with."

"He told me he was Riley Crown. How do you know his name?"

"I think you know why, don't you? What do you know about his plan?"

"I know he had trouble in Billings and wasn't going back. He never said he'd done anything wrong, he just wasn't going back. He had a lot of money, cash."

"So, what was the plan?"

She scooted up in bed, suddenly more alert. She spoke loudly. "Sheriff, I'm not looking to get anybody else in trouble. I met him in Bozeman, just a coupla months ago. I don't know him that well, but I don't want to make any trouble for anybody."

"Let's get this straight from the get-go. *You* are the one in big trouble, yourself. You intentionally shot a man today. You certainly could've killed him. Attempted murder. If he dies, it's murder. You'll be darn lucky if he doesn't die. One way or another you'll be in 27th Street for a long, long time." The Montana Women's Petitionary on 27th Street in downtown Billings was where all Montana's women convicts were warehoused and, while a modern, clean facility, it was already notorious for its spartan facilities and strict regime.

"You know Riley shot him too. Could be his shot that did it."

"That's not goin work. If you both shot him, you're both guilty of attempted murder or worse."

Carrie contorted her face and turned her head into the pillow away from Axel. He thought this might be the first time she had considered the consequences of her behavior.

He continued questioning her. "About the best thing you can do to cut your time is to help us understand this whole story and track him down."

As though offended by the prospect of going to jail, she turned back to face Axel and said, "I am not telling you squat. Dad told me he was going to line up a lawyer for me. Dad said I should answer all your questions, like it would work out better in the long run, but I'm going to wait for the lawyer. I don't want to go to jail."

"Well, I think your father gave you good advice, but it's up to you. If you want a lawyer and want me to stop I will. Like I said before. But you're only delaying the inevitable. Your guy, Riley Wellington, was supposed to appear in court last week, in Billings. Federal court. I'd say the FBI could figure out some federal crime that you might have committed by helping him, like harboring a fugitive, accessory after the fact. The feds, they don't know you, your family. They don't care. They would rather arrest you on some charge, get a judge to set a million dollar bail, let you sit in their lock-up and harass you and your family 'til they got what they wanted. And then take you to court, even if you cooperated. You don't want to be messing with those federal robots. I think you're better off co-operating with me than rolling the dice with them."

"No, I'm done talking. I'm not ratting on Riley. I'm going to sleep."

She again turned as far away from Axel as the heel stirrup allowed her.

The two sat in silence for a long moment.

Then Axel started talking to her back. "Somebody will catch him. They all make mistakes. And it *will* go badly for him. Certainly, worse than if he'd gone to court last week. Don't know if you can help him now, but you certainly can help yourself."

After a long pause, he continued, "Carrie, you shot a man this morning. There's no doubt you're going to jail. The question is for how long. The more you cooperate, the better chance you have of a shorter sentence. I'm not the prosecutor or the judge, but the more you can be helpful, the more material I have to convince them that you don't belong behind bars for the rest of your life. We will eventually find everything out. You can push the schedule and do yourself a favor."

She sank further down in the bed and started to quietly weep as though she finally understood what she had done.

Vicky came into the room balancing a bowl of ice chips, a Dixie cup of water and a small paper cup of pills. She looked at Carrie Baxter and gave Axel a grimace and a quick nod of her head towards the break in the curtains, suggesting that it was time for him to leave.

Axel stood up. "Carrie, we can talk later if you want. Think about it. The more we talk, the better."

Without turning her head towards him she said, "You bet." As Axel spread the cubicle's curtains to leave, she dropped a final word, "asshole."

Chapter 13.

As Axel stepped out of the cubicle his cell phone rang. It was Jennie Potts.

"What've you got?" He hurried down the hall.

"I went up to the Crystal Lake turnoff. And you were right. Wellington turned to go up towards the lake. I came back to the barricade and, just as I got there, up come two Grant policemen on ATVs. They said they were after a guy on a snowmobile who caused some sort of a hit-and-run in town. No injuries. On South Street. They said he was a big man on a snowmobile. I turned 'em back, like you said, but they said they'd be back with the chief. They spun out of here two seconds ago."

"You did the right thing. I'll talk to the chief. Warm enough?"

"Yeah, this machine puts out a lot of heat."

"How is the snow?'

"When I started out it was light, dry, semi-power, but then it came down real good and not so fluffy. It looks like it could go all day. Certainly not going to melt."

"Well, this afternoon we've got to make a decision about whether we go tomorrow or wait until Wednesday. Regardless, we have to line up the snowmobiles and make a few calls to get ready for this search, whenever. We got a lot of folks interested in our big boy. I think you can come in now. He's gone and we've got to figure out how to chase him down."

As Axel pocketed his phone Anne came out of a side door. "Hey, Sheriff, I hear you're messing with all my new patients."

"Busy morning. My word, don't you look *purdy* in your white outfit." She wore a knee-length, white smock, belted at the waist and had tied her auburn hair back in neat bun.

He looked up and down the corridor to see if anyone was coming. Seeing no one, he wrapped his arm around her shoulder and gave her a quick kiss on the cheek. She hugged him around the waist. They both squeezed so the two of them meshed together and his belted equipment smashed into her side.

She squawked, "Ouch," and he reduced the pressure of his hug.

"I guess messing with folks is what I do best. Sounds like you've been doing the same this morning. Spike looked pretty good going out the door."

"He's lucky to be alive. Another half inch and that bullet would have hit a femoral artery and he could have bled out in five minutes. We did all we could. He needs serious surgery and some kind of bone graft to put that leg together. It's blown apart. Never seen an x-ray like that. That balloon splint may hurt like hell, but it will reduce the internal damage and blood loss until they can put it together again." She looked at her watch. "He should be at the hospital any minute."

They stepped back from each other, but held each other's upper arms as though wanting to share a full embrace, but knowing they couldn't. Not here.

After a long moment she dropped her hand and asked, "So, what's with Marsh?"

Axel shook his head. "He's being as obstructive as he can. At the MP he told me he was going to get my job, one way or another. It's recorded on MP's closed circuit TV tape." He smiled and said, "Maybe I should run it as a TV ad. Marsh is all over this shoot-out, even though it's county. Now I hear he's got a legit reason to go after Wellington, the big guy driving Carrie Baxter's snowmobile. On his way out of town Wellington caused an accident on South Street. And he's wanted by the feds for skipping out on a trial date, *and* he's probably the driver that caused the semi crash down in Ice Box Canyon, that's county. So, he's got all three of us who want a piece of his hide. And he's heading for the mountains. But, I've got to keep Marsh outta this and find Wellington before he does."

"Honey, this case is not a referendum on you or the job you've been doing. It is not a race – first to the finish. You *are* the sheriff and you *are going to be* the sheriff. Nobody in her right mind is going to vote for Marsh, even if he's captured this guy already. And if he's working with the feds, that'll get screwed up. I can't imagine that that Marsh could cooperate with anybody."

Axel knew Anne was right on all counts. Marsh would only do things his way and the word *cooperation* wasn't in his vocabulary. But Marsh wasn't stupid, and he was working the case and getting traction. Axel glanced back down the hall towards Carrie Baxter's cubicle. "Well, she might know where Wellington's going, but she's not talking yet. She doesn't understand the trouble she's in. She could help herself and it could cut her sentence. Our boy's got a plan and she's got to know some of it."

"Let her think about it. Before she went under she was talking a blue streak. Bet she talks."

"There's a good chance she will. But when? We're burning daylight and Wellington is getting farther away every minute. We gotta get him before Marsh does."

"Axel." She stepped back and stared at her husband. "You're the right man in the right place. And you know it."

He quickly slapped his hat on his head and said, "Damned right, cowgirl."

Chapter 14.

Axel was on the move. As he left the clinic one of his county sheriff's pickups pulled in. It was Paul Ridge, his newest employee. Ridge was a local boy who went off to MSU and came back home with an engineering degree – well regarded, but not very useful in Grant unless one wants to teach high school or be a remote-employee writing computer code for a software company. Ridge really wanted to be a deputy sheriff. So far he had impressed Axel with his willingness to put in the hours and take every opportunity to get meaningful experience. He was curious, an attribute that already made him standout from the other deputies. He was a couple years older than Carrie Baxter, but Axel figured they knew each other. *Maybe she'll talk to him.*

Axel told Ridge where to find Carrie Baxter, and that he would try to rotate replacement deputies every few hours. Then Axel got into his own vehicle. He didn't start it right away – he just sat there thinking.

Ever since *Crestfallen* Axel was reluctant to deal with federal law enforcement, including the FBI, the U.S. Marshals, and Yellowstone National Park Police. He balked at calling the feds in, even on cases that had obvious federal aspects. When the Sheriff's Department had to work with the feds on a case, Undersheriff Ollie Macy was the department's liaison.

But Axel wanted to handle this case personally. He had new information on an FBI fugitive. He called Thorsten at the Billings FBI office. The conversation began with Axel introducing himself as the Sheriff of Rankin County.

Thorsten's response was cool and clipped. "I've heard of you."

From Thorsten's few words and his flat, almost uninterested tone, Axel knew Thorsten had heard of *Crestfallen* and that he was actively displaying his disdain for having to talk to the killer of Doug Burns, the undercover FBI agent.

Axel suddenly wanted to end the call as soon as possible. He reported on the MP shootout this morning and that Wellington was, indeed, one the shooters and the driver of the snow machine.

"Hmm, that all you got?" Thorsten grumbled.

Axel didn't answer immediately. He thought Thorsten should anticipate the solid confirmation that Wellington was in Grant this morning. He felt like saying, *"The world is a big place and your boy could be anywhere. And I am telling you where he was early this morning. Have a good day, jerk."* Wellington's whereabouts at a given time, even two hours ago, was solid information. If Thorsten didn't realize or appreciate that, then he could go looking for Wellington on his own. But instead, Axel said, "That's about it."

"So, tell me more about this gas station thing?"

"Well, what about it?"

"Why all the shooting?" Thorsten inquired.

Axel responded, "Do you really want to know?"

"I do, I do. It may help us find Wellington."

"Doubt that, but the way I understand it, the girl paid for the gas for their snowmobile, stole some cigarettes and ran. The attendant gave her a warning shot that ricocheted and grazed her leg. She grabbed a pistol off the snowmobile and shot back. In two shots she took out the station's windows. Her third shot hit the attendant in the leg. Then she dropped the pistol in the snow. Wellington walked back for it and the attendant, an old local guy, reappeared and picked up his rifle. Wellington shot at him a couple of times and hit him in the arm. Then they took off south on Broadway, State Route 176 towards The Flyover and the mountains. It leads to the Park."

"The scene's not in the city, right?"

"That is correct."

"So what's the chief's beef, he's a city cop, right?"

Axel was already weary of this question and answer session, so he said, "Talk to the chief. Lord knows how he thinks or why he does anything."

"I'll bet there's a story about the two of you floating out there."

Axel ignored the entreaty and replied, "Well, the city has a complaint against Wellington. It seems that in getting out of town Wellington somehow caused a traffic accident. So, the chief has a warrant out for him."

"On his snowmobile? Right? Where'd Wellington go?"

"Hey, come on, if I knew that he'd be in one of my holding cells. Nobody's seen him since," Axel said with a biting edge of annoyance in his voice. He had had enough of this banter with this unappreciative FBI agent. He had better things to do. In an attempt to wrap up the conversation he said, "That's about all I know for sure, Agent Thorsten. I figure Wellington cleared town on the snowmobile just before seven. Probably into the mountains between here and the Park. Below the treeline. We've got a seasonal gate across the only road to The Flyover. I sent a deputy up there. Looks like Wellington went around it and a few miles later, took a right turn-off the main road towards Crystal Lake. It's before the first switchback on the steep grade of The Flyover."

Thorsten responded, "Frankly, Sheriff, I can't see Wellington, a city boy, making it overnight in the mountains. But, I guess we need to find him and chase him down. So, what do you think?"

Axel didn't respond.

After a long silence Thorsten said, "What say, at first light, we all go out in a couple of snow machines to run him down? Maybe we get a 'copter up if the weather clears. Maybe a drone with a camera."

Axel had no reply. He was not eager to work with Thorsten, even if they had the same goal.

Thorsten continued, "Regardless, I'm coming down this afternoon and want to go out in the morning, whatever it takes. Can you line me up with a couple of snowmobiles? Got a guy from the Billings office who is coming down with me. I already asked the chief, but he struck out. We can't be having a federal felon running around. I gotta go tomorrow morning, for sure."

"So, now you're asking me to supply you with transportation, right? You're already pushing me and you're not even here yet. I guess you must work for the federal government."

"I can't deny it. If we could get helicopters, I'd get 'em. Drones, same thing. I didn't order this weather."

Axel pushed back in the seat of his SUV thinking of responses. After a long moment of weighing them, he said, "Well, Mr. Thorsten, we'll see what we can do. Probably better to get a couple young guys with big machines. And you and your guy can ride as passengers. Reduce the risk. And I don't know how much of this weather is going to hit the mountains. Usually they get more snow than we do. Wellington could be dealing with over two-feet of new snow. Snow could be drifting deeper in the open. But, it may not be too bad."

"Well, thanks. The chief told me he's talking to the county's search and rescue crew. Are they good?"

"The best, but they don't get much winter work. Mostly the snowmobilers go off in groups and take care of each other. But S & R knows the terrain. They'll help you."

"So, you're not going with Marsh?"

"You heard that right. I'm going for Wellington, but you gotta understand that I am not working with Marsh. He wants my job.

Running against me in April and trying to make me look bad at every opportunity. I don't want him in my business and I don't want to mess with his. As it stands, the Sheriff's Department will go it alone."

"Sheriff, listen, I do financial fraud out of Minneapolis, and Wellington's guilty as hell, but to me it sounds like you've got a stronger case than we do. What, attempted murder?"

"Yeah, you're right. I am going out after him, but I won't stop you and Chief Marsh."

"This could be a case of the-more-the-merrier, no?"

"Whatever, but me and my people are not going with Marsh."

Thorsten said, "Well, Marsh's called me twice already. It sounds like he's going to stay on the major trails and look for reasons to chase down some of the smaller ones."

"That's one approach. Whatever. He'll do whatever he does. But I want to go on record. You can count the Rankin County Sheriff's Department in as willing to assist the federal government to capture a fleeing suspect in the Harlan Mountain Range. But we won't be working with Marsh. No way. But, if you really need transport, we'll find you rides. Frankly, I can't believe that the chief couldn't find any."

"So, you're cooperating on your own terms."

"You might say that." Axel wanted to say *"I don't want you down here in the first place. And if you're going with Marsh, you're not going with me. So, you don't want me and I don't want you."*

Thorsten spoke up. "I want to go out in the morning. I'll let you know when I get to town. The guys in the office say we use the Matterhorn Inn. Probably late this afternoon."

"You do what you need to. Sheriff's Department's going to go out early."

Chapter 15.

Axel drove out of the clinic parking lot onto Route 34 going east, headed to the Sheriff's Department located on the first floor in the back of the old County Building on Broadway.

Three blocks west of Broadway, Axel passed a Grant police car, parked on his side of the road. As he came up to it, its light bar ignited and siren erupted. In spite of the slippery snow the car shot out onto the road – right behind him.

"What the hell ..." Axel scanned his mirrors to see who was driving, but the tinted glass preserved the driver's anonymity. Then he said out loud, "Fine, I'll pull over." The next hundred yards the road's right shoulder was blocked with either parked cars and trucks or piles of snow, so Axel slowed and crept to the side, but not all the way to the shoulder. The police car, its elaborate front bumper fitted with a deer-guard and tall push-bars, banged into the rear of Axel's slowly moving SUV. Axel stopped and the police car hit him again. *Wham!* Not a crushing blow, but a jarring punch.

Axel jumped out of the SUV, slapped his hat on his head and gripped his holstered pistol. The policeman had started to open his door, but still had his seat belt buckled when Axel yanked patrol car's door fully open. Axel stepped forward blocking the seated driver. He turned slightly so the driver could see his hand on his holstered pistol. Axel got the reaction he wanted. The young man put his hands up, threw his shoulders back and emitted a shrill involuntary, "Ah, ah!"

Axel took his hand off the pistol and leaned over into the car. He yelled in the policeman's face, "What in the hell are you doing, young man?"

He took a step back, giving the policeman some space, but not enough to get out of the car. Axel folded his arms on his chest and glowered down at him.

The policeman stared at the door handle, gripped the steering wheel and said, "Chief told me to bring you in. He told me to wait there 'til you came by and bring you in."

"Well, that's just not going to happen, scout. It's clever, though. Did he tell you *why* you were to pick me up?"

The cop was still shaking and now looked straight ahead over the steering wheel. He stammered, "No. No. No, he didn't."

"Well, I'd like to hear whatever it is from the chief, but in *my* office, not his. Ya know *he's* probably broken some law, just telling you to stop me the way you did. Tell you what, given our recent experience," he stepped back and swung his head forward to look at the vehicles' bumpers, "I'd like *you* to lead our little parade. I'll be right behind escorting you back to the police station. I'll stay and watch you park your squad car and walk into the office. Then I'll go to *my* office in the County Building, just like I planned and continue working on this morning's shooting incident. You tell the chief that. He'll understand. If he wants to talk to me or arrest me for something, he'll know where I am. You lead, I'll follow. Right?"

Axel stepped back further, gripped the door with both hands and slammed it closed before the policeman could reply.

The policeman opened the door again.

"I thought we had a plan? You lead, I'll follow. OK?"

"No, that's not it. I've got something to talk to you about. Something else."

Axel folded his arms and tilted his head. "Well, what would that be? If it's a county job you're after, I can't say you made a winning first impression." He leaned into the car to read the man's name embroidered on his jacket. "Would you agree, Mr. Aldridge?"

"No, or yes, I'd agree. But I need to talk to you about something else. Something with the chief."

Axel took another step back and looked at the snow piled up at the side of the road. "Well, I am not doing personnel work for the city. What's this about?"

"Actually, a friend wants to talk to you about something. Something the chief's doing that he thinks is wrong."

"That's pretty vague, wouldn't you say? Like I said, I am not in the business of supervising the police department. But, if your friend wants to talk, I can listen. Maybe steer him in the right direction. Tell him to call me up at the sheriff's office. I probably won't be there, so he'll have to leave a message and a return number. He doesn't have to leave his name, but tell him to say it's about … what? How about a flat tire? Yeah, a flat tire. I can be as vague as he is. I'll give him a call back sometime. Probably in a coupla days. After tomorrow. How's that?"

Aldridge nodded his head, "That's great. He'll probably call today."

"Well, today's a busy day, but we'll get to it. Now let's get out of the street."

Axel left the squad car door opened and walked back to his vehicle wondering what in the hell *that* could be about.

Aldridge backed up and then pulled out in front of Axel, who turned on his full light bar and escorted the police car to the station. He parked out front and watched Aldridge park and go into the building. As though to announce his exit, Axel flipped his siren and gave it a two-second burst. Then he turned off his light bar and slowly drove to the County Building, a formidable, three-story, eighty-year old limestone structure and his office.

Chapter 16.

Wellington eased the machine down off the crest of Sergeant's Corner and across the open field. This descent had been the toughest part of last summer's hike to the shed – loose scree was apt to slide with the slightest pressure. He had learned to lean into the slope and walk slowly and deliberatively, securing his footage and testing it step-by-step, before transferring all his weight forward. Today he maneuvered the snowmobile slowly while leaning into the slope, securing a foundation for the runners of the sled and its powered tred. To maintain control he aimed only slightly downhill, above his summer trail. Once across the field he planned to work his way down through the thin stand of trees back to the trail. The snowmobile crawled across the open field with minimal downhill slippage. His plan had worked. *This is good.*

He entered the trees and slowed down even further. Here the snow was somewhat protected from the wind, but was surprisingly deeper. He sank into the snow and slowly wove his way through the pines. But what he thought to be a snow-covered rise proved to be a large, snow-covered, rotting log, and the tips of both his runners embedded themselves into it. He dismounted and, using the log as a solid footing, pushed the heavy machine back. The only alternative route, to go straight downhill through the pines, was unacceptably steep. He decided to go over the log. He quickly found a smaller downed tree, dragged it over and pressed its trunk next to the bigger one to create a wide ramp. He stomped snow into the crease between the logs. Then he pushed the machine back further and re-mounted. He pressed the thumb accelerator down firmly. The churning track shot snow out the back as it propelled the machine up the snow-covered ramp.

The runners easily slid up the grade and flew over the top. But their flight only increased the height of their fall. Wellington's eyes widened as the machine's runners cut through the deep snow for a millisecond and plunged into the underlying frozen ground of a natural rise – a hard stop. He was thrown forward over the handlebars and into the windscreen. His face shield snapped off his helmet.

Later Wellington questioned what came first – the sound of crushed bones or the searing pain. His left wrist collapsed as though it were made of papier-mâché. His fingers were momentarily folded back against his forearm. The noise, like river rocks being tumbled together, travelled up his arm and reverberated in his shoulder.

Initially the pain was localized in his wrist, but it was soon overwhelmed by a stab of blue lightning that Wellington feared would take off the top of his head. He squeezed his eyes closed, cradled his left wrist with his right hand and fell off the sled. His involuntary, animal howl blasted out to the near wall of Mt. Elliott and echoed back. A wave of nausea followed. He vomited down the front of his snowsuit. His uncontrollable wail of agony continued through a second wave of nausea. His eyes widened in panic and then rolled back into his head.

Awhile later Wellington found himself lying on his back staring up into the snow-laden pines. Sweat and melted snow seeped into his closed eyes. Then, through what he took as a compassionate act of a merciful God, the pain slowly retreated. He fluttered his eyelids, and stared up into the gunmetal sky between the pines. Random snowflakes and clusters from the trees fell down on him. He yearned for more to land on his face to cool it.

He looked at his left hand, which felt only loosely attached to his arm. To his surprise there was no blood. He slowly rolled onto his knees, careful not to put any pressure on his injured arm, and pulled off his right mitten with his teeth. Then he gingerly gripped the left mitten with his bare hand and in a well-focused exhibition of strength and precision jerked the left mitten off.

This effort triggered a new wave of pain so intense that he feared that he might black out again. It only subsided when he slid his wounded hand into the snow. Once his hand and wrist were fully encased and numb, he tested them. The thumb, index and middle fingers fluttered normally, but the last two fingers had no feeling at all. He was afraid to turn his wrist.

The sweat on his brow turned cold and stopped running down his face. *This is how people die in the wilderness. I could lie here, in the middle of the mountains, go into shock and never recover – if I don't freeze to death first.* As he got colder, he felt the localized pain subsiding. He sucked in the cold, moist air in what seemed to him like his first full breaths of the morning.

Sitting cross-legged he gathered fresh snow with his good hand to cover the injured one. He could hear the solid *lub dub* of his heart and the wind in the trees. He would survive, but he knew he needed to stay still for a while.

As though a fog was lifting, he started thinking about how he got here – his penny stock scam. He bought the stock in abandoned mines for pennies and sold it for dollars. Simple enough. He and Ritter had only three ventures, a total of eight mines. Small potatoes, he told himself. *Christ, look at Bernie Madoff. He ran his Ponzi scheme up to $65 billion, before the feds caught up with him.* Wellington would buy all the stock of an abandoned or played-out gold mine on the Denver Exchange for virtually nothing. Ritter would poke around the mine and write a long, detailed report including the remote possibility of more copper, gold, or better yet, palladium or platinum, maybe even iridium. He didn't have to lie, just mention the possibility of more minerals. Wellington also required that Ritter's reports include an appendix that discussed every active mine in North America, each one's proximity and possible similarity to the inspected mine. He prepared a white paper on the metal's uses and the market rates for the last ten years. Their reports added credibility, whether or not anyone cared to read them. Then, with the documents in hand, Wellington went to work, selling the stock on the prospects of great wealth.

He'd always known the scheme wouldn't last long, but he had expected it to hold for at least another year. But, too many clients had asked too many questions. *And somebody called the feds.*

Wellington had cashier's checks drafted for each account's remaining balance, put them in the envelopes with the statements and mailed them. Some broke even: none had made any money. The next day he opened new personal accounts under various forms of his name, Riley Crown Wellington, R. Crown Wellington, and R. C. Wellington. Over the next month he transferred his portion of the firm's profit to them and then, every other day, withdrew just enough cash from each account, to avoid a visit to the bank vice president's office. His stack of cash was just over a million, seven hundred and fifty thousand dollars. He wouldn't steal any of Ritter's money, but he could kill him.

Wellington had always measured his life by his net worth. On any given day he knew the number. The last two years it bounced between one and two million. A million dollars might sound like a lot to most folks, but Wellington knew that in the volatile metals market it could be halved in an eye-blink. He thought, or rather hoped, that his operation was too small to attract the attention of the feds. He had been wrong.

He knew that if he was caught, he was going to a federal penitentiary. What money wasn't taken in restitution to clients would go in fines and lawyers' fees. And jail, even the white-collar colony at Littleton, just wasn't something he was going to do. And if they got him for killing Ritter, they might send him to a high-security fortress, where he wouldn't see the light of day. Jail was for bad people and he wasn't one of them; he was an Eagle Scout, a first alternate to West Point, Notre Dame B.A., Boulder M.B.A. and a youth adviser at the North Billings YMCA. Wellington told himself he was not a bad man and he was *not* going to jail of any stripe for any duration. He also knew he had done bad things and in fact he was guilty as charged. But he would escape justice or die trying. He had always known he would run. No wife, no kids, no parents, a pile of cash, fluent in Spanish – he could be anybody he wanted to be.

He would stay at Ruud's Lookout until spring, and then just keep going south. Maybe even down to Nicaragua or Honduras, he'd yet to decide which.

He pulled his lifeless hand out of the snow and considered his new situation. The feds *would* be on the hunt, and having lost one hand, he would be easy prey. He fell back into the snow and closed his eyes. Again, the cold snow eased the pain.

Chapter 17.

Arlyn drove for another five minutes and then turned left off State Road 34 onto the winding Bolivar Road that led into the foothills of the Harlan Range. The locals called the intersection Finerty's Corner after the roadhouse bar on the southeast corner. As he passed by, Arlyn whispered to the old log cabin, "I'll be back later."

Arlyn was pleased to see that, while unplowed, the road wasn't covered with deep snow. Apparently, the winds of the foothills had been at work and had already swept away the new snow. The road paralleled Black Crescent Creek, a spring creek that never froze over and, accordingly, was one of Arlyn's prime winter fly-fishing destinations. Arlyn knew every turn and back eddy of the creek. He knew the road well enough to avoid several snow-covered boulders on its margins. He slowed down for a bone-jarring irrigation ditch that cut across the road, just past the aspen stand on the right.

As Arlyn worked his way up the slope, he slowed to look at the creek's ripples and runs. He marveled at the fact that this part of town was only a thousand feet below the neighboring peaks and that it lay only seven miles north of the Wyoming border and Yellowstone National Park. Yet to drive to the Park would take at least three hours – back east to Broadway, then up through The Flyover's switchbacks and back down again.

The electrical job was simple enough – wiring a new horse barn with lights and junction boxes and installing a new submersible well pump.

Arlyn and Zak were at the creek by one o'clock. By two o'clock Arlyn had caught and released six trout, including a big-shouldered, fourteen-inch Yellowstone Cutthroat that somehow had wandered out of its natural range. He was pleased that he'd timed his efforts perfectly for a mid-day hatch of microscopic midges and that he was able to match-the-hatch with a hand-tied dry fly the size of a peppercorn. As he loaded his gear into the truck it began to snow again. Arlyn looked up to the sky and the dark clouds coming in over the Harlans and smiled at his good timing. *Now for a beer.*

Finerty's Bar was a virtual clubhouse for the ranchers of southwestern Rankin County and their hired hands. Few tourists had the courage to enter the bedraggled, century-old cabin. Over the years its ownership had changed frequently, but the new owners always kept the name. In 1883 Timothy Finerty had struck it rich with a Harlan Range gold mine and took his fortune on to Seattle. But, he returned a year later and started up the bar, only to disappear in the Harlans a month later. The last change of ownership was only six months ago, reportedly for a thousand dollars in cash and five calves to be delivered in October, ready for auction. Arlyn hadn't been there under the new owners, a young local couple who ran about three hundred head of cattle. He didn't expect that they had made any improvements.

For the last ten years Frank Dressler had been the barkeep – a man who had a low threshold for rancor. Frank was an Iraq War veteran in his late fifties who kept himself in shape hiking mountain trails – usually alone, as he seemed to hold a grudge against the world. Arlyn had seen him throw two fighting drunks out of the bar in a single toss.

There were four pickups in the parking lot, each one more mud-splattered than the next. Arlyn recognized one of them – a distinctive big, black Ford F250 with gold trim, a wrought iron deer guard and a full-crew cabin – but he didn't remember who owned it until he stepped into the bar from the entry room. It belonged to Ted Norris, the former husband of Ginny Norris.

Arlyn considered Ginny one of the most attractive women west of Billings – smart, thin, but chesty, with a look of innocence, a foundation of Western female assertiveness, the wisdom of a sage and opinions about everyone and everything – a classic former Montana barrel-racer. *Too bad Ginny knew she was a looker and liked to play with all the boys.*

Once divorced from Norris, she couldn't seem to get out of town or find a fellow who could keep up with her. Rumor had it that her divorce settlement kept her in fine style with a monthly alimony, a small house north of Grant with two hundred feet of frontage on the Vermillion River and a three-bedroom condo in Big Sky, an international ski resort town on the other side of the Park.

The problem, as most local folks understood it, was that, even three years after the divorce, Ted Norris felt cuckolded by every man that even looked at his ex-wife with a gleam in his eye. This put Norris at odds with half the men in south central Montana, a class that included Arlyn Cooper. Last year Arlyn spent one long night with her, by the end of which he wished it had not begun.

Last fall, at a bar on Broadway, Norris had hassled Arlyn about his so-called 'run-away weekend' with Ginny. Arlyn knew that Norris was still looking to punish him for his alleged transgressions. Arlyn and Ginny had moved on, but Ted Norris hadn't.

Norris was a short, solid man with the wide shoulders and a long scraggly mustache. Indoors and out he wore a wide-brimmed, black hat low over his shaved head. He owned one of the biggest cattle operations around, and hired a foreman and four full-time cowboys to run it. As a young man he had done a little calf roping and steer wrestling on the northern rodeo circuit, but since then he'd had acquired a thirty pound potbelly and now spent most of his time breeding and training quarter horses.

Norris sat in the far left corner of the barroom with his chair tipped back so its front legs were off the ground and the chair's back leaned against the wall. His hat dipped low to cover his eyebrows. He held a tall glass of dark liquor. Arlyn guessed it was bourbon. Norris was at a small round table with his ranch foreman, Jake Dickerson, a well-known local roughneck, and a young hired hand. The two were huddled over a pitcher of beer and several small glasses.

As Arlyn walked into the bar, Norris slowly nodded as though his latest prediction had just been confirmed.

At a table closer to the door were three men dressed in bulky, insulated bib overalls, unzipped down to the waist. Bundled as they were, they looked like a matched set, except for the unique arrays of dark splotches on their overalls and the size of the man sitting in the middle. Arlyn figured the fellow had to be at least six foot six, and three hundred pounds. The smell of oil and drilling mud overwhelmed the bar's usual sweet, stale beer aroma. The men slouched in their chairs as though they hadn't the strength to straighten up. They were oil field workers – itinerant drillers working the much-discussed fracking operation at the Lazy KZ ranch west of Grant in Tower County. Arlyn figured they were probably from Texas or Louisiana and smart enough to realize that drilling was not popular with the locals. They generally maintained a low public profile. Finerty's was a good place to do that.

Arlyn made his way to the bar, stepping around outstretched legs and muddy boots with a generalized nod of recognition and respect. He wasn't going to keep another man from making a living or enjoying his beer. To Arlyn's way of thinking if the oil was here, somebody, sometime was going to take it out. It might as well be these guys today. *Just don't mess with the trout.*

The bar itself was a century-old mahogany masterpiece. It had been transported from the famed Excelsior Tavern in Virginia City, with its mirrors, brass rails and a waxed deck, so smooth that Dressler could slide a mug of beer twenty feet from one end to the other. Arlyn put one foot up on the old brass rail and ordered a draft beer.

"Cold enough for you, asshole?" Norris bellowed from his corner. He'd run his words together. Arlyn recalled one of Arlyn's barroom maxims. *Watch out for whiskey drinkers. They get drunk before they lose their interest in fighting.*

Arlyn replied over his shoulder, "You betcha."

The first beer went quickly and slaked his thirst. He slowly sipped on the second, thinking about his dog in the truck and the long ride home. This would be his last.

Suddenly someone grabbed his left arm and squeezed. Norris leaned forward and breathed heavily on the side of Arlyn's face. The bourbon smell was strong.

"I assed you a question, cowboy." Norris yanked hard on the sleeve of Arlyn's coat.

Arlyn held his footing and turned his head towards Norris. "Yeah, it's cold. What the hell you think I said?"

Suddenly all eyes in the bar were on the pair. Arlyn could feel the hair rising on the back of his neck. *Norris was looking for a fight.* Arlyn shot a quick glance to the oilfield workers to see if they were with him if it came to an all-out brawl – Norris and his men versus Arlyn and whomever he could recruit.

The giant slowly nodded and said softly in a resonating baritone, "Slow day," as if that was reason enough to join in a bar brawl.

Norris shuffled closer to Arlyn, as though contending for his spot at the bar. Then he stepped back and without preamble slapped Arlyn across the face with the palm of his left hand – not a knockout punch, but a solid, full-contact slap, flesh against flesh. The sound re-focused the attention of everyone in the room.

Arlyn back-pedaled. "What the hell? You got a problem?"

Not waiting for an answer, Arlyn slammed his right shoulder into Norris's chest and pinned down his arms in a classic quarterback-tackle. He pulled Norris away from the bar and towards the cattlemen's small table. Norris pounded his fists on Arlyn's lower back. The seated cattlemen stood up and got out of the way. Arlyn pushed Norris against the edge of the table. Norris kicked wildly, missing Arlyn altogether.

Then the table collapsed and the two men slid to the floor. Arlyn straddled Norris, who was face-up with one arm stuck underneath him. With his free arm Norris grabbed Arlyn's near leg and rolled into him, pushing Arlyn off balance and onto the floor. Norris scrambled towards the bar. He spun around and sat on the floor with his back against the bar and his hands on the foot rail. He took deep breaths. Arlyn stood and, thinking the wrestling match was over, took a step towards Norris.

Neither man said a thing and the entire room was quiet, except for Norris's deep gasps for air. He looked up at Arlyn, smiled, and then suddenly propelled himself off the foot rail, slamming his boot in the middle of Arlyn's chest.

Arlyn backpedalled across the room into the overturned table. Jake Dickerson, Norris's foreman, who had been a spectator to this point, jumped up behind Arlyn and pinned his arms behind him.

Norris stayed on the floor, leaning against the bar.

The lead oilman, the one who was having a slow day, stood up. With one stride he was behind Dickerson. He reached forward, grabbed both of Dickerson's shoulders and dug his thumbs deep into the joints until Dickerson loosened his grip on Arlyn. Then the giant picked up both men with a bear hug and dragged them further away from the bar.

The second cowboy backed away from the fray.

As the oilman loosened his bear hug, he grabbed Dickerson's wrist in his massive, weathered hand and squeezed. He had full control of Dickerson's entire arm and demonstrated it by having Dickerson punch himself in the face. Then the giant softly asserted, "This is a two-man fight. Stay out of it."

Arlyn stepped away from Dickerson and turned towards Norris. Once again, all eyes were on them.

Chapter 18.

Wellington fluttered his lashes to sweep the snow out of his eyes. He had regained consciousness, but was confused. He took an inventory. He was alive, awake and could see. But where was he and why was he lying in this snowdrift? He was flat on his back, staring straight up into the dark pines and a heavy snowfall. His face was wet and cold, but why? *Can I move?* He slowly rolled his head back and forth, crunching the cold, fresh snow that had built up around him. When he lifted his left arm to wipe his face a searing jolt of pain threw him back into his molded bed of snow. He scanned from side to side without moving his head. *I remember now. My wrist.*

He could hear the machine still quietly idling. *How long had I been out?* He lifted his head, careful not to move his left side. The logs were there and the machine was nose-first in the snow. Heavy snow clung to the pine boughs and pulled them down. It was all familiar, but not inviting.

There was no question of turning around. He had too much to lose. The question was how to proceed. He raised his right arm to his face and wiped away the accumulated sweat and melted snow. *That was good.* It was the other arm that was the problem. He shifted his weight and brought his right hand across his body to gently remove his injured left wrist from its cast of snow. It looked like a preserved laboratory specimen – already shriveled and gray-white. He wiggled his left index finger. It moved, but its motion tugged on the others, and they painfully resisted. He rolled back to his right side and slowly, carefully, stood. At first he hunched over to protect his left wrist and then slowly rose to his full height. He cautiously surveyed the machine and his escape route – down the hill to the game trail leading out of the pines. With his right hand he unbuckled one of his packs on the snowmobile. He grimaced in pain, but told himself, *I can do this.*

He wrapped his injured left hand and wrist in a flannel shirt that he had he pulled from the pack. *One less shirt.* With his right hand he cleared away the accumulated snow on the machine. He found solid footing and, using his right shoulder, pushed the heavy snowmobile backwards out of the drift. Resting his left hand palm up on the steering bar to cushion it, he mounted the snowmobile and pressed down lightly on the accelerator. He moved forward slowly around the drift and wove his way through the pines. With one eye on the trees and the other on his hand he slowly guided the snowmobile back to the game trail. Emerging from the trees, he looked at the odometer and was pleased to see that he had only four more miles to travel.

Between the heavy snow and his injured wrist the journey was slow, but he soon reached the last switchback. It angled up to Ruud's Lookout and the shed. *Only three miles to go.* He pressed the throttle harder and the machine responded with a thrust that pulled the front-runners up off the incline. When he cut the throttle the runners slammed back to the ground. In spite of the pain caused by the jolt, he was again pleased and surprised at the machine's strength. *Tyler really did create a super sled.* He slowly climbed the narrow, undulating trail, ever mindful of the steep drop-off on the right.

Ron Boggs

From the top of the last rise he could see the shed. *Only two hundred yards to go.*

His pleasure was short-lived, however. Arriving at the shed he examined his wrist. It had already begun to swell and discolor.

Chapter 19.

During Axel's five-block transit from the police station to the County Building the character of the snowfall changed from a light, sparkling amusement to a serious, pelting blizzard – *a March dump.* The cloud cover was a solid dark mass slowly sliding down the Vermillion River valley from the mountains. *Good thing Spike got out when he did.*

From across the parking lot he could hear, but not see, the county plows and sanders preparing to hit the main roads for the second time today. Both of the Sheriff's Department's new snowmobiles were in the machine shed. Jennie Potts had returned. *Good, I can use her.* He would need to have more deputies out on the roads this afternoon and tonight to deal with the inevitable accidents and stranded motorists. *Gotta figure out who's going where tomorrow.* The glass-bulb thermometer next to the building's rear door, the Sheriff's Department entry, registered fifteen degrees.

In contrast to the whirlwinds occurring outside and inside Axel's head, the office was calm. Ange Clausen sat at her desk and was reconciling last week's staff schedule with the payroll-hours reported. It was a manual calculation on a large sheet of yellow accountant's paper. Even after more than seven years on the job Axel continued to be amazed at the amount of administration his staff required. He wondered again when the county would computerize their payroll operations.

He stood quietly, hat in hand, in front of Ange's desk while she finished her work. He felt no disrespect. If he interrupted her now, it would take her an extra five minutes to redo the calculation of Ollie's overtime. He knew because he had done such calculations himself. He glanced at the Montana Highway Patrol monitor behind her desk that gave the Rankin County weather report – *six to twelve inches of new snow, more at higher elevations.* Ange finished Ollie's report, put a red check mark by his name and looked up at Axel.

"What's up, boss?"

"Right now, I need to talk to Jennie." He scrunched up his mouth as though lost in thought.

"'She checked in a few minutes ago. I think she's back in the washroom. Want me to go get her?"

They stayed in place for a moment and then he said, "No, but send her into my office when you see her. We got a boatload of things going on."

"How's Spike?"

Axel smiled knowing she probably already had several reports from her local network, but wanted to hear yet another – this one from the husband of the treating physician. Whatever he said would be broadcast within ten minutes. He needed a comprehensive, irrefutable response. "Not as good as I'd hoped. His arm's OK, but Spike and his shattered femur are on their way to Billings. Anne says he's lucky the shot didn't hit an artery. Good thing he got out before this weather arrived.

"Don't know what Jennie told you, but she had a good morning ride. She told me she spotted Wellington's tracks and followed them up to the turn for Crystal Lake. Then, back at the barricade, she stopped a pair of city cops. They were after Wellington. They're lucky she stopped 'em. They wouldn't get very far on their ATVs. Not in this snow." He swung his head towards the door. "Got about twenty feet of visibility now. They'd be lost in an hour if they didn't fall off the road."

"What about Thorsten?"

"Yeah, I talked to him. Treated me like a hostile witness. He says he's coming down this afternoon. Going out with Marsh and with the S & R. Ben Jones. Thorsten's out of Minneapolis." They both knew the special meaning in his last statement – FBI Minneapolis, the home of the undercover agent whom Axel shot a year ago last October – but neither said a thing. He swallowed hard and continued, "Do you have Butch Parker's transcript of the truck accident? I want to check on exactly what he said about the driver of the Silverado. I'm hearing a lot about 'big guys' today. And I think they could all be the same guy! A one-man crime wave in Rankin County. Fancy that."

"Transcript's on your desk. What's with the cops?"

"S'pose I should call the chief and find out. Apparently, our big guy caused a wreck on the way out of town."

Ange looked up at Axel and said, "On a snowmobile? Really?"

When Axel didn't answer, she continued, "Carrie Baxter. She OK?"

"Well, Vicky stitched her leg all right. But she's in a lot of trouble. You know her parents very well?"

"Sure, everybody does. Baxters've been here for a hundred years. During the sixties, her grandmother was a County Commissioner and ran a local stockyard. They were behind an effort to get a slaughterhouse going."

"Yeah, I just can't figure it. Stupid move, shooting back at Spike. At least she has admitted that she was a shooter, but she's not fully cooperating yet. She will. And I'll bet my bottom dollar that her driver, the other shooter, is the guy who drove the semi off the road. Ruthless. *And* he *is* the guy the FBI is looking for. Baxter clammed up about his plans in the mountains. But, I gather it's somewhere 'tween here an' the Park."

Axel again scanned the weather monitor and frowned. He stepped away from her desk, pointed to the monitor and headed towards his back office while continuing to talk. "Weather's not going to get much better tomorrow."

Back in his spartan office he stood behind his desk and flipped through the transcript. Butch Parker was the north county rancher who witnessed the semi-tractor crash in Ice Box Canyon. Parker said that he didn't get much of a look at the driver of the Silverado as their pickups were side-by-side. He only knew that he was a big guy – a big, big guy in a white Silverado.

Still standing, Axel picked up his desk telephone and called Marsh at the police station. Marsh started right in. "Well, you son of a bitch. Your girlie deputy stopped my boys from catching a federal felon. Hope you're proud of yourself. I'd call that interference with an authorized law enforcement activity. Abuse of power. Obstruction of justice. You know, don't ya, that that guy and his machine caused a wreck down on South Street an' he was on his way out of town. We'd a caught him, too. We tracked him to the barricade and we'd have caught up with him for sure. Hell, we'd a brought him in. Feds want him, you know. Damned straight. Now with this weather that boy is *gone*. Gone to God knows where. I got a warrant out for him and I've called the county search and rescue an' we're going after him, first light tomorrow."

"Well, Leslie, I just heard that you've been looking for him. We didn't know about your traffic accident. Anyway, he'd probably had a good two-hour head start on you. My deputy did her job, what I told her to do. The way I look on it, we probably saved you a second mission to rescue your boys after their four-wheelers got bogged down or the boys got lost in this blizzard. Not much is going to move today. Tomorrow either." Axel said nothing further and considered the information that Marsh didn't know – the semi accident and Carrie Baxter's arrest. He said nothing about either one.

After a moment of silence Marsh started in again. "Don't think for a minute that because you're sheriff, you can do anything you want. I'm going to pursue this obstruction of justice thing. That'll nail your ass to the wall. Circuit court, your home turf. See how you like your buddy Judge Barr from the other side of the courtroom. Right, Sheriff Cooper?" He paused and when Axel said nothing, he added, "You'd better enjoy that title while you can. This is gonna make you look like you're soft on crime, maybe even hooked up with Wellington, like his local protector. If you think this election's over, you'd better think again, boy." He paused and then spat out, "You're going to be a loser."

"Chief Marsh, talk to you later." Axel hung up.

Chapter 20.

Fielder used his cell phone while sitting in his personal pickup in the employee parking lot. "Talked with Kenner. We're sending out a couple of rookies to clear out your elk. Snow's not too bad here. I think I got to Kenner. I could tell he wasn't against the approach. Never heard of it. Like we were spending Monopoly money – outside our budget."

Marsh answered, "Damned bureaucracies. Hell, it takes me months to buy a new vehicle. City council acts like I am trying to steal something. How long you think this deal could take?"

"Federal government, you never know. But, I got a draft of an application ready to go. Maybe take a week to file once Kenner gives the green light. I'm asking for a hundred and sixty acres – down the draw, over the crest of that east-west ridge where the snow is usually pretty thin and melts fast. Figure about two grand an acre. Over three hundred grand, all told."

"On the market I'd get half that – not the best pasture land. So, I figure we got about a hundred and fifty to split?"

"Sounds good to me."

"They are going to put up fences, ya think?"

"That'd be a first. Most of our boundaries are National Forests, so there's usually no need. Seems to me you could keep grazing cattle on it, less of course the elk came down the hill by themselves."

"That'd be a bitch, like they read the application and knew that the Park was bigger and they had more land to roam around."

"I think we're giving them too much credit. They'll just keep doing what they do. Hell, yesterday we had a herd going down the road towards Gardner. They just take the easiest path at every step."

Chapter 21.

Breathing heavily, Norris stayed on the floor. He reached up behind him and grabbed the front edge of the bar, pulled himself up and slowly scanned the room as though looking for a weapon. Arlyn stepped back towards the door and away from Norris and Dickerson.

The scene was again set – either the fight was over or the second round was about to begin.

The giant oilman had ensured that it was Arlyn and Norris, *mano-a-mano*. Norris moved to his right and Arlyn stepped away from him. The hunched-over men circled, like prizefighters, assessing each other.

Then Arlyn stopped, held up his hands at shoulder height, palms out, and said, "I think we're done here. No?" He straightened up and flipped his chin toward Norris, waiting for an answer.

"Fuck yourself, you pansy-assed flatlander," Norris spouted from his crutched stance. Then he straightened up, cocked his arm, and threw himself at Arlyn. With all his forward momentum he launched his fist. Arlyn saw the haymaker coming and back-pedaled out of range into the pile of toppled chairs. Norris's big swing threw him off balance, and Arlyn, without a wind-up, stepped forward and smacked Norris on the side of his head with a short, powerful jab using only the base of his open palm. Then he backed off and waited for Norris's next move.

As his legs collapsed, Norris fell away from Arlyn. He initially crashed into the jumble of chairs. Then he slid off the chairs in stages, as though he were a multi-story building demolished by synchronized dynamite explosions. His right shoulder hit the floor first. His head whipped back and hit the brass foot rail with a hollow *thump*.

Dickerson snatched the handle of a shattered beer pitcher off the floor and brandished the thick shard of razor-edged glass like the saber of a marauding pirate. Then he lunged towards Arlyn.

Arlyn backed away, stumbling over the chairs. He fended off Dickerson's swing, forearm-to-forearm, but Dickerson's wrist glanced off Arlyn's arm and hit his shoulder. His glass sword scraped across the back of Arlyn's head. The thin bevel of the glass peeled away a portion his scalp, instantly creating a bloody flap. Arlyn remained standing as blood gushed from the wound. He slowly eased himself to the floor next to Norris and put his hand up to his bloody head.

Pitcher in hand, Dickerson took a step towards Arlyn as though to decapitate him. But before he could take a second step, the giant oilman leaped forward, grabbed Dickerson's arm and slammed it on the edge of an upright chair. The glass weapon hit the floor and shattered. With the strength and poise of an Olympic wrestler, the oilman lifted the attacker and threw him towards the front door, away from the bar. Dickerson bounced off the door, back into the arms of the oilman. Then the giant slammed him towards the bar. Dickerson's shoulder hit the front edge of the counter, and he landed on the floor next to Arlyn, who was leaning on Norris. With one hand the oilman held Dickerson down. For a long moment the four men were frozen, as though they were modeling for a statue.

At that moment Frank Dressler came out from behind the bar carrying a shotgun. He pointed it at the floor. In a low, commanding voice he said, "That's enough. Move slowly with your backs to the wall."

The men at the tables stood and complied without a sound, as though they were relieved that the fight was over. The giant backed into the corner with his mates. Dickerson grabbed the edge of the bar, pushed himself off of Arlyn and moved to the opposite corner. Arlyn had one hand on his bleeding head and put his other hand on Norris's shoulder and pushed himself up.

Norris lay face down and didn't move. The damage was easy to see. Behind his right ear on his shaved scalp was a bloodless, cylindrical cavity – an indentation in his skull that looked like it could have been made with a baseball bat. Dressler knelt down and turned Norris over. The stiff body rotated in one piece, like a big, heavy sack of seed. *Thunk.*

The still air was saturated with the tang of blood, the sulfur of raw oil and the sweat of outdoor workmen.

All eyes were on Norris's pale face and its frozen, vacant stare. The men didn't move, except to quietly shuffle between the chairs to get a better angle. There was little question that he was dead. Dressler knelt down and put two fingers on Norris's neck, checking for a pulse. Dressler shook his head.

As the observers quietly backed further into their corners, Dressler stepped behind the bar, punched 911 into the phone and talked to the CED dispatcher.

Arlyn stayed in the center of the room with his hand on his head. Blood oozed through his fingers, ran down his arm and dripped off his elbow. The ranchhands and oilmen made room for him in the suddenly over-crowded bar. Somebody slid a chair behind him and another gently guided him into it. He said nothing. His head bobbed back and then he arced forward. One of the oilmen caught him before he fell off the chair.

From behind the bar Dressler brought out a fresh cloth towel roll. With his pocketknife he sliced into the roll to create a long bandage a half-foot wide. He did it with the exacting efficiency and skill of one who had prepared for this day. He had one of the oilmen hold the end of the bandage roll against the back of Arlyn's head while Dressler re-positioned the bleeding, loose skin. He then pulled the cloth tightly around Arlyn's scalp. The striped turban grew thicker with each rotation. After the third go-round, Dressler sliced the bandage roll crosswise and snugly tucked the tag end into the bandage.

Dressler got behind Arlyn, grabbed him under his armpits, and pulled him off the chair onto the floor in the corner away from the gawking men. Arlyn lay back and rested his head on the wall. Dressler positioned a folded coat under his head. No blood seeped through the bandage.

A long twenty-four minutes later, the Rankin County emergency medical team arrived – as did Police Chief Leslie Marsh.

Chapter 22.

Axel was still at his desk when the direct CED call came in.

"Sheriff, it's Chief Marsh."

"Hey, I thought we had agreed to meet in court with your obstruction of justice complaint. Whataya' got now?"

"You'd better listen now 'cause you're going to hear a lot of different stories about this. Bunch of oilmen and cowboys." He had a serious, gruff tone to his voice.

"Doesn't sound too good, whatever. So, what's going on?"

"Well, Axel, I am out at Finerty's and they just put your brother in the EMT van going to the clinic. He's got his head cut up pretty bad."

"What the hell?"

Leslie Marsh cleared his throat. "You know Finerty's? Out west on 34, the edge of town. Bar fight." There wasn't really a question and Marsh continued, "Arlyn got hit with a broken glass pitcher. Got a big gash on the side of his head – scalped, peeled back his skin, I guess. The barkeep, Frank Dressler, bandaged him up pretty good. EMTs are probably halfway to the clinic already. Can't be more than a coupla miles." He paused and Axel heard him swallow hard. The line was quiet to the point that Axel wondered if they had lost their connection.

"I'll check with Dispatch. Hold on." Axel cupped his hand over his CED phone and shouted out, "Ange!" She came running to the door of his office and he said in as calm a tone as he could, "Call Dispatch. Arlyn's in an EMT van coming in from Finerty's. We need an ETA. Keep at 'em 'til you get one and tell me as soon as you do."

Ange nodded and ran back to her desk.

Axel took his hand off the phone and said to Marsh, "I'm back."

"The EMTs figure he'll be all right. He walked to their van on his own. Had his wits about him. They didn't even remove the towel Dressler wrapped around his head.

"Ted Norris, you know him?" Marsh didn't wait for a reply. "Well, Arlyn knocked him down, and he hit his head on the foot rail and died."

After a long pause, Axel said, "Norris died, right then and there?"

"Yeah, never moved. Might of broke his neck."

"And *then* Arlyn got cut?" *There had to be more to the story.*

"Yeah, I don't know everything. They wrestled a bit and then Norris took a swing at Arlyn. Aryln countered and knocked him down. Norris fell and hit his head. Died on the spot. Coupla cowboys and some oilmen saw it all." Marsh stopped, coughed, and said, "I am arresting Arlyn soon as I can. Manslaughter."

"What the hell! Marsh, that is absolute horseshit, and you know it. This was a bar fight." Axel waited for a reply and when none came, he continued, "You just said that Norris swung first. This smells of a Virginia City vigilante necktie party. *We got our horse thief. Let's string him up.*" He was suddenly standing, clutching the big phone, pacing behind his desk and uncomfortably warm inside his office.

"So, this is some bad-ass, clever election stunt?"

"No, sir. There are already a couple versions of the fight going 'round. Regardless of who you believe, we absolutely got ourselves a dead man here. This was no playground fistfight. It's got to be something – manslaughter, negligent homicide, assault and battery. Hell, I read those Academy books. It's got to be something."

"How'd Arlyn get cut?"

"Jake Dickerson jumped in, picked up a chunk of a broken beer pitcher and smashed Arlyn with it. Took a slice of the left side of his head. Lot of blood. No guns. No knives."

"You arrest him? Dickerson?"

"Can't say that I'm going to."

"Marsh, damn it, why wouldn't you arrest him. If you want a cold-blooded act, it would be Dickerson attacking Arlyn after the fight's over? Right? But, maybe 'cuz Dickerson is your star witness and ripe to say that Arlyn attacked Norris? Christ, this is absolute crap, from start to finish. When's the last time you heard of any charges coming out of a bar fight. Hell, your boys break up bar fights once a week and nobody gets charged. For charges to stand against Arlyn, he would have had to jump off a stool and smash Norris with a hatchet as he walked in the door. Did he do that?"

"Can't say that he did, but we still have a dead man in the City of Grant and somebody's responsible. I'm a chief of police doing my job. I'll let a judge and jury decide if he's guilty."

"Bullshit, you can't do this. You arrest Arlyn and you *will* regret it. You're not a one-man justice machine. You talk to Webber?"

Harry Webber was the part-time Rankin County Attorney, who had a private practice in town. He handled county prosecutions and the more serious city cases. For the last four years Harry Webber presented all of Axel's criminal cases. They were batting one hundred per cent and, while they had had their disagreements, the two respected each other. Axel shook his head in disbelief and said, "Webber won't take this. This is bullshit. Just another Rankin County election stunt."

Marsh jumped on the word *stunt* and shot back, "Hey, I got witnesses and a dead man. Webber will support this. He's not going to balk. And ya better have somebody pick up Arlyn's damned mutt before I shoot it."

"Right." Axel clicked the disconnect button on the side of the CED phone.

Chapter 23.

Axel immediately called Harry Webber's cell phone. Webber answered on the first ring but whispered, "Ax, been meaning to call you. Heard you've had a suspect in custody. Slam bam. You want to try this case yourself – seems pretty straightforward. Carrie Baxter, yeah? That's tough. Hey, I'm in Billings, in the middle of an evidence seminar."

Axel replied, "Marsh is saying he is going to arrest Arlyn, my brother. Bar fight, out west at Finerty's. Ted Norris got knocked down, hit his head and died."

"You serious, Ted Norris died? Can't imagine that he'd ever be in a fight that he didn't start. Christ, we haven't had a bar fight go to trial since I've been prosecutor. Wait a minute, I got to get out of this crowd."

Axel waited, holding the phone to his ear and hearing the shuffle of people moving about and the hubbub of distance conversions.

In a louder voice Webber continued, "OK, I'm out in the lobby now. How'd it happen?"

"So far, I only know what Marsh told me. They wrestled around a bit. Norris took a big swing, missed and Arlyn hit him on the side the head and knocked him down. Head hit the foot rail and he was gone."

"Witnesses?"

"Yeah, some oilmen and a coupla of Norris's guys. And Frank Dressler, the bartender. Then there's Arlyn, of course. One of Norris's men scalped him with a broken beer pitcher."

"Say what? After Norris went down? Arlyn's OK?"

"I haven't seen him yet, but he apparently walked to the EMT van. On his way to the clinic now."

"Good, I hope he's all right."

"Know in half an hour."

"Well, if they're fighting, and Arlyn knocked him down and he hit his head and died, I can't see prosecuting him for Norris's death. While I can't stop Marsh from arresting Arlyn, I can get him released to you. Personal Bond. That good enough for now?"

"So, he wouldn't go to jail at all, right?"

"Well maybe, but short. Once you give the document to Marsh, he has to hand him over to you. Course, Arlyn better show if there's a trial or your ass is in a sling."

"There won't be a trial. Marsh is just looking to make the Thursday edition of *The Courier* – with the arrest of my brother. Probably conjure up some headline about the Killer-Coopers."

"Yeah, great."

"Arlyn's going to the clinic now. What does it take to get him assigned to me?"

"Well, first Marsh has got to arrest him. Then you deliver an executed Form 8., I think it is. I will call Michelle and have her type one up and stamp it. Take ten minutes. You can pick it up. I'll tell Marsh. It's Arlyn with a *y*, right?"

"Yeah, great. It's A-R-L-Y-N. Is Marsh going to respect this Form 8.?"

"If he ever expects me to take one of his cases to circuit court, he sure as hell better. I'll call him as soon as I get off the phone with Michelle."

"Good. Tell Michelle I'd like to pick it up this afternoon after I go to the clinic. So, there's no rush. Arlyn's going to be at the clinic awhile."

"Understand now, this would not stop a trial from being scheduled. You got some witnesses that support self-defense?"

"I will. But once you hear the whole story, I'll bet this is a case you're *not* going to want to take to trial. It's going to be over before it gets started."

"Get those witnesses."

"Got it, thanks."

The men hung up.

Axel stared out the window at nothing in particular other than the accumulating snow. He tried to imagine how the fight went such that Arlyn knocked Norris down and then got hit with a broken beer pitcher.

Ange came to the door. Axel looked up at her and she whispered, "Five minutes."

Axel waved his hand at her to acknowledge the report and looked at his watch.

"Ange, wait a minute. I need to talk to you."

Chapter 24.

Ange was still in Axel's office when Jennie Potts knocked on the open door.

"Sheriff?" she asked.

"Come on in. I need to talk to you and Ange. Is Ollie around?"

From the doorway Jennie replied, "No, I think he's still at the MP with the forensics guys."

"Still?"

"Right. A lot of shots fired."

"Need your help. Come on in. Sit down, ladies. This could take a while."

The women sat in the two wooden armchairs in front of Axel's desk.

"So, here's the short version. Brother Arlyn was in a bar fight out at Finerty's, west end of town. Ted Norris." He looked at Ange, who nodded indicating that she knew the man. "Norris died and Arlyn got cut up. He's coming into the clinic. Marsh says he is charging him with manslaughter." He looked up at Ange again, and then at Jennie, as though confirming the gravity of the situation.

"But, he's not going to be locked up for long, not if I can help it. I talked to Webber and he'll issue a form that releases Arlyn to my custody. So, he won't go to jail before trial, if there ever is one. Michelle upstairs will be typing up the form as soon as Webber talks to her. Marsh has got no reason to charge Arlyn. It's just an election stunt. But, he can arrest just about anyone he wants."

Ange glanced at her watch and nodded.

"I'm going to the clinic, meet Arlyn's EMT van." He turned to Jennie and said, "I gotta think that the best witness is gonna be Frank Dressler, the bartender at Finerty's. Can you track him down and have him come in tomorrow for a recorded interview. Or go out to Finerty's on the edge of town. We need a clean, irrefutable record admissible in court, if need be. I want you to conduct the interview. I'm too close to Arlyn. Go through the process by the book, A to Z. Don't be afraid to ask the same question three different ways. Take breaks if you need to come up with new questions, but let him talk as long as he wants. Get everything he says on tape and announce everything – where you are, who you are, what time it is, and when you start and finish. When you take your breaks and when you return. All that stuff. Marsh may interview him later and we want to make sure that we've got all our bases covered. No surprises can pop up later. Got it?"

Jennie looked puzzled and said, "Yeah, tomorrow? Aren't we doing the search tomorrow?"

"Well, we were until about a minute ago. Too much snow. I changed my mind. Ange, you got that, we need to put everything off for twenty-four hours. We're going *Wednesday* morning, seven o'clock."

"You bet. We can slide."

"This snow is going to continue. Let's do the same set-up. Meanwhile Jennie, you interview Dressler, by the book. Comprehensive. Got it?"

"Absolutely."

"I don't think there's anything else we can do now." He stopped, turned and peered through the window at the near-whiteout conditions, as though he was looking for something in particular.

Then he turned back to Ange and Jennie Potts, and said, "And I gotta believe our missing shooter is the fella that caused the semi accident last week and, I guess, the police think he caused a wreck in town this morning after he dumped Baxter. The FBI is after him for missing a court date on some fraud complaint. Two FBI guys are on their way down from Billings and going after him. Name's Riley Wellington. FBI's working with the S & R and Marsh and going out the first thing tomorrow, assuming this blizzard runs its course. Can't imagine that it will. But I kinda like the thought of Marsh lost in a late winter snowstorm. They won't find Wellington. We'll have the whole field to ourselves on Wednesday."

He paused and again looked back to the window. Turning away, he said, "You got to admire the FBI's arrogance. They are going out with Marsh, right? But asking us for a coupla snowmobiles or jockeys with machines that'll take 'em out. I told him we'd try. We're certainly not offering ours – save ours for Wednesday. Potts, you and me."

Potts interrupted, "We're not all going out together?"

"I don't know when Marsh is going, but we are definitely *not* going tomorrow. Period. Anyway, we are going to be looking in different places. Not that I know where Wellington's hideout is or anything, but we're not going with Marsh, and we might have some resources they don't. For now, we're going to play nice with the FBI and see if we might scare up a coupla snow machines for them. We're looking for two machines, or better yet, two guys with machines that want to earn a hundred bucks carting a couple of FBI agents through the east slope of the Harlans. This is for Wednesday. If Marsh goes tomorrow, he's on his own and I don't know how the FBI is going to go with him. Check that, let's not mention the FBI. That'd get folks all riled up. I can see Hank's headline on Thursday now – *MP Shoot Out!! Rankin County FBI Manhunt.* We don't want that." Hank was the editor of *The Rankin County Courier* and a long-time friend.

Axel continued, "With the weather and the mountains, it will be rough enough. Probably ten, fifteen degrees, could be three feet of new snow, and fifty miles or so of scooting around. Probably a long hard day. I'd like you two to find the biggest, baddest machines you can with guys that can take 'em apart and put 'em together again. There are no tow trucks out there. Probably not the kind of guys who are looking to help out law enforcement on a regular basis, but somebody who's got the equipment and can use the money. Know what I mean?"

Ange answered, "Sure, there's folks in town who can handle themselves in the woods. Have good snow machines. Not pretty-boys, but they can get the job done."

"Find the two best. Need to round them up this afternoon. Can you do that?"

Jennie Potts looked over at Ange, and said, "Right. Can do."

Ange fluttered her eyelashes and twisted her head at Potts' response, then looked to the floor. Then she slowly raised her head and, as though already working on a list, said, "Sure, we know people. But, I'd have to think a bit. I don't run in those circles. Could take a few calls."

Axel stood, effectively adjourning the meeting, and said, "You're ahead of me. Do the best you can." He looked at Potts and then at Ange. "Now, I'm going to the clinic. Ange, first can you call Ben Ackermann. You know him right? A west side rancher. And ask him to pick up Arlyn's dog at Finerty's. Dog's name is Zak. We'll get Arlyn's truck later. Tell him about the fight and that Arlyn'll be over later in the week. We got a lot going on."

Jennie stood and headed for the door. Ange stayed seated and said, "Is Arlyn all right?"

Jennie stopped at the door to hear the answer.

Axel put on his coat and over that a long rubberized slicker. "Well, I'll know more in a while. Can't be too bad off, he walked to the EMT van. Say, who's the guy that worked on our old snow machines. Local kid. What's his name? Taylor something?"

Angie replied, "You mean Tyler White? Runs a small engine shop out of his garage. Friend of my son, Ryan. He's a whiz with motors and knows all the trails. He'd be a good guy to ask. I think he spends a lot of time in the backcountry. He runs a snowcat on the mountain for a regular paycheck."

"Yeah, that's him. One good prospect, no?" He didn't wait for an answer. "Probably doesn't have the newest equipment. But put him on the top of the list. Jennie, can you go talk to him now, after you set up Dressler?"

"Yes, sir."

"Wednesday, we need at least two extra machines that are reliable. Don't even ask about tomorrow. We're going Wednesday." As he zipped up his slicker he continued, "And I'll bet the ski mountain's got a machine they could loan us for the day. Maybe a driver? And they have jumbo snowcats for grooming, no? I'll try and get one from the mountain and get somebody to drive it up to Crystal Lake. They're pretty big. Hold three or four people, no? Make a good field headquarters. Up at the lake."

"I can check it out," Ange offered.

"Well, maybe I should talk to management. Make it an official request. Yeah, I'll do it. I want you, Ange, to be our information hub. Who's in, who's out for Wednesday. Whether we get a snowcat or not, we will also need a CED receiver, amplifier and mini-switchboard. Everybody needs a receiver. We have to be able to communicate out there. I remember a demonstration of something like that back when they set up the CED – a closed network that could operate in remote areas. That's what we got here, no?"

"CED? Ok, but I might need a little time," Ange answered.

"Well, you work on that? And keep track of who's on first, and Jennie, you're going to talk to Dressler and Tyler, right? I'll call up to the ski hill."

Jennie said, "You bet, boss."

Down the hall the phone on Ange's desk rang and she left Axel's office to answer it. Jennie went back to her desk.

Chapter 25.

Ange was off the phone by the time Axel walked up to her desk on his way out. He was thinking about how harsh the wintery conditions would be on Wednesday. He started talking while looking out the window. "Boy, it's going to be tough. Cold. Two, three feet of new snow. We can't get broken down thirty miles out. We'll need good strong machines. Helmets, extra gas." He turned towards Ange and said, "You can start your list with Jennie Potts and me on the two county machines. Ours are singles. Should we meet here or up at the barricade?"

"Better here, we can round up extra supplies and make calls at the last minute."

"Good idea. What say, six-thirty?"

"That would be good, but dawn's not until seven lately."

"OK, let's say meet at six-thirty, launch at seven? No need to go crazy with this. Tell Jennie we'll need everything we've got for winter survival."

"Got it, boss." Then she pointed to the desk telephone.

"What's that? Oh, I guess we'd better call everybody ... Marsh, Jones and Thorsten and tell them about our change. Thorsten says he's driving down this afternoon, but I doubt it. Anyway, he'll have to decide what he wants to do. I'll check back later." He put on his hat, turned to the door and said, "Right now, I'm gone. Arlyn should be at the clinic in two minutes. Can't say I can help him out, but I want to be there."

"You bet."

In the thirty minutes he had been inside the County Building the storm had gotten worse. Standing outside the office door, Axel could not see the county garages at all. His nearby SUV had been pelted with a new inch of snow. The snow whipped around in circles as it buffeted off the buildings and stung his face. A roll of thunder stopped him in his tracks. *What the hell?*

His cell phone rang with Anne's ringtone. He didn't answer it. He wanted to get out of the weather and into the relative tranquility of his vehicle. And he knew he couldn't get his gloves off and dig through the layers to get to the phone in the front pocket of his jeans before the call went to voicemail. He cleared the windows, climbed into his SUV, started the engine, and turned on the wipers. Then he took off his gloves and called Anne.

She started right in. "Arlyn's coming in. Big scalp cut."

"Yeah, I heard. I'm on my way over now. What do the EMTs have to say?"

"Stable. Low fluids, but his pressure's rising. Could have been worse. We can handle it. Got the OR set up for him. Take an hour of sewing. We'll put him under just to simplify things. Keep him still. Not too heavy. Take only another hour or two to clear out of his system."

"Sounds good. I want to see him before he goes under."

"OK, then you better get your fine self over here right quick. And Carrie Baxter wants to talk to you."

"Good timing."

As he drove slowly through the unplowed snow on Route 34, Axel looked to the west in vain for the incoming EMT van. *Not yet.* He parked in front of the clinic's main entrance and left the engine running. He turned the vehicle's heat register to maximum with the fan pushing the hot air to the windshield and kept the wipers going. He left the vehicle to enter the clinic.

With his head down he shuffled through the blizzard. Between the double doors he raised his head and was surprised to see Anne in the lobby. She'd never come out to greet him before. He swallowed hard, expecting bad news. Her eyes were wild and wet. *Had she been crying, melted snow, what?* She held out both hands to hold his.

He looked at her knowing something was wrong, "Honey, what's up?"

"They're off the road, a mile out. Just this side of the Cenex station."

Axel spun around, back towards the doors. "I'm going to bring him in. Emergency entrance."

"Axel. It'll only take ten minutes to get a tow truck out there. He's stable. He can handle it."

Axel crashed into the outer pair of automatic doors – they didn't open fast enough for him. On his way out he yelled over his shoulder, "He'll be here sooner than that."

Axel quick-marched through the deep snow and opened the rear door of his SUV. He flipped the back seats down and tossed his equipment up to the front passenger seat. He said out loud to no one, "Ten minutes, my ass."

Once he had cleared the back of the vehicle, he clambered into the driver's seat, flipped on all the lights and sirens and put the transmission in four wheel drive – low. He couldn't go over twenty, but he'd have better traction.

The van was only a few feet off the road but nose-down in the culvert where the snow was halfway up the side of its doors. One of the rear doors was open and the engine was running.

Axel thought to himself that with the engine exhaust going into the van, Arlyn was likely to get asphyxiated before he bled to death.

Axel planned his approach. He'd have to close both lanes of Route 34 and he'd back up to the van – facing west. Once loaded up he would have to drive west, away from the clinic, loop through the Cenex station and then back east to the clinic. He called Ange. "Arlyn's EMT van is in the ditch – this side of Cenex. Need a deputy out on 34 to block eastbound traffic. Goin' to transfer Arlyn to my vehicle. Got someone close?"

"Ollie's here. Jennie's out talking to Tyler. Everybody else is out of town, north in the canyon or east."

"Send Ollie, now. I'm going to go past them and then back up to the edge of the road facing oncoming traffic, so he'd better get here fast."

The driver of the EMT van had turned off the engine, pushed his door halfway open against the deep snow and slipped through the narrow opening. As Axel drove by he saw that the driver was out of the vehicle, high stepping to the rear. Once there, he pulled its doors fully open, as if he knew Axel's plan. In his rearview mirror Axel saw Arlyn, his head wrapped in a white towel. Arlyn was off the collapsed gurney and sitting on the floor, with a second attendant holding up an IV bag with a tube running to Arlyn's arm. Axel would have two passengers.

Axel started to back up. The first EMT in his white shirtsleeves waved Axel back, up to the edge of the unplowed road. Axel felt one rear wheel dip off the pavement. *Far enough.* He set the emergency brake. The crunch of the tires on the new snow vibrated the whole vehicle. His SUV and the ambulance were still five feet apart.

In his rearview mirror Axel saw Arlyn and the second EMT work their way out the back of the ambulance to stand in the knee deep snow. With Arlyn between the two EMTs, the trio pushed their way through the deep snow.

Dark blood covered the front of Arlyn's shirt like a large bib and there was a streak of bright fresh blood across the headdress. Arlyn caught Axel's eye and slowly bobbed his head as though to say *I'm doing OK*, but he said nothing.

Just as Arlyn and his IV attendant flopped into the back of Axel's SUV, Ollie, with all lights flashing, came to a stop in the westbound lane. There he got out and sorted the accumulated traffic to give Axel a clear path to the west.

With the two passengers aboard, Axel yelled, "All in?"

"Ready", responded the EMT.

"Here we go," Axel said as he eased off the emergency brake and again set the transmission in four-wheel drive - low. He applied as little gas as he could to get the SUV moving forward without slipping. It slowly clawed up the incline and onto the road heading west. Axel drove slowly, hunched over the steering wheel, weaving between the stopped vehicles on either side of the narrow, unplowed road. He had precious cargo.

Finally, Arlyn spoke. "Sheriff, you're goin' the wrong way. Clinic's behind us. And, if you don't mind, I'd rather have Anne do the stitching."

"Hell, I thought you were dying."

"You're not the only one. Not too many guys have been scalped in Montana and live to tell about it."

"Anne's ready for you. After all this, you'd better cooperate."

"What makes you think I wouldn't?"

Axel was pleased to hear his brother in such good spirits. Perhaps, in spite of all the blood loss, he was not hurt that badly.

"'Cause I've known you all my life. And *I* came out all the way out here to rescue your sorry ass, that's why. You've been particularly uncooperative with me since you were twelve."

"What are you saying? I owe you something? Forget about it. I taught you how to walk. Remember? Hell, I can crawl to the clinic from here. I'm just doing this for Mickey, my new hero. A bona fide first-responder. Without messed up folks like me he'd have to go work for his dad on the ranch up on the Highline. One thing though, you had better give Mickey a ride back to his ambulance. And help him and Roy get their van out of this ditch."

Axel took a peek at Mickey in his rear view mirror. "Mickey looks to be a very competent young man who can fend for himself. Pretty resourceful guy, I'll bet. But they'll need a tow truck to pull that van out. And the next time the plows come by there's going to be a new four-foot wall of snow to get through. Mick, call George Rampart. Tell him I said to put you at the top of his list."

Mickey responded, "Great."

"Spike OK?" Arlyn interrupted.

"Off to Billings. Anne might have the latest."

As Axel approached the clinic's side transport door three staffers came out to assist in the delivery.

"Here's your welcoming party. Now you behave yourself."

"Yes, captain."

"I'll check in with you later."

The clinic staff delicately loaded Arlyn onto their gurney and wheeled him inside. Axel stayed in his SUV. After Arlyn was inside Anne appeared at the door and waved Axel to come into the building.

Axel thanked Mickey, shook his hand and told him that if Rampart's tow truck couldn't pick him up, Axel would get a deputy to give him a ride.

Chapter 26.

Axel parked in front of the clinic and sat for a moment thinking about Arlyn and their ups and downs over the years. He turned his head towards the building and saw Anne waiting for him. He grabbed his hat and jumped out of the SUV. As he passed through the first set of doors, Anne blurted out, "Arlyn's going to be OK. It's just that the skin's peeled back."

"Great, nothing internal?"

"No. It was a good clean peel. I can just put the skin back in place and sew it up. The EMTs did a good job, but I'd better get to it. The sooner, the better. And Carrie Baxter's ready for you. She called for me and asked me to tell you that."

"Did her dad show up? She told me she was going to get a lawyer."

"No, she's had no visitors. She's up on the second floor now. Back corner. I think she just figured out what a deep hole she dug for herself this morning."

Axel was relieved. He was certain that Carrie could help him find Wellington.

"Can't fault her for that. Anything new on Spike?"

"No, other than that he arrived safely. I'll have someone call Billings."

"Thanks, Hon." He squeezed her hand. "Take care of Arlyn, he's the only brother I got. He was a wise-ass coming in, so he can't be in too bad a shape."

"I'll assign the best seamstress we've got. We'll even use the clean bandages and sharp needles."

"Why is everybody so clever all of a sudden? I thought I married a serious person." With a playful smirk on his face, he swung out his hand as though to swat her on the rear. She jumped out of the way and he pulled his hand back. They once again smiled as they drifted off in separate directions.

Axel took the back staircase to the second floor and, as he walked down the hall, tipped his hat in acknowledgement to Paul Ridge stationed outside the door to Carrie Baxter's room.

"Anything new, sport?"

"No, sir. Still here."

"Well, we're stretched pretty thin. But, let's do this together. She may be more relaxed with you. An' you might have some good questions." He slowed down and stopped outside the room. "Hey, you familiar with the hiking trails 'tween here and the Park?"

"Somewhat, spent a coupla summers with Montana Outdoors Adventures, guiding city kids on hikes into the mountains."

"Good, got a snowmobile?"

"No, but I could probably get one, my uncle's. Polaris 600. Maybe two years old. What's going on?"

"Hmm, we'll talk later. OK? Could use you Wednesday in the mountains. See if you can line up that machine, OK?"

"I'll give him a call."

"Good." Axel nodded towards Carrie Baxter's door. "Bring your notepad. We may want to record some questions and answers."

Axel opened the door and the two men entered. Carrie was sitting up in bed and looked up from her magazine. She no longer had an IV in her arm and her leg was no longer elevated. She had her leg outside the thin blanket. Her color had returned, her hair was rearranged, and she looked ready for discharge. The bandage on her leg was smaller than Axel had expected. She appeared to be a different person than the damaged, fearful child he had talked to early this morning.

As he entered, Axel held up his hands – palms forward. "Carrie, before you say anything, I need to remind you that anything you tell us can and will be held against you in your criminal proceeding. You remember what I said earlier."

"You bet."

"This here's Deputy Paul Ridge. You two know each other?"

She answered first. "Yeah, I thought that was him. Grant's a small town. Think that Paul's sister was a year ahead of me at school."

"Yep," Ridge said.

"Well, we'll have plenty of time to talk about the shooting. Lucky for you, Spike Reynolds flew out to Billings General before this storm rolled in. You coulda killed him, ya know." He shook his head.

She said nothing, but bowed her head.

Axel continued, "My main concern, right now, is Riley Wellington and where he might be headed. Seems he's a popular guy with Montana law enforcement. A wanted man. Missed a court date last week in Billings. Federal. Some kind of stock fraud. We have the FBI coming down. And I think he's the guy who caused Saturday's wreck in the canyon. And, if he did, he caused the death of the driver. Heard about that?"

"Yeah, our ranch is just this side of the canyon. I didn't know the driver died."

"This morning. I just heard. Wednesday morning we're goin' to be out looking for Wellington, 'tween here and the Park. We tracked him past the barricade out to Crystal Lake. Do you have any idea where he's going?"

"No, he never told me."

"What did he tell you about where the two of you were headed? Had you heard about this trip before, or did it just come up overnight?"

"Riley's been coming down since the summer and going into the mountains to prepare a place to stay. Chopped wood, canned goods, pots, pans – like he was fixing up a cabin for the winter."

"Know where he was taking the stuff?"

"No, just that he had some kinda building in the mountains. He said that it was ready – firewood and food. Enough so we could stay for weeks."

"How many weeks?'

"At least until the snow melted and we could hike out to get an old truck in Princeton."

"A truck in Princeton? His truck?"

"No, well yes, I guess it's his now. He made a deal."

"A deal?"

"He made like a deal with Tyler White, a guy here in town." She looked at Paul for confirmation. He nodded his head, but said nothing. She continued, "Traded his new pickup for a snow machine and some old battered-up truck. Tyler took the old truck up to Princeton. Before The Flyover was closed for the winter. Don't know anything else about the truck, but Riley said Tyler had rebuilt the snow machine. Riley called it a bulldog. He said it had a special belt for heavy snow."

On hearing the name *Tyler White* Axel tried to keep a straight face. Only an hour ago he'd assigned Jennie Potts to talk to White.

But Axel thought maybe he could get more information out of Carrie Baxter, so he pretended he'd never heard of Mister White.

"Tyler White, is he in town now?"

"He was this morning. We left his house about five-thirty."

"Where's he live?"

"Down near the old school."

"Did White ever go with Riley on these supply runs? You ever go with him?"

"No. Neither of us went. Riley always went alone. Keep the location secret."

"Did you ever know of anybody to go with him? Did anybody ever meet him there?"

She shook her head and said, "No, it was like a big secret – he didn't want anybody to know. Never talked about it."

"Did he hike it in? Use an ATV?"

"I think he would load up an ATV, drive it in as far as he could, unload the ATV and then haul the stuff in from there, maybe two or three trips back and forth. Mostly he would go one day, stay overnight and come back the next and then go back to Billings. I'd usually see him coming and going. Sometimes he'd stay out two nights."

"OK, so let's back up with how it is that you know him, in the first place, and what you think he might be up to."

She put away her magazine. Then staring straight ahead she said that she first met Wellington at a party last June – at Jenkins' Covered Wagon Ranch, one of the dude ranches on the Yellowstone River east of Livingston.

"Wait, I thought you said you met him in Bozeman?"

"That's where I really got to know him. I first met him at the party at Jenkins'."

"Whose party was it?"

"Well, Bud Estes and some other guys from Billings."

"Who would they be?"

"I really don't know them. I came with Sue Frederickson. She's from Grant." She looked at Paul, who again nodded his head, acknowledging that he knew Frederickson. He wrote a note on his pad.

"And you met Wellington there?"

"Actually it was after the party. Sue met him during the party and asked him to give us a ride home. He gave us a ride back to Grant from Jenkins' and then he went home to Billings."

"That's pretty far out of his way."

"Well, I think Bud asked him to give us a ride. We were pretty wasted and Bud didn't want us staying overnight. So when Sue asked, he readily agreed."

"So, how many times did you see Wellington since then?"

"About six or seven. He came over to Bozeman a coupla times this fall."

"You're not in school now, right?"

"Yeah, staying with my parents."

"How about Frederickson? She see him?"

"I don't think so. She's in Bozeman."

Paul Ridge made another note in his book.

"You have White's address?" Axel asked.

"No, I don't know the number. He's down on Bryce Street on the corner, 'cross from the old school. Has a big garage – a shop in his garage."

"You know why Wellington was taking this trip?"

"No, told me he was in a hurry, that's all."

"Why were you going?"

"Get out of town, I guess. Like I dropped out of school and didn't have a job. Living on the ranch was boring. I talked him into taking me last night. Bad idea, huh?"

"Appears that way to me. So, Riley Wellington drives down from Billings, stays with Tyler White and takes off this morning for the mountains? You both left White's this morning. And went straight to the MP?"

"Yep."

"Wellington know anybody else in town?"

"No."

Axel looked over at Paul Ridge, silently asking if he had any questions for Carrie. Ridge said, "He left you at the clinic, right? Which way did he go afterwards?"

"We were almost down to South Street before he turned around and dumped me at the clinic. I am sure he went back down Broadway headed for the barrier and up The Flyover."

Axel looked back at Ridge and Carrie and said, "Well, that's all we've got for now. We've got to check you out here and transfer you to the County Building as soon as we can."

"Yeah, right," she said with a note of sadness. "Yeah."

After leaving the room Axel asked Paul what he knew about Tyler White.

"Well, I don't know him very well, but it's a small town – can't avoid anybody. He graduated high school the same year I did. Sixty-two in our class. Grew up with him. Not a bad guy, sort of a townie, but not a troublemaker. Now, I see him around a lot. Driving 'round town. Not a drinker or a doper or anything. I think he works pretty regular on the ski mountain, grooming." He looked out the window – a solid white picture with the wind pushing the snow left to right. "In the summer he picks up work with ranchers, cutting hay, repairing mechanical stuff. I've heard that if you have a small engine problem – lawnmower, bush hog, chainsaw, power washer, whatever – he's your man. Seems he's always rebuilding somebody's old car. The local story goes that his dad died a while ago. Mom got remarried and left town. Gave him the house, I guess. He's kinda around a lot. Owns an old Ford, sunbaked black. Could be the one he traded with Wellington. I really don't talk to him that much, but it's a small town and everybody knows everybody's business."

Axel, thinking of *Crestfallen*, replied, "Tell me about it. *Often wrong, but never in doubt.* Think we'll be talking to Mr. White right quick. He was already at the top of our list of folks to work with the FBI."

"Why's the FBI involved?"

"It's a long story. But for now, I need you to stay here. Check with your uncle. We can probably get him a couple hundred bucks from the feds."

"Really?"

"Paul, we're gonna go into the mountains after Wellington. You can count on a day with the FBI Wednesday. Look good on your resume. Let Ange know how it works out. Call her on your cell. Not CED."

Back in his SUV Axel called Ange to tell her about another possible snowmobile and ask if Tyler White was on the team. Ange reported that White told Jennie Potts that he couldn't go, claiming the blizzard would have him grooming the ski mountain for days.

Axel responded, "I think we need to talk to that boy. Hope she did better with Dressler?"

"I think she's set it for tomorrow morning. I didn't get any particulars."

"Well, I'll check with her. And I haven't really talked to Ollie today. Can you call him about working a double shift? He could check out now, work tonight and then take tomorrow off. Have him call me on the cell if he has questions, or if anything unexpected came up with the state's forensic guy. One more thing, we gotta have somebody relieve Ridge and sit with Carrie Baxter until we can jail her. She's ready. At this point, we need every deputy. Gotta have everybody available, what with this storm and the snowmobile-run Wednesday. I'll talk to Anne about Carrie Baxter checking out." Axel smiled to himself knowing Anne would try to hold Carrie at the clinic for as long as she could.

"Ange, can you do me a favor? I am going to White's house now, but I need to pick up that form from Webber's office upstairs. Michele should have it ready. Could you go get it?"

"Sure boss, I'll call her now."

Chapter 27.

Axel parked four blocks from Tyler White's house. He left his pistol belt and CED phone in the vehicle. He did not want to be recognized. Too many visits by law enforcement vehicles and the neighbors would start talking. Further, he would rather Marsh not know about this meeting. White was Axel's asset and he wasn't sharing. He pushed his cell phone into the front pocket on his tight jeans and placed his broad-brimmed hat upside down on his slicker in the back of the SUV. He wore his Carhart waistcoat and gloves. A blue woolen stocking cap over his ears completed his outfit.

He walked hunched over into the wind-driven snow. Axel felt that White could make a difference and he laughed at himself for being so pleased that Marsh didn't know a thing about him. While he tingled with anticipation, he told himself to be cautious. He really needed to enlist Tyler White and didn't want to start off on the wrong foot.

From a block away Axel spotted what he figured was Wellington's white, late-model Silverado pickup. It was inside an oversized garage that had one of its overhead doors open to the weather. A man was clearing the walk, conscientiously pushing the snow off the pavement with a walk-behind motorized plow. He was small, just over five-and-a-half feet tall and, Axel figured, even with his winter raiment he couldn't have weighed over one hundred and forty pounds. He wore a Navy pea coat, a wool hunter's cap with the earflaps down and had a short, well-trimmed beard. Axel figured that this fellow, even with his beard, could pass for a high school senior.

Tyler's small stature made Axel think of Ulysses S. Grant, the successful Civil War general for whom the town was named. He wondered if Tyler rode horses – Grant was an expert horseman.

As he approached Axel noted that the weather was changing, the temperature had risen, the wind had moderated, and distinct, gray clouds had replaced the solid black thunderheads of the morning. The snowfall continued but had lost its ferocity. Axel was afraid that the storm, while less intense, had stalled over Grant and the east slope of the Harlans and the snow would just keep piling up.

Over the rumble of the plow's engine Axel identified himself to White and asked if they could go inside. White nodded agreement and motored the plow back to the garage.

Axel took a close look at the Silverado and said, "Nice truck."

Tyler White made no reply, but closed up the garage and pointed the way down the plowed sidewalk around to the front door. As the men stomped the snow off their boots in the front entrance hall, Tyler offered coffee. Axel declined.

The house was minimalist: a neat, one-story frame with hardwood floors. Axel figured it was built in the late forties or early fifties long before the coalmine closed down. It had been rehabbed recently and was decorated with a few well-placed pictures. As they walked back to the kitchen, Axel glanced at several framed prints by Remington and a Charlie Russell charcoal, maybe an original. In the corner of the dining room, on its own pedestal, was a small bronze of a bucking horse. Certainly not what Axel expected of a twenty-five year old, bachelor mechanic.

White again refused to join Wednesday's effort to locate Riley Wellington. He was working tonight and tomorrow night, he said, starting at five o'clock each afternoon. Because of the snow he said he would probably work a twelve-hour shift both days. And he wouldn't lend anyone one of his snowmobiles. "They're my babies, 'n somebody else would just screw 'em up and get themselves stranded in the outback. They're not going without me. And I'm not going."

Axel nodded, thinking of an effective reply.

They sat at the kitchen table. Axel couldn't get over how clean and meticulously maintained the house was. It looked as though some real estate agent had prepared it for a showing to prospective buyers. Tyler obviously took great pride in his home. Perhaps this was something Axel could use to his advantage. White, like Carrie Baxter, had a lot to lose.

Axel started slowly and deliberately. He had to make certain Tyler understood that he was very close to several serious crimes and needed to distance himself from them.

After a long, quiet moment Axel said softly, "Tyler, I understand you have a job, and they will want you up at the mountain. All this new snow. But, you *need* to be with me first thing Wednesday morning. Let me tell you why."

Axel laid out what he knew of Riley Wellington, Carrie Baxter, Wellington's involvement with the FBI, the MP shooting, the semi accident, the driver's death, and the wreck on South Street that Wellington caused while leaving town. He also explained that any reasonable person would suspect that Tyler knew something of Wellington's plans. He said that the lopsided swap of an old pickup and a re-built snowmobile for a full-dress, late model Silverado might be sufficient for one to assume that the Silverado's new owner was involved in planning Wellington's escape. And the recipient of the bargain might also know the reasons behind it. He also suggested that the Silverado, now parked in Tyler's garage, might itself be evidence in charges brought against its previous owner. He wondered out loud why any seller would deliver the swapped-out, old pickup to Princeton in September, months before he would receive the Silverado. Certainly, the seller would have asked why Wellington wanted an old truck in Princeton and then planned to disappear for a few months, if not forever. Axel concluded his inquiry with a simple, "No?"

Tyler did not respond, but squirmed in his bent hickory chair as though he'd suddenly discovered he was sitting on a jagged rock.

"You never wondered what he was up to?"

Finally the small man spoke, "Sure, I wondered. Anybody would. But I saw a city guy with a lot of money who offered me a whale of a deal. And I took it. Drove over the pass with my old Ford in September, just before The Flyover closed. I knew he wasn't about to tell me his plans, so I didn't ask. Simple as that."

"Where's the truck now?"

"I parked it in a friend's garage up in Princeton. Gave him a coupla hundred dollars. He starts it up and runs it for ten minutes every day. Make sure the battery's good. I told him Wellington would come by sometime in April, early May. The truck's there now. I talked to my guy a coupla days ago."

"Wellington tell you when he would pick it up?"

"Just like I told my friend. April, early May."

"Can you give a name, phone number? We'll see if it's still there."

"Sure. Can't imagine that it isn't."

Axel stood up and walked around the tidy kitchen. As he examined the cupboards and their contents he started talking, "Rankin County's got nothing against you and I'm willing to assume you knew nothing of Wellington's federal charges and his flight from them. But, it's really hard to image that you don't know any more. Didn't have more curiosity. The FBI may have a different opinion than I do. I'm sure they have all kinds of laws against helping a fugitive escape. It would be easy for them to make some allegations, and they've already got their own lawyers lined up. Doesn't cost them anything extra. They usually go big, like accusing you of being a partner in Wellington's stock swindle. And, after they scare the hell out of you, they make some more allegations where they might actually have some evidence. The feds could even take the Silverado as evidence. And by then you've spent all your cash on lawyers. You've lost, even though you're innocent." He stopped as if to let his last statement soak in. Then with a nod at White, he continued, "But there's another route. I figure working with the feds to capture Riley Wellington would speak volumes to most law enforcement folks, the FBI included. 'Specially if we found Wellington."

"Think so?"

"Let's put it this way ..." Axel secured Tyler's attention, but continued cruising around the kitchen. He cast his eyes around the room as though appraising its contents. He stopped in front of a glass-doored cabinet that held a stack of gold-rimmed dinner plates. He slowly turned back to face Tyler, who had been watching him closely. Axel stroked his whiskered chin and said, "It would be a hell of a gamble if you refused."

Tyler slowly nodded, as though acknowledging Axel's perspective. Neither man spoke for a minute.

Then Axel proceeded as though Tyler had formally agreed. As for Tyler's work obligations, Axel said he would handle those with the manager of the ski mountain. He was already planning to call about borrowing a big, treaded snowcat to serve as a command center. He had never asked the ski mountain manager for help before, but did not think he would be turned down. And Tyler just might be the best man to run the big, awkward rig.

Axel watched Tyler relax as he processed Axel's argument. He stopped shifting in his chair and put his elbows on the table and held his head in his hands, staring at the tabletop.

Without looking up Tyler said, "I told you I never knew any of this 'til just now. Wellington was a rich guy who wanted a super snowmobile and offered me a great deal." He looked up at Axel and, as though he was making a solemn oath to a packed courtroom, he said, "That's all I ever knew." He shook his head after he stopped talking, underscoring his plea of innocence.

Respecting Tyler's assertion, Axel held back his response. After a long silence he asked, "Well, now that you know more of the story, what do you think?"

"I'm not into lawyers and allegations and stuff. And I don't want to be. I've done nothing wrong. You make it sound like I'm trapped."

"I haven't accused you of anything. But frankly, I think I've given you some good advice." Axel sat down across the small table and stared at Tyler. "And, damn it, I need your help. I am not a backwoods mountain man and I'm certainly not a snowmobiler. A little help would go a long way. I can call your boss right now."

Tyler raised his head a bit, nodded again, and looked Axel in the eyes and whispered, "OK, do it."

Axel leaned back and slid his cell phone out of his front pocket. "Would Andy Holiday be the man to talk to?", referring to the ski resort's general manager.

"Yeah, if you want a snowcat, he'd be the guy."

"Right."

Axel called Holiday from Tyler's kitchen and got full cooperation – without explaining why he needed the equipment. The hill was going to be closed tomorrow – too much snow. Tuesday was usually a slow day anyway. Tyler was not to report in this afternoon, or tomorrow, so he'd be fresh for Wednesday morning. At six a.m. Wednesday Tyler could pick up a snowcat at the grooming crew's garage. Axel figured that he could drive the eight-foot wide machine out to Crystal Lake. He would need an escort through town and somebody to open the barricade. The pieces were falling into place. Axel concluded the call with, "Thanks Andy, Tyler will be there Wednesday at six." He ended the call and turned to Tyler. "You got that, Wednesday at six? You've got a coupla good snow machines yourself, right?"

"Yeah. With an hour's work, I could have three."

"Two will be enough. Could you recruit a guy to drive the second one without having to tell him the whole story?"

"Sure, but how am I going to get the cat and snowmobile up to Crystal Lake?"

"We can certainly get somebody to drive your snowmobile up to the lake. Can't do too much damage on such a short trip. You leave the snowcat at the lake and drive your rig. Right?" Axel didn't wait for an answer. "Call Ange Clausen at my office and give her your buddy's name and tell her you're coming too. I figure you can get the two machines over to the County Building sometime tomorrow. Right? Wednesday you drive the snowcat up to Crystal Lake. It stays there. So, unless there's a change, one of my deputies can escort you up to the barricade. You can go straight to Crystal Lake and wait for us. The snowmobiles are leaving the County Building at seven. So we'll meet you before seven-thirty. Ange'll be expecting you to call this afternoon. We gotta be ready to go Wednesday morning."

As Tyler showed Axel to the door he said, "I really want to keep the Silverado."

Axel looked back at the small, young man and replied, "Then let's find Wellington."

Chapter 28.

As Axel was getting settled into his vehicle, a call came through on his personal CED line. He sat and looked at the receiver and the small flashing, amber light. It couldn't be Anne or Ange. They would call on his cell. It was either the CED dispatcher or someone who got the number from the dispatcher. *And it better not be Marsh.* He picked it up.

"Cooper here."

"You're one hard guy to get hold of." It was Thorsten.

"One of my New Year's resolutions – be unavailable. Let my people make their own decisions and learn from them. How did you get this number?"

"Come on, the federal government still has some influence, even in Rankin County. I need to talk to you."

"I should warn you, I don't do psychiatric counseling. How's it going with the chief?"

While Axel felt he was playing with the man a bit, he really did wonder what Chief Marsh was up to and the nature of the combined resources of the FBI and the Grant police team. *Were they still planning to go tomorrow? Maybe the FBI could get a helicopter up.*

Thorsten parried with, "Sheriff, I want to talk to you first. Before the chief."

"But working with him tomorrow."

"Well, it's not going to be tomorrow. That's my point. And I will work with everybody – whoever, wherever – I need to get the job done. Nothing personal. Nothing political. You two can have your own spat without any help from me. I have no dog in that fight."

"Well, what do you mean it's not going to be tomorrow?'

"We turned back just after I called you earlier. That canyon road was just too much. Two feet of unplowed snow over icy hard–pack. Even the four-wheel drive on the Tahoe couldn't handle it. We'd end up in the river, for sure. Should make it tomorrow. Go out Wednesday morning. Maybe have a helicopter."

"Still working with Marsh, though."

"Yeah, but I want to meet you before I see him. I'm going be at the Matterhorn. Say eleven o'clock. Can I meet you in the restaurant tomorrow morning?"

"I can't do that. Mr. Thorsten, you may know Mr. Wellington, but you don't know the City of Grant or Rankin County. That check-in clerk at the Matterhorn is going to call her three closest relatives and four besties to tell them the FBI is in town. Your black Tahoe and federal tags will probably give you away before you even park it. And that Minneapolis haircut - it might as well be an illuminated halo marking you as an angel come to help us poor, backward rural peasants." Axel had never laid eyes on Thorsten, but had a well-developed model of a mid-western FBI agent. "And they serve booze at the restaurant. Even in the morning. A full bar. And I can't walk into any bar at any time in central Montana, but that half a hundred people will be telling me about it the next day. '*Gee, I didn't know you drank. How many did you knock back at lunch, Sheriff?*' So I'm not going there. Just what is it you're dying to know? I think we got you some snowmobiles if you need them. We are not going out tomorrow either. This storm may still be here tomorrow. Wednesday's plan is to be at the County Building about six-thirty, leave at seven. We'll have rides and drivers for you. Talk about multi-jurisdictional cooperation. But, I want you to understand that I'm not going with Marsh. You're going with him, so I really don't care when you go."

"Well, it looks like I need you for transportation, right? If Marsh wants to go out tomorrow, I'm not there. So, I'm going when you're going. I thought that you'd help us find this guy. You're messing with me, right?"

"All I'm saying is that these snowmobiles we found for you are leaving when I leave and not before. So, basically, your ride is leaving Wednesday, and I hope that works for you. Hell, you're not going to be here until tomorrow, right? So, what are we talking about? You coordinate with Marsh. You do that. I'll check the weather between now and then, and then we can plan. OK? And if there are any surprises, call me back in a couple of hours. You've got the number."

"Right."

Axel shook his head and said out loud to himself, "What the hell was that about?"

Chapter 29.

After Axel pulled into the clinic parking lot, he called back to the office to get an update on the weather. *No change.* He noted the wind had died but the snowfall continued as though it was on a mission to envelop the whole town under a pristine white blanket.

He was feeling better about the search for Wellington. Waiting a day wouldn't hurt them, as Wellington couldn't get very far in this snowstorm, if he wasn't at his destination already. The Sheriff's Department would have a competent team including Tyler White, who may have some insights into Wellington's hideout. They had rugged equipment, and maybe the wind-blown mountain snow would not be so deep. Regardless, the weight of the day was getting heavier. As he finished his second banana sitting in the parking lot, he tried to count the times he had been to the clinic today. *Was this the third or was it the fourth? Maybe only three.* He put his cellphone on airplane mode, stuffed it in his pocket, and clambered out of the SUV.

The receptionist directed him to Arlyn's room – down the corridor, third door on the right. In the room there was a pile of Arlyn's well-worn, bloody clothes in a plastic bag on the chair, but no Arlyn. Axel trotted back to the receptionist. "He's not there," he said apprehensively.

"Well?" the receptionist said. By her tone Axel could tell she was not concerned. "He's around somewhere. He was up and walked by here a while ago. Frankly, he surprised me. Can't have gone too far." She flipped her gaze to the front doors and the piles of snow on either side of the walkway and continued, "He certainly did not leave the building."

Axel wasn't so sure. "I'm gonna look around." He turned and quickly moved down the hall, checking on every room. Then he went up the back stairs.

Arlyn was on the second floor. He had pulled up a chair in the hall and was talking with Deputy Paul Ridge. He had a bright white bandage around his head, an IV in his arm and a four-wheeled trolley to suspend the bag of fluid. He wore a hospital gown and sat with his knees spread and his underwear revealed.

At the top of the stairs Axel was winded, but blurted out, "Arlyn ... damn it, you are definitely flunking Hospital 101. You can't be walking around ... Christ, how much blood did you lose? How many stitches? Has Anne seen you out here?"

"Ax, slow down or you'll be the one needing medical care." Careful of the IV line in his left arm, Arlyn put his palms out in front of his chest and said, "Look, I'm doing fine. Just catching up on the news of the day with my new friend Paul here." He sat down again. "Look. I'm sitting down. Go get yourself a chair. Sit down, so you don't fall down. You've heard that before."

Axel circled around the IV trolley and squeezed Arlyn's shoulder. "Damn you, Arlyn. You're such a pain in the ass."

Arlyn replied, "Thanks, but remember, it's your ass. You don't have to be riled up. Anne did a spectacular job. Fifty-seven stitches an' I'm feeling no pain. No pain. But that operating room is kinda creepy. All those electrodes and computer screens. Don't want to go *there* again. Paul told me about the shootings at the MP. Guess I'm not today's only casualty."

"Busy day."

Axel flipped his thumb towards the door to Carrie Baxter's room and asked Ridge, "She tell ya anything worth repeating?"

Arlyn jumped in and answered, "Your law officer here won't let me near her. I know I could squeeze it out of her."

Ridge shook his head, *no.*

Axel stood right in front of Arlyn. "You don't know the half of it." Then Axel turned to his deputy, and said, "Paul, how'd you do with your uncle?"

"Good to go. He's got two good sleds – singles. Six hundreds. They can handle deep snow and a steep grade. Pleased to help. I got a driver for the second one, Lennie Walters. Good guy. But, my uncle said he would drive if you want him."

"You guys have done this kind of stuff before, right? You heard we're going Wednesday, not tomorrow? I don't think anybody's going anywhere between now and then."

"Oh, yeah. Ange called. And sure, I spent a lotta time on the snow in the Harlans. Had a '95 Yamaha that kept losing its tred. Lotta mechanical work out in the woods. At night."

"Well, sounds like experience to me. Frankly, I'd rather have you young guys driving, no offense to your uncle. We'll take Lennie on your recommendation. The ski mountain is lending us a snowcat. Shouldn't take any more than twenty, twenty-five minutes to get to the lake. Tyler White is on board."

Ridge responded, "Good."

"Ange's got somebody coming out to relieve you."

Axel turned to his brother and said, "Arlyn, can I carry you and that IV rig back down to your room? Those painkillers are going to wear off. Then you are going to have real problem."

"What, *me* be a problem. Has that ever happened?"

"Not since last Wednesday, as I remember it."

"Wednesday, I can't remember anything special about last Wednesday."

"Seems that's the problem. I'll see you to your room. Right?" Then he raised his voice, and repeated, "Your room, remember, downstairs."

"Sure, whatever."

Chapter 30.

Axel delivered Aryln to his room. Arlyn positioned the IV trolley next to the bed and climbed in.

"Pretty nice. Late afternoon nap," Arlyn said as he pulled his gown around his knees to slide in under the heavily starched sheets.

"Did Anne want you to stay overnight?"

"Yep, considering the weather and all, I think I'll just stay here where it's cozy and warm. I'll face reality tomorrow. Hey, what about Norris?"

"Cold and stiff. The EMTs wanted nothing to do with him. Barkeep called a mortuary in Billings."

"Holy crap. Just gone. Gone."

"And I better tell you now, Chief Marsh is looking to arrest you. Manslaughter."

"Fuck, you kidding me? Norris started it. I wasn't like I knocked him down and then pummeled him. Hell, I hit him once, he fell over and hit his head. Come on, mister law enforcement, this isn't right."

"We can't stop him from arresting you, but I am getting papers to have you released to my custody, so you won't have to spend much time in jail. I talked to Harry Webber. I don't think this will ever see the light of day, but Marsh can arrest you."

Arlyn sat up in bed and tilted hid head "Hey Ax, is this a part of Marsh's election campaign? New headline, *Another Cooper Killing! Three in Two Years.* That may turn peoples' heads and sell papers, but it's bullshit if you ask me."

"I think you nailed it. Never heard of anybody in a bar fight being brought up on charges."

"Hey, what happened to Zak?

"He's OK. Ben Ackermann is gonna pick him up at Finerty's. Probably has him already."

"Ben will spoil him I'm sure. Zak's probably happier than ever."

"Now, your truck is probably under three feet of snow, out at Finerty's."

Arlyn put his hand up to his bandage and, as he slipped back into the folds of the pillow, said, "The least of my worries."

"Take your nap. I'll check on you later." As he left the room Axel pulled out his cell phone.

He had a long voicemail message from Frank Dressler, the bartender at Finerty's. Ange had given Dressler the number. He reported that Dickerson and some of Norris's ranch hands had just left the bar, and "I'm afraid they're looking for Arlyn. They left here about a quarter past five. Two pickups. I've already called Marsh to let him know. He said he was sending out a couple of squad cars to the clinic. Can't say much about the road conditions or whether either of them will ever make it, but they're after Arlyn. Headed east on 34."

Axel looked at his watch. It was just about five-twenty-five. He scanned the parking lot and Route 34, a blank white canvas with drifts of windblown snow in the foreground. No signs of any movement, including Marsh's city police. *They had better get here before Dickerson.*

He asked the receptionist to find Anne and have her meet him by the transport door. The snow had stopped for the moment and the wind was down, but light flakes eddied in the corners of the building, glistening in the building's outdoor lights. They added a sparkle to the flat light of early dusk. Axel went out the transport door and tromped through the big drifts to the parking lot and his SUV.

He swung the vehicle up to the curb, put it into reverse, and went up and over the curb into the deep snow. At the transport door he parked the SUV and retrieved his weapons belt and a scoped Winchester 7 mm rifle.

Anne was waiting for him when he came in the transport door. She looked at his weapons belt and massive rifle and frowned. "What now, Ax? What's going on?"

He set down his rifle, took her hand and looked into her eyes. "'Fraid we got trouble, Hon. We've got some cowboy-vigilantes coming over from Finerty's to snatch Arlyn. Norris's men. Could be here at any time."

Anne wasn't impressed. "Well, they can't be coming in here and grabbing a patient. This is a hospital. My hospital. You really think they're going to try? Try to take Arlyn out of here and then what? Kill him?"

"Never know. Jake Dickerson could just walk in here, pull a gun, and demand the release of Arlyn. What are you going do? They are coming. And we can't stop them before they get here, but they're not getting Arlyn. Period." He slapped his holstered nine-millimeter pistol.

"Sheriff, you can't hold them off yourself?"

"No, ma'am. Marsh's city cops will be coming over. Can you put this building in lock-down mode? All the doors secured?"

"They can't shut us down. With this snow we're going to have some action ... traffic accidents, heart attacks, you name it."

"Well, Honey, this is not going to take long, but it could be ugly. Drunks with guns. I gotta get Arlyn and Carrie Baxter out of here, now. They're both good to go, yes?"

"He's OK, but we'll have to pull the line. She'd be checked out if she weren't under arrest."

"Figured."

"We've got an ASP, an active-shooter-protocol, from Billings General, our overloads. I'll pull that off the computer. It probably says to lock the doors and call the police."

They quickly went up to the reception desk and Anne called Vicky to get Arlyn and Carrie Baxter ready to move. Then she moved to the computer and started typing.

Axel walked over to an electrical panel on the sidewall of the front entryway and flipped the locking switch for the double doors. Then he punched a button on his CED phone and asked for Chief Marsh.

When the static cleared Axel asked Marsh, "You coming to the clinic?"

"Two units on their way. Three guys. Going full out with SWAT gear and shotguns. They should be there any time. Where are you?"

"I'm at the clinic with Anne, Arlyn, and one of my deputies. Probably three or four patients and as many staffers. We're not ready for a siege. I'm hoping your men can head off these bad guys."

"Right. You gonna let them in?"

"Your men? Damned straight. Counting on them. More'n likely it's gonna be a demolition derby in the parking lot. It's got to be your guys."

"Never seen anything like this. The rescue squad could park a fire engine cross the entrance."

"Yeah, good idea. They may not make it out here in time. But, what the hell. Give it a go."

"Won't hurt to try."

"Go for it. I'm staying inside with firepower."

"I'll be out straightaway."

"You bet. Call if you need me." Axel punched the disconnect button on the CED transmitter.

Anne had listened to Axel's half of the conversation and asked, "So what's he doing?"

"He's sent three cops in two squad cars and a fire truck. Those juiced up cowboys could be here any minute. You've got Arlyn and Carrie Baxter. Any other patients in beds? Where's Arlyn?" he said as he looked down the corridor.

"Nobody else in beds, but I do have three people in the ER with cut fingers and chest pains."

"Well, can they stay here with you? Away from the windows. I gotta get Arlyn and Baxter out of here. Figure we can load 'em in my truck."

Anne responded, "Sure," and turned towards Arlyn's first floor room, calling for Vicky at the top of her lungs.

Axel smiled. *She understands.* He shouted over her calls for Vicky, "Anne, I'll meet you at the pad. Paul's gonna drive 'em in. Pronto."

Anne spun around and saluted. "I'm with you, Sheriff Cooper! This is outrageous. Nobody's raiding my clinic."

Axel went into one of the north-side patient rooms to see if there was any movement in the white outdoors and was surprised to see that the snow had started up again and was carried by a strong southerly wind and drifting across Route 34. *What the hell?* He ran out to his SUV.

A few minutes later, Anne had Paul Ridge and the two patients ready to load up. She helped turbaned Arlyn, without his IV trolley, into the front seat, and Ridge loaded Baxter with her bandaged leg into the back.

Axel got out of his SUV. He turned to Ridge and said, "You're driving them to the County Building. Call me if you have any trouble." He glanced at Arlyn, who looked worse than he did ten minutes ago. Axel turned back to Ridge and continued, "But don't take your eye off Arlyn. He's not going anywhere."

Arlyn raised his arms in mock-surrender.

"And if he gives you any trouble, you lock him up too."

"You bet, boss," replied the young Montanan.

At the slam of the door, Ridge put the SUV in gear and took off with his damaged, but precious cargo.

In spite of the heavy snowfall Axel stood with Anne and watched the vehicle make its way through the parking lot and out to Route 34. After a moment he heard the wail of the approaching police cars.

"Gotta go, Hon."

Axel threaded his way through the snow, walking in the tire tracks and out to the parking lot. The first police car swung off Route 34, fishtailed down the drive, and stopped two feet from the boulders on either side of the clinic's front walkway. The second car pulled up behind the first. The driver of the first car jumped out and ran up to Axel. He was Aldridge, the young cop that had pulled Axel over earlier in the day. Now he wore a combat helmet with a face shield and a suit of black Kevlar armor that, Axel thought, made him look like a cartoon character.

The young man stepped up to Axel and respectfully said, "Sheriff."

Axel looked him in the eye and said, "Mr. Aldridge, I think we've got two pickups with three or four guys coming in. Drunked up and looking for trouble. They're after my brother Arlyn, but he's already gone." He pointed back to the sloped driveway. "I think you guys can stop them out here. I'm going to be backup, inside the clinic in case they get that far. These front doors are locked." He looked out over parking lot and the four snow-covered cars.

"Can we get one vehicle near the driveway and another right here? But facing the highway. Here by the boulders? I got one unit over there." He nodded at Paul Ridge's county pickup. "Why don't you move it closer to the door and flip on the light bar. Keys should be in it. The more apparent manpower we can show, the better."

"Got it. So, how do you see this going down?"

"Good question. Two pickups. We got a bunch of pissed off cowboys. Looking for a guy they think killed their boss. But

I don't see them coming out with guns blazing. They're going to see that we're here en masse and bang – it's over. Like some general said, 'We wanna be the firstest with the mostest'. There may not even be any arrests. They start shooting, that's another story. Gotta be ready for that." He tapped the man's Kevlar chest protector.

"S'right, Sheriff. I gotta check in with the Chief." The young policeman gestured toward his vehicle.

"Glad you got here pronto. Let me know if Marsh's got new ideas." He knocked his knuckle on his CED phone sticking out of his coat pocket. "Go direct, number twenty-three."

Aldridge turned back to his vehicle and said, "Yes, sir. Here we go."

"Roger that."

Axel entered the clinic by the transport door and checked in with Anne. She had Vicky, the receptionist, two other staffers and three patients in the pharmacy in the inner core of the building. They all sat on the floor. Vicky opened the door a sliver as Axel walked by. "We're doing the tornado drill," she whispered.

Axel held the rifle out of sight. Over the heads of the front row of occupants, he called to Anne, "City cops are here. I truly don't expect much. This could last five minutes, but you never know."

"Right, Sheriff. We're staying here, 'til you come get us."

The setting sun had found a crack in the otherwise solid cloud cover. Its last rays reflected off the bottom of the clouds creating an eerie soft pink hue on the western horizon. Through a patient room window Axel spotted two pickups coming east. Slowly. Any experienced trooper would know that here were two inebriated drivers clinging to each other for protection. The first one wandered like a small plane in a headwind and repeatedly smacked the roadside snow bank, sending up a plume of dry powder. The second was under better control but followed the first by only ten feet, much too close to be able to respond to any sudden re-direction, especially on the snow-packed pavement. Indeed, as the first truck took a sharp turn into the clinic's parking lot, the second braked hard but clipped the rear bumper of the first, knocking it off course. The first slid sideways down the entry ramp, pushing up a mound of snow ahead of it.

The police cars flipped on their light bars and nudged forward, just enough to crack the icy bond between the tires and the snow. A policeman ran to the county vehicle and got its light display going as well.

The lead pickup backed up and turned to face the three law enforcement units in their full display. The second pulled up right behind it, as though it had second thoughts and hoped to hide in the shadow of the first.

After a moment, the first pickup swung slowly out into the parking lot, away from the clinic past the county vehicle. The second followed twenty feet behind. The two turned and crept forward quietly through the snow, keeping the law enforcement vehicles at a safe distance.

With no warning the second truck suddenly looped around the stationary county pickup, accelerated with jets of loose snow shooting out of its wheel wells, slid through a hard turn and dove straight towards the clinic's front entry. It sideswiped a boulder, sending up a shower of sparks before squaring up with the doors. It paused as though to catch its breath and then roared forward, into the glass doors.

Initially the first set of doors held together, absorbing the impact with a giant spider web of deep cracks through the thick glass. But after several seconds of the truck's persistent push, the doors and their frames fell to the floor in a single cacophonous flop.

Axel had scooted up towards the front of the building until he was just outside the first patient room. He set the rifle on semi-automatic and activated the scope's laser beam. He squatted and duck-walked a few feet to his left behind a small computer desk. Expecting the vigilantes' pickup to breach the second set of doors momentarily, he cradled his rifle on the top of the desk. His target line was two feet inside the second set of doors and about three feet off the ground – just the height of the engine.

The invading pickup lurched back and forth to align itself with the second set of doors and then it accelerated under full throttle. The doors initially slowed the truck to a crawl, but ultimately gave way under the truck's steady push. As it breached the doorframe and slowly moved into the building itself, Axel shot. He tattooed the hood with four holes – six inches apart. With a fifth shot Axel flattened the right front tire. Halfway through the door the pickup stopped abruptly. The passengers were thrown forward by the jarring stop and then thrown back into their seats. Axel quickly shuffled back into the patient room and once again took aim – this time at the man in the passenger seat. The scope's laser beam illuminated the truck's side window and cast a red glow over the face of the passenger, who turned towards Axel.

Other than that, no one moved. That was just fine with Axel. He wasn't interested in shooting anybody. He could wait for the city police to apprehend these guys.

Axel had been deaf to the arrival of a city fire truck and a third police car, but now they were in prominence as they swung their piercing headlights across the clinic's walls, illuminating the pickup. An old squad car cast a revolving red beacon that repeatedly scanned the reception room's far wall.

Outside the policemen quickly snared the other pickup and took its three drunken cowboys into custody, handcuffed them, and put them into the police cars.

With a shotgun in one hand Aldridge crept across the shattered glass of the entryway. He crouched behind the pick-up's tailgate and slammed the rear fender loudly with the butt of his gun. Axel caught his eye and the two nodded at each other. Axel held the laser beam on the truck's passenger.

The young cop again slapped the gun against the body of the truck.

Both front doors of the truck opened a crack. Axel watched intently as the passenger-side crack widened, ever so slowly. He felt his heart pounding in his chest. *Either it's over or we've got ourselves a gunfight.*

The situation was familiar to Axel. It was *Crestfallen* all over again. He told himself that *if a man shoots at me, I shoot back.* It was an order to himself. But he wasn't convinced. Axel knew that he wasn't going to shoot first, but he could not convince himself that he was going to return fire. Then he re-formulated his own rule-of-engagement; *the man gets the first shot, if it's close, I'm going to shoot back. If it's wild, I will hold off. If he takes a second shot, I'll return fire. He's got one free shot.*

As Axel moved to his right to steady his rifle against the doorframe, Chief Marsh, without an overcoat or body armor, squeezed past Aldridge to the side the pickup. His pearl-handled pistol was holstered, but prominent nonetheless. He slapped the rear fender of the truck with his open hand. Then he shouted, "You boys get the hell out of that truck. Hands high."

He paused. No one moved. Marsh continued, "You're leakin' gas all over the damned floor. Now git outta there! Mind if you're holding a weapon, we're gonna shoot you dead. Now move."

The passenger door opened slowly and a man silently climbed out with his hands in the air. Fingers splayed apart – no weapon. Jake Dickerson, with Axel's red laser beam illuminating his chest, elbowed the door closed behind him. Then the driver got out. Hands high. Marsh stepped back, away from the truck. He signaled Aldridge and another patrolman to move forward. They cuffed the two men and slow-walked their captives out of the building. As Marsh turned to follow them, he nodded to Axel and said, "Good shooting, Axel. You stopped em cold."

As Axel moved to the front of the battered pickup, Marsh turned back and growled, "Arlyn here? I got my warrant – manslaughter. Figured he'd still be here."

"Leave Arlyn alone. Go lock those cowboys up. You've got enough business for one night."

"So, where is Arlyn?"

"Can't say as I know for certain. Not here though, I can tell you that."

"Well, he's a wanted man. My warrant will be on the Montana Highway Patrol report running tomorrow morning. You see him, you better tell him to turn himself in. If he's doesn't show by five o'clock tomorrow, I'm calling for a statewide manhunt. You hear me? I'll have every lawman in the state looking for him. Hate to see him compound his problems by running." Marsh turned away from Axel and took two steps over the shattered glass, stopped and turned back and spit on the floor and without his eyes leaving the floor said, "But, then that would support my conviction that the Coopers think they're above Montana law."

Axel regripped his rifle and squinted his eyes in a focused scowl. He slowly bobbed his head and sternly said, "Get outta here. I've had enough of your crap today."

Marsh turned away and walked out to the parking lot.

As Marsh walked to the parking lot, Anne peeked around the corner to see the devastation of her beautiful clinic – smashed up glass doors and a disabled pickup in the reception room. Windblown snow had started to accumulate on the floor of the entrance.

Anne held her hands over her ears as she screeched. "Oh, my God. Oh my God. What happened? Oh, my God."

Axel laid his Winchester on the floor and hugged her as she sobbed hysterically. He assured her that no one was hurt. He explained the sources of the noise and damage and that Marsh and the city police had the situation under control – except for the gasoline leak that was starting to smell up the whole room.

Axel helped as best he could. But he couldn't extinguish the thought that he could have done more to protect Anne and her domain. It left him feeling like the entire scenario somehow supported Marsh's election contention that the Montanans of Rankin County didn't need Axel Cooper.

In two hours the disabled truck was removed, the front entrance was sealed off, and the floor was cleaned up. While Anne calmed herself by attending to the clinic's patients, Axel drove to the County Building. Anne stayed at the clinic throughout and left only when all the patients, carpenters and cleanup crew were finished. The night shift arrived and assured her that they could handle whatever else might need to be done. A city snowplow shoveled a path from the parking lot to the transport door.

At the County Building Carrie Baxter had settled into one of the cells and Arlyn had behaved himself. He was, in fact, sleeping in Axel's chair at his desk, holding his little, white bag of prescription drugs.

Axel reported to Ange, Ollie and Arlyn on the cowboys, policemen and Marsh at the clinic. The group's reaction was muted. No one wanted to reinforce a positive assessment of the Grant Police Department's behavior.

Ange had stayed late and taken her usual competent, comprehensive approach to the logistics for Wednesday's expedition into the wilderness. She had even prepared a summary sheet assigning drivers and passengers to the available equipment.

Further, she had secured extra snow machines, if needed, from the local electric power cooperative, her husband's employer. She had also gone grocery shopping and put in an order for special early-morning delivery from the local bakery.

Tyler White would drive the wide-track, slow-moving machine down from the ski hill before daylight, and out to Crystal Lake. Ange had contacted Clark Thorsten of the FBI in Billings to make sure he could handle one of Tyler's snowmobiles at least as far as Crystal Lake where Tyler would take over. The FBI agent had proudly proclaimed that as a native Minnesotan, he could handle any snowmobile. But, he was concerned that the roads would be clear tomorrow for the drive down from Billings. Ange assured him that no snowstorm would shut down Rankin County for two days straight.

She also reported that Hank Anderson, editor of *The Rankin County Courier*, had called three times to get a quote from Axel for Thursday's weekly edition. She told Axel, "You'd better call him, or he'll go with whatever Marsh gives him."

"Well, if Marsh tells the truth it won't be half bad. The police did a hell of a job today on short notice. Marsh talked Dickerson and his driver out of their truck. Unarmed. Impressive."

Axel called Hank and they chatted amiably for a few minutes. Hank finally asked about the raid at the clinic. Axel resisted Hank's entreaties to give him an on-the-record, minute-by-minute account of who did what and claim some of the credit for a job-well-done.

"If you talked to Marsh, you probably got the whole story. I was inside the clinic and stopped the pickup after it crashed through both set of doors. Marsh talked the guys out of the truck."

"How'd you stop the truck?"

"It wasn't me so much as four shots from an elk rifle into the engine block. And one in a front tire."

"That'd stop about most anything."

Axel was ready to end the call when Hank asked, "Do you have anything to say about the fight at Finerty's?"

Axel referred him to Frank Dressler as the most impartial witness to Norris's death and Arlyn's injury. After a thoughtful pause, Axel added, "Did Marsh tell you he's looking to arrest Arlyn, manslaughter?"

"Are you serious? No, he said nothing about that. Strange, he usually likes to crow about such things."

"He's got to know that it won't see the light of day. Webber won't even take it to court."

"I am not putting anything about that in the paper. I got enough this week. What with the MP shoot out, the Ice Box canyon crash, Carrie Baxter, the fight at Finerty's, Norris's death, the vigilante cowboys and the weather, I'll only have enough space to squeeze in a few ads."

"Right," Axel chortled knowing full well that most of the newspaper's revenue came from advertisements, rather than the retail sales. Any news would be edited to fit into the space left after all the ads were positioned in the eight-page weekly.

Axel said, "Appreciate you holding back on the warrant. We're gonna get it quashed. I gotta talk to a few folks, Webber included. Had enough crap from Marsh today."

Axel and Arlyn made it to Axel's house just before ten o'clock – a long day for both of them. Arlyn was unimpressed that Marsh had a warrant for his arrest. "Don't prove a thing, 'cept he's an asshole and we all knew that already. I can wait to turn myself in, can't I? Like twenty-fours, OK?"

"No, the warrant's live. They could serve it at any time. Stay here tomorrow. But a Grant policeman may come knocking on the door with the warrant. Marsh said he'd give you to five o'clock before he start looking for you, but I don't trust him. I am going to be talking to Webber first thing tomorrow. There's got to be a way around this."

"Well, I've been in jail before. Can't say it's a pleasure cruise. They've got to set bail. Need a judge for that, no? How long you think that would take?"

"Arlyn, you're not going to jail."

"Good", Arlyn replied and smiled. "Ax, this is not the end of the world. I can handle it. Can you?"

"We'll see."

Anne met them at the back door. While Axel got a quick cheek kiss, her response to Arlyn was more extensive; she helped him off with his coat, sat him down at the kitchen table and with professional precision examined his eyes and the head bandage. She took his pulse and declared him 'on-the-mend'. She gave him a glass of water and a small green pill, which he took without question. He declined their basic dinner of mac-and-cheese with ham and went straight to bed in the small guest bedroom.

Axel ate standing up leaning against the kitchen counter, while Anne emptied the dishwasher. Axel and Anne talked about the raid at the clinic. Her position was simple – we were lucky – those crazy, drunk cowboys didn't hurt anyone. The clinic was in the city so Marsh had jurisdiction and he and his police did their job. Axel had prevented the situation from escalating into a violent confrontation and saved his brother and Carrie Baxter from harm. He had done his duty.

But Axel was not convinced that he had done all he could.

"Ax, you just don't get it, do you? You are the best sheriff, the best *man,* this county's ever seen and you are going to win this election regardless of anything Marsh does or doesn't do. Forget that he's even in the race." She stepped close to him, put her hands on his hips and hooked her thumbs into the belt loops of his jeans. She looked into his eyes and said softly, "You, you my dear, are the best thing to hit Rankin County since *Star Wars* was at the Bijou."

He started a reply, "Don't you think ..."

She drew her hands forwards and slid her fingers down to the inside of his belt buckle. "I do think. And what I think is that I am going to have to show you just what I mean. It seems my words aren't getting through."

Axel pulled his head back. With his eyebrows raised he struck a puzzled, lopsided grin. "Honey?" he whined.

"That's right, dear one." She tugged at his belt and pulled him forward as she back-pedaled. As they shuffled towards the bedroom, she slowed down. She took one hand off his belt and ran it down the inside of his thigh as she whispered, "I think you're beginning to understand. Quick learner."

Chapter 31.

In spite of postponing the search for Wellington, Axel was up before dawn. He shaved and dressed in his official uniform of black dress boots, tan slacks, brown, open-collared shirt, brown car coat and his distinctive gray broad-brimmed hat. He was out the door before Anne or Aryln woke up. His mind was already churning. The highest order of business was to get to Webber on Arlyn's possible manslaughter charge. His hope was that even if Marsh arrested him, the county prosecutor would not take the case to court. He had routine things to sort out at the office. Certainly with this weather there would be some county road wrecks. And he needed to secure the arrangements for tomorrow's search for Wellington.

On his way out of the house he grabbed a broom to sweep off the foot of new snow that encapsulated his county SUV. There was still a light wisp of snow in the air, but it wasn't readily apparent if it was new snow or just a wind-driven rearrangement of last night's contribution. Once again, Axel beat the city plows out and slowly crept through town. Axel figured that the total snowfall since yesterday morning was close to three feet. Several open lots had drifts of more than four. He couldn't help but wonder how much had fallen on Mt. Elliott and Riley Wellington, wherever he was.

The thermometer by the back door of the County Building said twelve degrees. No chance of any snow melting today. Axel pushed open the door and startled Ollie who was seated at the front desk – Ange's station during the day shift.

189

"Boss, what are you doing here at this hour?"

"Everybody's got to be someplace. I'm here," Axel replied with a broad smile.

"Hey, after last night. Figured you'd be sleeping in."

"I could say the same of you. What, you working double shifts? What time did you finish up yesterday afternoon?"

"I checked out after the tow truck pulled the EMT van out of the ditch. Caught some sleep and was back about eight. Quiet night, grabbed some shuteye in cell three."

"How's Carrie Baxter doing back there?"

"OK, at last check." He looked over at the internal cell monitor screen and turned up the volume knob. He looked up at Axel and said, "Sleeping now. Had a visit from her father about eleven."

"Good, I hope he talked some sense into her. We need all the help we can get in finding Wellington. I think she's got more to tell us. Ya know, she just blew Spike away. Pretty cold. If he dies, she's up for murder. Have you heard anything new on him?"

"I've got nothing."

"I'll check with Anne later. I'm sure she'll be checking." He took two steps around the front desk. "Guess I'd better write-up last night's escapade, while it's still fresh."

"Tell me again, how many did the police take in?"

"Well, I counted five total. The two in the pickup that crashed through the doors. Marsh did a good job of talking them down. Quite a scene. Coulda been ugly. They were armed to the teeth. I guess the other truck had three guys."

"Copper told me that you stopped the pick-up cold."

"Well, four shots to the engine block will stop just about anything. Used that Winchester. I swear that thing could shoot through a brick wall and still go half a mile. Hey, what do we have for weather today?"

They turned to the Montana Highway Patrol weather monitor. The Rankin County weather forecast was for a clear sky by mid-afternoon and continued temperatures in the teens. Again, Axel considered that it had been a smart decision to put off the search for a day. He said, "A good day to work indoors. Any traffic problems yet?"

"Not yet, but we'll get 'em. No doubt about it. County plows were out all night. We've got three of our units out now. All quiet, so far."

"Could be bad later. What time you off?"

"Well, now that you're here, I am ready to go."

"That's good, wrap it up. I'm here for a while. See you tomorrow."

"Thanks. Hey, here's something for you." He handed Axel a pink telephone message sheet.

While Axel looked at the small sheet Ollie said, "Guy wouldn't give his name, but left that cell number. Said he needed to talk to the sheriff about a flat tire and hung up. Just a while ago."

Axel looked at his watch. He nodded his head and remembered that the young city policeman, Aldridge, who pulled him over yesterday, had a friend that wanted to talk to him. *Strange, but there had been more bizarre approaches, like the fellow who sent him an anonymous Federal Express package full of empty bags – bags that he said had once held marijuana. He said that the bags had blown over to his property from his neighbors'. And then he did not give me his name or address.*

Axel went back to his office and called the number.

It was answered on the second ring by a husky voice, "Yeah?"

"This is Sheriff Cooper. I've got a message to call this number."

"Yeah, right. Thanks for getting back to me. I gotta talk to you. I appreciate that you are a busy man."

"I am all yours. What ya got?"

"No, I don't trust the phone. Got to be in person. Face-to-face."

"Well, I am at the office in the County Building."

"No, that's not going to work either. I got some very sensitive stuff on Marsh and I am a dead man if the wrong people find out I'm talking to you."

"So, you want to meet me to tell me something about Chief Marsh, but don't want him to know about it, right?"

"That's about it."

"What's your name?"

"I just want to do this whole thing once. I don't want you snooping around asking about me before I get the story to you. People would find out, and who knows where that will lead. This is serious shit."

"Well, we deal with a lot of that. This is a public office and what we do ends up in the newspaper with everybody having an opinion about it and sometimes folks go to jail based on our investigations. Sometimes they go for a very long time. For starters though, you have to understand that I don't supervise the police department or its chief. And in case you hadn't heard, Chief Marsh happens to be trying to get my job. Maybe you're working for him and this is all a set-up to make me look foolish or worse. If we're going to meet, we'll do it on my terms, if you don't mind. There are other folks you can go to if you've got problems with the chief. And I can tell you who they are."

"Name's Victor Pepper, Vic. Live in town. Run a bar."

"Mr. Pepper, tell you what, it's still quite early. But, I've got a bunch of things I need to do right away. Could you meet me here in town somewhere at say, eleven o'clock?"

"Sure, but it's got to be private."

"How about the clinic. It's so public, it's private. I'll get there early. See you drive in. You sit down in the emergency room waiting area without checking in. I follow you in and we go off to a private room. I would have to have someone with me. I need a witness. Can't have you telling people some crazy tale about what was said. I'll try to get a state trooper – they would be the ones to investigate, if it came to that. In fact, I can set you up with somebody in the Billings office right now. Straightaway."

"No, that won't work. I want you there. I trust you. As for the clinic, there're too many cops come through there. And with what I heard about last night, they'll probably be swarming."

"Well, OK, you're right. I got another spot. The opposite end of town – my brother's ranch. About eight miles east out State Highway 34. Right before you cross McNally Creek. He's got a mailbox with his name on it. Should stick out above the snow. And he's got a big heated garage. You can pull right in. But, I warn you, there'll probably be more than two feet of snow in the driveway. You can handle that?"

"Yeah, out east of town?"

"Right, just under eight miles. South side of the road. Last milepost before his place is seven. If you get to number eight, you've missed it."

"Yeah, that sounds fine. What time?"

"Like I said, how about eleven o'clock. And I'll have someone with me, so don't freak out about that."

"Well, I got to trust somebody."

"Guess so. We all do."

"If you're not there by eleven-thirty, I'm leaving, and then I'm not going to meet you anywhere but here in my office. You got one shot."

"Eleven o'clock."

"Right, take care."

Axel shook his head as he hung up the phone. *The things I do. What's this about?*

Axel's call to Ham Frazier in Helena was not routine. Ham was the long-serving assistant commissioner of the Montana Highway Patrol and acted as its chief operating officer. The commissioners, who lasted an average of eighteen months, were usually budding career politicians who worked with the legislature and governor to set the MHP's staffing and funding levels. They typically ran through one legislative session and then moved on. Ham was not political and he did not aspire to his bosses' position. He enjoyed his virtually unchallenged authority and worked to maintain it through any number of special relationships, private exchanges and shared secrets. Throughout the state's law enforcement community Ham was well regarded and often indispensible.

Ham and Axel had a private, higher-order, multi-dimensional relationship. Years ago Axel was a trooper living in Grant with a young wife dying of cancer. Ham needed an extra trooper in Kalispell, more than three hundred miles away, and he chose

Axel. Ham presented the re-assignment as a take-it or get-fired proposition. Axel resigned and stayed in Grant to comfort and support his wife through her slow decline and agonizing death. Ham had never apologized or even acknowledged the harshness of his demand. But, from Axel's perspective, he had made innumerable, subtle moves that had benefited Axel in his role as Rankin County Sheriff. Ham never announced that he was extending special treatment, and Axel never acknowledged it.

Nonetheless, Rankin County had more Montana Highway Patrol manpower per mile of state highway than any other county, easing the burden on Axel's staff. Rankin was among the first Montana counties to secure an allocation for the advanced training for first-responders. Rankin was the beta-testing site for the state's consolidated countywide communications equipment, the CED system in use today. New Rankin County Sheriff's Deputies always seemed to secure their first option for scheduling attendance at the Montana Law Enforcement Academy. Last year Axel was appointed by the governor as the county sheriff liaison to the Montana Highway Patrol oversight board – perhaps the handiwork of the quiet, but influential Ham Frazier. And after *Crestfallen,* Ham had been Axel's indefatigable advocate and liaison to the governor and U.S. Senator in repelling the personal assault of the FBI and the U.S. Marshals Service. Ham always returned Axel's infrequent telephone calls.

Today, Ham was at his desk. After discussing the weather, the MP shootings, Ted Norris's death, Arlyn's scalping, last night's thwarted raid on the clinic and an overnight wreck outside Missoula in which a semi- tractor trailer entered the freeway going seventy miles an hour and sideswiped a tandem that refused to yield, Axel made his pitch. He said, "Ham with all that going on, do you have an extra body nearby that could be in on a meeting late this morning? I got a local guy who's got a complaint against the Chief Leslie Marsh, here in Grant. Wants to meet me, face to face, but won't say what it's about. I had to pry his name out of him. Ya' know, I can't touch this. This is your bailiwick, right? I tried to have the guy contact you directly, but he'd have none of it. He wants me at a private meeting. Frankly, it could be a set-up. Marsh has told me he'll do anything to get my job."

Ham grumbled unintelligibly into the phone as though he were analyzing the request and in conclusion said as much to himself as Axel, "So, the boy wants this today of all days. Would you miss out on anything if you took this meeting today? Anything important?"

"No, not really. 'Cause of the snow, we postponed a manhunt into the Harlans for Wellington, the federal fugitive. Marsh is involved and brought in the FBI. Today we're open for traffic accidents and secret meetings."

"Never liked these sort of things. Hell, can't he just walk into your office?"

"He's afraid Marsh would be all over him. Said he'd be a dead man."

"You know this guy?"

"No, says, he runs a bar in town. One of our eleven, can't say which one, but it should not be too hard to get a line on him."

"Bartenders – usually pretty well known. How 'bout this, we've got a rookie out of Billings. Wet behind the ears. Just out of the Academy. He's on the six-to-three shift, but he'll probably be doing extra hours today. I see he's on the road. Turned in two accident reports already. I'd have to clear it with his boss in Billings, but we could probably have him in Grant by ten-thirty. Could you get him back on the road by noon? He hasn't handled anything by himself but road wrecks. You'd have to coach him, but he's fully qualified. Actually, might be a good experience."

"Yeah, back on the road by noon. I am meeting this guy at Arlyn's, out on Route 34, east of town. He could meet me there and leave straight away."

"What time?'

"Say 10:45 at Arlyn's, 786 State Route 34. East of Grant going to Cody. He's got a big, heated garage. I could meet him there. Caller is coming at eleven."

"OK, I will set it up. I'll call if we can't get the trooper there on time."

"Great, thanks, Ham."

"Hey, this is what I do. Be safe."

"Roger that." Axel hung up the phone and stared at the pink slip. *Probably a waste of time. At least the road will be plowed.*

Axel looked at the clock – nine-fifteen – and called Harry Webber's office to learn that he was in court in St. Vrain all morning and wouldn't be back until noon. He asked Michele, Webber's assistant, if she could book him for a one o'clock meeting in Axel's office. She agreed.

Axel's next call was to his home number. After four rings, Arlyn answered, "Cooper residence."

"Hey, You still in bed?"

"No, as a matter of fact I'm trying to figure out how your fancy coffee pot works. Need a little caffeine."

"The secret is to push the black button on the right side. Lid unlocks and pops up. You found the bag of ground coffee? Anne's gone?"

"Never saw her. I got up about eight and she was gone. I got the coffee bag. Looks strong – like it could straighten my hair and clear out my sinuses with just one cup."

"It'll put a sparkle back in your eyes."

"Just what I need."

"How are you feeling?"

"I am doing fine. No pain. Slept some. But looking out the window, I think I'll stay here, if you don't mind."

"No and plan on spending tonight too. Save you an early ride in from the ranch. And you'd make my wife happy. She doesn't like to let go of her patients. You gonna be up for a sleigh ride tomorrow?"

"Wouldn't miss it for a box of Cracker Jacks."

"Good, We can use you. I gotta go. The feds are coming in."

* * *

Clark Thorsten arrived at nine-thirty. Ange offered and delivered a cup of coffee to Thorsten while he waited. Then, according to plan, she brought him into Axel's office while Axel was in the cell block talking to Carrie Baxter.

Thorsten claimed to have had a county escort down State Route 176 off the freeway – a Rankin County plow escort. "I couldn't believe it, we got off the expressway and who's doing a U-turn in front of us on 176 but this big orange snow plow with a sand spreader. Twenty-seven miles an hour, but a clear, skid-free highway. The whole way." Ange replied that he probably had a quicker trip into town than half the folks in the county.

Axel looked into his office and saw Thorsten sitting on the edge of the un-upholstered chair in far corner – as far from Axel's desk as he could get. He had thrown his heavy, navy blue overcoat on one of the other chairs. He was a small, middle-aged man, with narrow shoulders and a buzz cut of sparse, white hair. He wore a loose dark suit with a blousy, white shirt. No tie. Thorsten was leaning forward, gripping a smart phone so tightly that the tendons on the back of his hand stood out. He stared at the screen. When Axel knocked on the doorframe, Thorsten rose quickly and took a step sideways to stand next to the chair.

Axel's first thought was *my God, he's afraid of me.*

Thorsten looked up and in a weak, dry crackly voice said, "Sheriff?"

"You're right there, Mr. Thorsten. And today I'll be sheriffing all day."

Thorsten didn't approach him, or offer to shake hands. He asked, "So, how's your brother?"

Axel smiled in response to the question. *He remembered.*

"Amazingly well by all appearances. Startling, actually. Fifty-seven stitches in his head, and he's as good as new."

"Well, that's good to hear." Thorsten stepped in front of his chair.

Axel walked to the front of his desk and leaned against the front edge. Whatever Thorsten had to say, he wasn't jumping into it. Axel continued the dialogue about Arlyn, "Sure is. But we'll have to talk to my wife for the full medical opinion. She sewed him up."

"Oh, she's the doc here?"

"Yep, she's living her dream – rural emergency medicine. She runs the clinic."

"Ah, the clinic. I've already heard stories about last night. Sounds pretty wild."

"We had some cowboys who wanted to take the law into their own hands."

Axel took a deep breath and asked if Thorsten had seen the chief yet.

"No, this is the first place I stopped. Actually, I had my Billings minder drop me off. He's checking us into the Matterhorn."

Axel walked behind his desk, gripped his desk chair and dragged it towards the door. He sat down, leaned over and flipped the door closed.

Thorsten also sat down, leaned back and said, "Just off the phone, trying to get a helicopter for tomorrow. They'd have to fly in from Seattle tonight, but this weather's now swung west. It doesn't look good. They're telling me it's too risky. Can't count on it. Otherwise, how do we look for tomorrow?"

"Boy, a helicopter would make the search a two-hour proposition, no? They could spot Wellington's encampment two miles out. But helicopter pilots are a special breed – very particular about when they will fly. But then I guess they got reasons – those things don't glide too well."

"It sounds like they don't want to come, least not until Thursday."

Axel rubbed his chin, considering just what to tell this federal agent. He began cautiously. "That's too late. Don't know about the other folks, but we're all set for the morning. My group, I mean. And we've got a jumbo snowcat from the ski hill, holds three or four. We can take it up to Crystal Lake, about seven miles past the winter road barricade on The Flyover, the mountain pass to the Park. It's too big for the trails that splay out from there, but we can use it as a field headquarters. And we got a few good, big snow machines plus the Department's two singles. Five hundreds. Trail machines. Probably enough equipment for six or eight guys. I figure we can put you on one of the tandems and your partner on the other. I've got drivers for both of them – local guys, who know their way around the backcountry. Hope you've got some cash?"

Axel stopped and looked at Thorsten. He again considered telling him about Tyler White and White's relationship with Wellington, but he again decided against it. *What gain was there in telling Tyler White's story now? Thorsten's meeting Marsh later today, he'd probably relay the story to him. They'd both be all over White in a heartbeat.*

"The government pays its bills."

"You *are* going with Marsh and the S & R crew. Right?"

"What do you mean?"

"Well, we talked about this. The Sheriff's Department is not working with Marsh. So, the way I see it, we got two groups – my people and Marsh's contingent of police with S & R support. I figure each group's goin' to have to split up to go two or three directions, so combined we'll have five or six groups blanketing the east slope of the Harlan Range between here and the Park."

"So, what's with you and Marsh? Seems I walked into the middle of a spear-throwing match. I'm not looking to get impaled."

"Good idea. Let's just say, I want my job. And so does Marsh. Vote comes up next month. Lately he's been out to make me look bad, one way or another. Says he'll do whatever it takes. Hell, I've even got that on videotape. He'd love to find Wellington and hand him over to you – just to get one-up on me. The city's warrant against Wellington is so weak as to be non-existent. It's based on a minor wreck that Wellington might have caused on his way out of town. Nobody hurt. A fender-bender. Can't say most of the law enforcement establishment would be eager to go into winter mountain wilderness looking for that guy – especially after a major dump of new snow. No, Marsh is doing this to make himself look like a hero and me look like a fool. Period."

"And yours? Your reasons?"

"I got 'em. Boils down to the fact that I like my job and think I'm pretty good at it." As sheriff, Axel usually didn't have anyone asking him *why* he did anything. The hair on the back of his neck bristled. Then he took a deep breath and concluded that he needed to relax, there was nothing to be gained by alienating the federal agent, even if he was working with Marsh. Axel started up again. "Wellington's my guy. Ran a semi off the road in the canyon a couple of days ago. Rolled the cab and trailer. Driver died yesterday. And yesterday Wellington took a coupla' shots at the MP attendant. As did his girl friend. You heard about that, right? Both my cases. You see the boarded up station on the way in?" Axel turned away from Thorsten and looked through the window at the slow, sparse traffic. The sky was brighter. The snow had stopped and the wind was down. *Not what the forecast said.* After a moment's pause, Axel said, without turning back to Thorsten, "And frankly, I would hate for Marsh to find your fugitive and win the election because of it. It would be a sad day for Rankin County. The man's just not up to it."

"And you'd be out of a job."

Axel turned away from the window and its fuzzy white panel. "It's more serious than that. I'll survive. I was a state trooper before and I can be one again." Axel stopped abruptly. He didn't know Thorsten and he had already said enough, probably too much. He stared at Thorsten, wanting some answers from him. He wanted to ask him why he was here.

Axel started up again, "So, we've got rides set for you. We are working the same plan that we had for today. Leaving the County Building at seven o'clock. I imagine that Marsh has got a timetable and logistics set up, right?" He paused and Thorsten shrugged his shoulders. "If they're going before seven, you're going to have to catch up with them if you're on one of our tandems." He paused. As almost an afterthought he said, "So anyway, why the rush to see me, if you're going with them?"

Thorsten looked up at Axel, he tossed his smartphone from one hand to another and back again. Scooting to the edge of his chair, he hunched over with his elbows on his knees and said, "Yeah, I am OK for tomorrow. But let me tell you, I'm with the

FBI, twenty-five years. Minneapolis. I just do financial cases. An accountant. I'm working the Wellington case, 'cause it's stock fraud. I cover everything financial between the Twin Cities and Spokane. Here's the point, everybody in the Minneapolis office knows your name. You're the man who shot Doug Burns. Lots of folks have cautioned me about you – everybody from the FBI – Washington, the U.S. Marshals Service, and, most enthusiastically, your neighbor, Chief Leslie Marsh. They say I shouldn't talk to you, let alone work with you, rely on you, trust you. But this case is mine and I'm working it my way. As they used to say, I needed to see *The Elephant* – experience the real thing. I knew Doug. He was a good man."

Axel had listened long enough. He blurted out, "And I am the elephant?" *This was absurd.* He stepped up to a six-inch stack of papers and folders on his desk, smiled slightly. But then he clenched his teeth and with one arm swept the stack off the desk. Papers flew in all directions. He waited until the last pieces fluttered to rest. Then he turned towards Thorsten and cocked his head forward and shot him a piercing stare and held it long enough to cause Thorsten to squirm in his chair. Then in a firm, loud, but controlled, voice Axel said, "How many times do I have to re-live the worst day of my life?" He paused. Thorsten's cell phone fell off his lap and then he pushed himself back further into his chair, but said nothing.

Axel held his stare and shouted, "You ever been shot at? You ever shoot anybody?" Axel leaned further forward and peered into Thorsten's eyes for a long moment. Thorsten shook his head, *no.* Then in a softer tone Axel said, "It trues you up, makes you realize there is evil in the world. I live with this every day. Everybody knows what I did. They may not be too judgmental to my face, but they sure as hell think about it and like to talk. It's who I am to those folks. And me too – it's in my bones."

He chuckled, "Now I see why you sat over there. I hope you're satisfied. Did I live up to my billing? You want photos?" He walked back to the door and then spun around towards Thorsten and said, "Yes, I shot Doug Burns. I had two guys running straight at me. Both had rifles. One fella shot at me from fifty feet and missed by inches." Axel flicked his hand past his ear and lowered his voice. "And they kept coming. You hear that?" Then he whispered, "They kept coming. And nobody." He stopped and looked at Thorsten's wide-eyed, frozen face again. "Nobody told me about any undercover agent. I saw two killers. And I was their live target."

Thorsten looked at the papers strewn across the floor and then up at Axel, but said nothing.

"You read the transcript of the Senate hearing?" Axel said and then paused a moment. Thorsten had no response. Axel continued, "Read the newspapers? *The Rankin County Courier*, it told the story straight, but like the Kennedy assassination, the moon landing, 9/11, or Earp's gunfight at the OK Corral, some folks keep wanting to make *Crestfallen* into more than what it was." He paused again and again Thorsten had no response. Then Axel said, "I suppose the Bureau wrote its own report. I've never seen that. You read it?"

Thorsten sat back in his chair as though he was the focus of a blast of air. He shook his head in short vertical vibrations, *yes.*

After inhaling deeply, Axel continued, "Can't say I want to, but I'll bet it has something to say about how undercover agents should behave. Does it say anything about undercover agents shooting at law enforcement officers, or running around with bad folks who do?"

"Suppose it does," Thorsten said in a dry crankily voice.

"It better or somebody's done you and every other FBI agent a gross disservice."

Axel turned towards the door.

But he wasn't finished yet. With one hand on the doorknob, he eyed Thorsten again and said, "I bear the lifelong burden of being the man who was in the wrong place at the wrong time. I swear it was shoot-or-die. And I shot. And I live with that burden every ... every day of my life. I never knew Doug Burns, but he is in my bones. Do you know when this happened?"

He didn't wait for an answer. "I'll tell you. October 15th, year before last. Today's March 19th, right? That makes it just about five hundred and twenty-one days ago. Does that help you understand who I am? Before another one of you folks comes out here to figure me out, they'd better talk to a Bureau psychiatrist to learn what killing an innocent man feels like, day after day." He paused and let go of the doorknob. He stepped towards Thorsten as though to shout something in his face, but he backed off and turned away again. "I'm outta here. Enjoy the office."

He walked through the door and, as quietly as he could, closed it tightly behind him, as though sealing the matter of *Crestfallen* and Doug Burns.

Walking towards the front office, Axel looked at his watch. Ten o'clock already. He looked up and there was Arlyn sitting in the chair in front of Ange's desk.

"Pretty funny hat."

"What are you yelling about in there?" Arlyn replied.

"Sheriff business. Beyond the comprehensive of the mortal man." He turned and smiled at Ange who was pretending not to listen.

"A lot a stuff is beyond me, but I'm cool about that."

"Smart man. Hey, how'd you get here?"

"Walked, hell it's less than a mile. With this snow I probably made better time than anyone who doesn't have a snowmobile. Figured with my new celebrity status, I might get a free breakfast at Rosie's."

"How'd that work out?"

"Well, she had a coupla of cold pancakes and a some overcooked bacon. But, the price was right. Hey, can you get me a lift to my truck at Finerty's? Gotta get Zak. He'll get spoiled if don't get him back today."

"Anne clear you for driving?"

"Well, she never said I couldn't. I'm off those drugs. Can't say they did much anyway."

Axel turned to Ange, "I haven't seen Jennie Potts yet. She around?"

"She was in and out while you were in your office."

Ange flipped her head back, just as Thorsten came out of Axel's office. With his head held high as though he was trying to catch Axel's attention, Thorsten walked out of the office wearing his blue overcoat buttoned to the throat and a matching ear band. He held his hand out and said," See you tomorrow about six-thirty, right?"

The men shook hands and Axel turned to Ange and asked, "We all lined up for the morning?"

"Right, boss. Mr. Thorsten is to ride with Tyler White. Seven o'clock blast-off."

Axel walked Thorsten to the door.

Arlyn had intently watched the exchange and as soon as the door was closed said to Axel, "Must be Mister FBI. You still fighting with them? Thought you and Ham won that battle."

"Let's just say, they're still fighting with me. Enough of that. Let's get out of here." He turned to Ange and said, "We're going out to Finerty's. Pick up Arlyn's truck. Has Potts set up the interview with Dressler?"

"That's where she is now, I think. Brought out Phyllis, the court reporter. Judge Barr postponed everything today because of the weather. Dressler wanted to have the interview before he opened for the day. While it's still fresh."

"What is it the kids say? *Brilliant?* Ang, I'm taking Arlyn out there now and then I'm going out to Arlyn's place east of town. Should be back by twelve-thirty or so."

Arlyn looked at Axel and said, "You're going to my place?"

"Right, as soon as you tell me how to open the garage door. And I don't want you to go there for a coupla hours."

"Really. I can't go to my own house?"

"We'll talk about it on the way out to Finerty's."

Chapter 32.

A Montana Highway Patrol car was parked in front of Arlyn's garage when Axel pulled into the driveway. He pressed Arlyn's remote control opener and the wide garage door opened. He drove towards the garage and waved his arm out the window to the trooper.

During the entire trip out, past innumerable roadside snowdrifts, Axel considered this meeting was a waste of his time. *Never should have agreed to it.* There were just too many things to do today. And the weather – a two-day March dump. Today was not a good day for an irrelevant, blind inquiry that will probably lead nowhere. The state legislators had been wise in not letting county sheriffs investigate local police. Too much opportunity for friction and personal vendettas. He smiled as he reflected on the scene yesterday at the MP station with Chief Marsh in full dress with his pearl-handled pistol. *Yeah, that was friction. And yet, I agreed to meet with some guy I never met to talk about Marsh. Eight miles out of town, the day after the worse storm of the season. I could have had him come in to the County Building through the property records door. Meet in my office.*

But, he also knew that he had a strong, personal reason for being there – any truth to Pepper's complaint against Marsh, whatever it was, or even a public inquiry would harm Marsh's election bid. A public prosecution would stop Marsh in his tracks. Axel recognized that he simply couldn't avoid the intrigue and excitement of being one of the first to know. *Maybe Pepper's got something.*

Once in the garage Axel called to the trooper, "Move up to my bumper, we've got a third vehicle to squeeze in here. Appreciate you being on time. On a day like today. Hope this isn't a bust. Name's Axel Cooper."

"Sheriff, I am Jim Milliman. Out of the Billings post. Hope I can help."

"Well, Mr. Milliman, let's find the thermostat and heat this place up."

Near the side door, Axel found the control panel and turned up the propane heater and with the remote control closed the garage door.

Milliman wore his head shaved and it seems to Axel that his outset ears were pasted on at right angles as an afterthought – Mr. Potatohead. The circular, flat-brimmed, campaign hat added a comical touch. *But then who didn't look peculiar wearing a hat over a shaved head.* He hoped that this rookie trooper could handle the interview. Axel was there as a witness, not an interrogator.

After a quick glance at his watch, Axel said, "Milliman, here's all I know. We got a guy, Victor Pepper, a bar owner in Grant, who wants to talk about some activity of the Grant Chief of Police, Leslie Marsh. Pepper should be here any minute. Don't have a clue what he's going to say. The point here is, if there is a crime, it's yours to investigate. The Montana Highway Patrol. I cannot be involved. I don't have jurisdiction. But, Pepper said he didn't want to talk unless I was here. So here I am. But, you are carrying the load. I am not leading any investigation into Chief Marsh. Got that?"

"Yeah, but what do I do?"

"Simple, at this point, just listen to his story. Make him fill in the gaps. Ask questions as they come up. Ask what proof he has. Ask for specifics – time, date, place, people involved, paper trail. Any documentation. Names of witnesses. You gotta take perfect notes. Write down everything he says. Next week Pepper may have a different idea of what he said here today. People lie and they change their stories. So, your notes may be evidence. Never know. Also, they're good for your boss. Bill Ramsey, right? He'll be the one to decide what to do with Pepper's story. You'll write-up your one-page Form 312 incident report and attach your notes to it."

"Never done anything like this."

"All you have got to do is be a good listener. Ask questions that keep Pepper talking. We're not arresting anybody today. And, whatever Pepper tells us, we're not marching out of here on a rampage. You tell him 'we'll be in touch'. No matter what he says, got it? He'll push you on what you are going to do and when. They're all in a hurry, thinking we've got nothing else to do and they have just given us all the facts we need to go arrest somebody. But, you can only say, 'we'll be in touch.'"

"Right."

Just then the men heard the crunch of the cold snow under a heavy vehicle. Axel pressed the garage door remote control and a snow-covered blue pickup came into the garage. Axel closed the door behind it.

Victor Pepper jumped out of the truck with an insulated metal coffee cup in one hand and the other extended for a handshake with Axel. The men shook hands. Pepper looked around the garage and said, "Thanks for setting this up. I think this is private. I see we got ourselves a trooper." He flipped his head towards Milliman.

Axel put his hands up, and said, "Mr. Pepper, let's slow down here. We are all here. Chief Marsh is not. We're here at your request. But, if we're going to make anything of this confab, there are a few things you need to know. Ground rules. OK?"

Pepper shook his head, and Axel introduced trooper Milliman.

As he did with the trooper, Axel explained that the state investigates and prosecutes police activities. The county does not. Milliman took over and promptly asked to see Pepper's drivers license. He recorded the details and, at Axel's suggestion, the three moved to the far corner of the garage, near the propane heater, where Arlyn had stored a stack of lawn chairs. The men unfolded the chairs and sat down.

Pepper's story was simple. Two years ago he opened a new bar in Grant – The Sawmill on south Broadway. He bought a liquor license from a fellow who was retiring. Axel knew the prior owner, but said nothing. The license allowed the bar to serve liquor only until midnight. Several other bars in town have licenses that let them stay open until two in the morning. And there were two other bars that also had midnight licenses.

Pepper described competition in Grant as 'pretty tough' and said, "The cops were making it tougher." After about a year of operation, uniformed Grant policemen started coming into the bar two or three nights a week at about eleven-thirty. They milled among the customers. They usually arrived in pairs and stayed through the last call and midnight and only left when all the customers were gone. Never talked to anyone, even though some of them knew the customers. Some folks would leave as soon as the policemen appeared. Pepper said, "No one wants the police to see them drinking, right? Not a party anymore." He reported that it got so that by midnight all the customers were gone. Pepper said that he often missed out on a couple of hundred dollars during the last half-hour. "Some weeks I lost over a thousand dollars in the till. That would be about three hundred bucks profit." He had called the chief of police to complain, but his calls were never returned. He never went to the police station.

Then one afternoon, Friday November 23rd last year, Chief Marsh walked in. He wore a dark blue, full uniform with a pistol on his hip. Pepper had never seen him before. There was no one else in the bar. Marsh asked to talk to Pepper in the back room. They went back to an open area by the beer cooler. There Marsh laid out what he called a *program* – for $200 cash a month, Marsh would call off his cops and Pepper could stay open until two, like the other bars. Pepper was amazed since his license was issued by the state Liquor Control Board, and he understood there were only so many two o'clock licenses per county based on the population. Pepper said, "He stepped towards me, flattened his hand on the top of the grip of his pistol – it just sat there like a plate on a tennis ball – and said with a sneer, 'Son, this is between you and me. You and me. Understand?' He repeated it several times, 'you and me'."

Pepper told Marsh that, in fact, he didn't understand and he didn't know how the city police could change the state license. Pepper said that Marsh backed off and repeated, 'This is between you and me, boy. And I can have six cops in here at eleven if I want. Every night. You understand that?'

Milliman interrupted Pepper to ask that he repeat the date and the exact statements that he and Marsh exchanged. Milliman looked up at Axel as though he was checking in to see if he was doing all right. Axel nodded his head as the young trooper continued to take notes on his folio pad in his lap. The garage was silent except for the hiss of the heater.

Axel sat back in his chair. While he had his own questions and wanted more background on Pepper, he was not going to interrupt. Milliman was doing his job. Everybody conducts interviews differently and Milliman was getting the story – an amazing one at that. Victor Pepper presented himself as honest, but naïve. He had his story organized – *perhaps, too well organized*.

Pepper continued. He and Marsh made a deal. Marsh collected two hundred dollars a month on the afternoon of the first Friday of the month, his cops stay away and Pepper stayed open until two.

Milliman interrupted, "So, how many times have you paid him?"

"Well, I first paid him in December, so, I guess it's four times, December, January, February and March. Cash."

Milliman asked, "Do you have any record of those payments."

"Well, I made notes and put them in the paid-invoice pile. We count the payments as expenses for the IRS. So, I guess we have records, our own. But Marsh never gave us nothing. Suppose he could've come back the next day and say he needed to be paid. And I'd have no proof."

"But, you did make a record of each payment?"

"Oh yeah, a little sheet off a note pad with the date and a handwritten note says two hundred bucks to Marsh. Labeled 'em *Security.*"

"But, you wrote these notes the same day you paid him?"

"Oh, yeah."

"And they all have Marsh's name on them?"

"Yeah, sure."

"You personally wrote these out, right?"

"Yeah, so what's the big deal? I wrote them out by hand on the day that I paid Marsh. I'd write two hundred dollars, Marsh, Security and the date. Usually a little three-by-five note card."

"The big deal is that they would support your story."

While still sitting in his chair Pepper swung his whole body towards Axel and then back toward Milliman. He cried out, "Story? This isn't some made-up story. This really happened. I am not paying Marsh anymore."

Axel interjected, "Is that why you called me?"

"Yeah, I am done with Marsh and his payola game. He came to me last week and said that starting in June, when The Flyover opens and the tourists come to town he's raising the rate to three hundred. A month. The balls he's got. It's like I'm working for him."

"Do you know if he's done this to anybody else?"

"No, but there's only a coupla other midnight bars. Abernathy's and The Snag. He could be shaking them down too."

"Did you ever talk to anybody else at the police department about this? Anybody else collect the cash?"

"No, it's been like he said the first time, him and me."

"Who else knows about these payments? Anybody?"

"Yeah, my wife, Sandra. She does the books, the taxes. The reports to the Liquor Commission."

"But, these payments aren't itemized on any public record, no?"

Pepper looked confused and drew his answer out as though thinking about its consequences, "Nooo, no where." He looked at Milliman and Axel and spurted, "What? You think I made this up? Cause I didn't itemize this ... what?" he appeared to search for the right word for several seconds and then said, "Extortion, that's what this is, extortion."

Milliman turned to Axel and Axel replied to Pepper, "It's just a question. No need to be concerned. You did or you didn't. Doesn't mean anything by itself. How 'bout this – we change the topic. Tell us about yourself. How did you come to own a bar in Grant? Where you're from, that sort of stuff."

Victor Pepper relayed that he was from Glendive, Montana, the only son of a railroad engineer and a homemaker. He had two older sisters who married local cattlemen. He had a goal since high school of getting-out-of-Glendive, a pretty sleepy place as he described it. He went to a local community college for a year and a half, but quit because he wanted to make some money. With the local Bakken shale oil boom at the turn of the century he signed on as a laborer. Over ten years he worked his way up to foreman of a hydraulic fracturing and horizontal drilling team. He worked fourteen-day shifts – fourteen consecutive days of twelve-hour days – and then fourteen days at home. He lived at the company's trailer camp a half-mile from the work site and on his days off usually went back to Glendive to stay with his parents. He traveled the country some as a bachelor and worked on an oilrig in the Gulf of Mexico for two years. And he assiduously saved his money. He married a girl from Billings, whom he met in Louisiana, and they decided to start a business back in Montana. Grant was close to Billings and his wife's family and looked like a good place for capturing some tourist dollars. He found owning and running a bar easy work, but long hours and a lot of staff turnover. "Some weeks you'd think I was back on the Bakken, the hours I put in."

He looked at Milliman and said, "You got my address – a small frame house up by the new high school. Own it outright, no mortgage. Near the river, which is nice."

Axel had heard enough, Pepper had something here. It would take some checking around, but his narrative made sense. He didn't seem the type who would make up this scenario, for whatever reason – including further extortion or inducement by Marsh. He appeared to have some money, so he wasn't telling lies for a small payout from Marsh. Trooper Milliman had some solid information to present to his boss. The case would be investigated. Axel looked at his watch. He had a one o'clock meeting back in the County Building with Harry Webber. He turned to Milliman and said, "Think we got enough to get started, no?"

Milliman flipped through his six pages of notes and said, "Sure, I think we got a lot of good information here. I'll have to boil it down for my supervisor." Then he turned to Pepper and said, "Hold on to those invoice slips. They could be important."

He gave Pepper his card and continued, "If I haven't contacted you by Monday, you call me. We should have a handle on this in a couple of days, and we'll see where we go from there."

Pepper stirred in his chair and with a whine of irritation said, "So, what are you going to do? What do I do until then?"

"Well, we'll be in touch. Don't change your behavior. Don't talk to anyone about Marsh – other than your wife – and she shouldn't talk to anyone either. Pretend this meeting never happened. We'll be talking to the Liquor Control Commission, maybe the other barkeeps in town. Your name won't come up. We will not talk to Marsh."

Milliman turned to Axel, who shifted his eyes to Pepper and said, "Trooper Milliman's your man. I am out of this case, so don't try to bring me back in. You wanted your meeting, and you got it. The Highway Patrol folks will take it from here. Got it?"

"Yeah, but do you guys believe me? Can't you do something about this right now?'

Milliman interjected, "We'll talk by the end of the day, Monday. Stay cool."

After Victor Pepper left, Axel turned to Milliman and said, "Good job. You've got a good presence – assertive, but not too strong. Good questions. You got some good information. You may have a hot one. And I'm serious, I absolutely want out of this case, now. I don't want updates, e-mails or my name brought up in anything that's public or could be subpoenaed for trial. I don't want my name in the papers. This is yours. You got a pretty good file started and the guy seems credible. More than we get with most traffic accidents, eh? Good luck." The men shook hands and Trooper Milliman backed his patrol car out of the garage, fishtailed across the open yard, and turned east – away from Grant. Axel smiled and thought that wherever young Trooper Milliman's going, he's headed the right direction. Going away from Grant was a good idea. *If this story's true, you never know what Marsh would do to quench it. And if it's not, he'll go ballistic knowing that someone was spreading false rumors about him.*

The snowplows and sanders had been up and down State Route 34 several times since Axel's drive out an hour ago. The snow had stopped, the wind was down and the clouds had brightened. *Tomorrow's going to be a great day.*

Turning into the county lot, Axel noted that it was plowed clean and two of his deputies were working on clearing snow off their vehicles. The Department's snowmobiles had already been swept clean and were idling quietly.

The front desk was empty, but Ange had left a note for him in the middle of her desk reminding Axel that she had an early-afternoon doctor's appointment and that in the paper-clipped envelope was the signed Form 8. remanding Arlyn to Axel's custody if he were arrested. Axel examined the form and tucked it into the inside pocket of his jacket. He went back to his office to discover Harry Webber seated in one of the wooden arm chairs amongst the array of papers Axel had swept off his desk before walking out on Thorsten.

Webber's greeting was, "Nice décor, Sheriff. I moved a coupla papers that were on the chair." He pointed to a small pile of papers on the desk. "Hope you don't mind. Nobody at the front desk, so I let myself in."

"Mi casa es su casa, Harry. Find anything interesting?"

"I didn't even look. Figured you had some things I shouldn't see."

"Well, we did get the Form 8. from Michele – thank you very much." He padded his jacket pocket confirming its presence. "But I can't say Marsh has made any moves to arrest Arlyn. Not yet, but he said that if Arlyn doesn't turn himself in by five o'clock he'll start a manhunt. I sent one of the deputies out to interview Dressler, the bartender."

Webber snapped his head in disbelief and said, "What? Why'd you do that?"

"I wanted to get to Dressler, before Marsh corrupted him. Get the straight story."

"Axel, this isn't a county case at all, you know that, right? It's a city case, if it's anything."

"Well, he's *is* my brother. And I am not going to let Marsh push him around. Marsh'll use Dickerson's version of the fight to push a case against Arlyn. It wouldn't surprise me if they negotiated a quid pro quo involving Dickerson's testimony against Arlyn in return for reducing his charges coming out of last night's raid. You heard about that?"

"Sure. Dickerson is in Marsh's jail. Don't know if he's been charged at all. I haven't seen a referral from Marsh. But, you can't be running a parallel investigation trying to establish Arlyn's innocence. Certainly not on Rankin County time, with county resources."

"I'm after the truth. Sue me, I'll reimburse the county."

"Axel, the system doesn't work that way. This shop is not Axel Cooper's Detective Agency."

"Harry, I hear what you're saying, but I want the truth. Before the stories start mutating into half-truths and outright lies."

"So, who's interviewing Dressler?"

"I send out Jennie Potts. She's good on getting facts. And we got a tape recorder and Judge Barr's court reporter. He closed the courthouse today."

"My God Axel, if this ever goes to trial and Arlyn has to use the transcript, we're going to have one hell of a circus – the judge's court reporter and a sheriff's deputy as witnesses for the defense. Never seen that. And I'd have to give you a public tongue lashing about exceeding your authority, squandering public resources, all that kind of bullshit."

"So, this is what? A mild reprimand?"

"This, dear friend, is a private, informal conversation during which I first learned of your transgressions. And that the door is closed. Maybe I don't yet know what you did."

"Well, Arlyn's case is never going to come to trial and you know it."

"You'd better pray on that. And you better be ready to share whatever you find. I want copies of Potts's notes and the transcript. Hell, I'll even pay for it. Enough of that. One thing I know for sure is that Carrie Baxter *is* going to be charged. I've heard from her Billings attorney already. Got anything more from her?"

"No, not really, but initially she was an open book. I'm sure she'll come back around. I just hope that Spike pulls through. It would be a double tragedy. Hey, want some coffee?"

"No, but I'll take a glass of water."

"We've got plenty of that."

The two men stood and walked out of Axel's office to the vacant deputy's lounge down the hall towards the cells.

Pointing to the gray steel door with a wired glass window Webber asked, "Baxter down there?"

"Yeap,"

They leaned back in the reclining, upholstered chairs – Axel with his coffee and Webber with a large glass of water. There were few people that Axel could talk to who appreciated the necessities and hardships of his role, and Webber was one of them. They discussed the Baxter case, the bar fight, Spike's health, Norris's death, Dickerson's raid on the clinic, Riley Wellington's whereabouts, the semi trailer accident, tomorrow's snowmobile search, Arlyn's injury and Chief Marsh. Axel said not a word about Victor Pepper's allegations against Marsh. *We'll know soon enough whether the Montana Highway Patrol thinks they have a case.* After a while, two afternoon-shift deputies came into the lounge and interrupted their privacy. Webber wished Axel well with the search as Axel walked him to the front desk.

Webber turned back to Axel and patted the outside of his suit coat, and said, "You might just want to give me that envelope."

"What, don't I need it to give to Marsh?"

"Yeah, but let's make it a little stronger."

Axel pulled out the envelope and handed it to Webber. On the top of the Form 8. Webber wrote "Pre-arrest filing. Do not take Arlyn Cooper into physical custody." He dated and signed his statement and handed it back. Axel slowly read the note.

"So, I bring this down to the police department? And what, they don't arrest Arlyn?"

"That's right. Arlyn's in your custody as of this moment. Hope you know where he is and that he's not leaving the county any time soon. And just to be sure, on that form, have the highest-ranking police officer in the office, maybe Marsh himself, sign and date the form to acknowledge that they got it. Eliminate the chance for Marsh to say that he never saw it. Then have them make us two photocopies. One for you, one for me. Remember though, Marsh can still try to make a case out of this."

"Oh, yeah, I got that part."

As Webber reached for the door knob, Axel grabbed it, and said, "Harry, thank you. Thank you."

"Good luck tomorrow."

As the door closed Axel put on his overcoat and hat. He then took the long, snowy, five-block walk to the Grant Police Department. He returned with copies of the amended form with the dated signature of Sargent Thomas Rialto.

Chapter 33.

Axel was fully alert at five in the morning and processing the events of the last forty-eight hours and the logistics of the coming day's campaign into the eastern edge of the Harlan Range in pursuit of Riley Wellington. In the bathroom a new array of thoughts took over his mind. *What if Marsh actually found Wellington? And how would Anne react to Arlyn going out into the mountains on a snowmobile only two days after she had put fifty-seven stitches into his head? What if the FBI backed out?* Looking into the mirror he whispered to himself, *"I need Arlyn – fifty-seven stitches, head dressing and all. The FBI won't help. They're just here for the kill. Marsh won't find Wellington. Hell, we're going to go and whatever happens happens."*

By six o'clock the brothers were ready for the day with full snowsuits and, for Arlyn, a headscarf, goggles and hooded parka. They crept out of the house before Anne had even opened an eye. They were excited. Axel couldn't help but think back to their innumerable early morning deer hunts during his first years in Montana. *Then it was Arlyn leading the hunt. Today it's me and the quarry is human.*

Outside the sky was clear and the pre-dawn monochrome light was dissolving as the sun edged its way over the east bench. *So far, so good.*

As they approached Broadway, the sun was throwing spears of light and color into the gray and white town. It started in the tops of snow-laden cottonwoods and slipped down their trunks as the sun rose. The thermometer on the local bank said fifteen degrees. Axel took that as a good omen, thinking the day could warm up to thirty in town and into the twenties in the mountains. He drove south on Broadway past the County Building without slowing down. In the SUV Arlyn turned towards Axel, but said nothing. The pavement was plowed to South Street. There Axel revved the engine, shifted into low gear, and crashed into three feet of unplowed, fluffy whiteness, and then pushed out to the barricade that blocked winter vehicle traffic on The Flyover into the Park.

He unlocked the gate, swung it open, secured it, and jumped back into the SUV. Then Axel turned to Arlyn, who had yet to say anything since he got in the vehicle, and said, "You ready?"

Arlyn pulled the drawstrings on his hood and said, "Bring it on! Why wouldn't I be?"

"Hey, I'm serious. You don't have to do this. I can take you back home now, back to the clinic. Hell, you can go back to the office, the jail – whatever."

Arlyn moved his head slowly to face Axel. "Bro, I missed the excitement at the clinic. There's no way I'm going miss it today. And if Anne gets pissed, I'm blaming it all on you. You shanghaied me from the warmth and comfort of my bed to put me at death's door wandering around uncharted, alpine wilderness."

"Well, you got one thing right. We need a story for Anne, but I think it goes something like, 'I couldn't hold Arlyn back, he was begging me to take him along, and he assured me that without him, we'd never find Wellington.' But seriously, are you OK with this? Maybe you had enough excitement Monday at Finerty's."

"Well, yeah, I've still got a headache, but who wouldn't? It's no worse than if I'd stayed too long at the bar."

"I'd say you nailed it – you stayed too long at the bar."

"Fine, great analysis, jerk. But I want you to understand that Norris was on me from the moment I walked in. A minute was *too long*. You got that?"

"Yeah, I got it. Are you good to go? You feeling alright?"

"Hell, I slept well again last night. I'm not bleeding. It wasn't that bad. I think I can help you, so I'm going to do all I can."

"Good. I'm not going to ask you again."

"Well, don't then. Can we get more coffee at the office?"

Axel nodded his head, put the vehicle in gear and drove slowly back towards the County Building. At South Street he asked, "So, where would a fellow go from Crystal Lake to hide out for the rest of the winter?"

"Well, he's got to be set up at an old lumber camp, a shed, a lean-to, a cabin – something permanent like that, right?"

"That's what Carrie Baxter said. Said he had a building."

"When you go to think about it, you can't get east of the Vermillion River from here. So, we sort of have a triangle with the Vermillion on one side, the Ginger on the other and the Park as the base. There's no place to hide in the Park. And we have two mountains in the triangle, Pinecrest and Elliott. Most likely he's up a small creek, back into a deep valley on one of them. Out of the wind. Certainly, below the treeline. He'd have a fitted-out miner's cabin or shed from an old logging camp. So he's probably in a place someone else built, a while ago. Feeding a potbelly stove for six weeks – have to have a lot of pine. Plenty of choices, but I gotta figure his place is pretty substantial. It's away from the main routes. He can't have some random snowmobiler see smoke coming out of his chimney. Pinecrest is pretty raw – rocky, not much protection."

"So, think we should focus on Elliott?"

"Probably. Pinecrest's hardly worth the time. I figure he's gonna be on the backside of Mt. Elliott in the Ginger River drainage. The higher slopes of both of them are nothing but bare rock, open plateaus and talus fields – slabs on a moonscape. Hell, and on the east side of either one you could see him from the road. And the treeline on the near side of Pinecrest can't be more'n a couple hundred yards above the lake. Not much room to hide."

"You keep thinking and talking to me."

At six forty-five the County Building's parking lot was a swarm of pickup trucks and indistinguishable humans in bulky snowsuits, helmets, mittens, face shields, goggles and moonboots. Axel recognized Paul Ridge and Ridge's friend Lennie Walters, a well-known local tradesman. They had matching shiny silver machines. The two Sheriff's Department units were out of the garage, running at low idle – warmed up and ready for Axel and Jennie Potts. Then there were the two massive machines that made the others look like juvenile editions. Axel presumed they were Tyler White's custom work.

A county pickup truck with its tailgate down had a huge, stainless steel coffee vat, a box of water bottles, bags of sandwiches and a big electronic device with a large twelve-volt battery and a headset. Axel figured it was the CED amplifier-transmitter. As Axel drove by, Potts closed the tailgate and hurriedly jumped into the truck. Axel figured she was off to meet up with Tyler White and his snowcat.

Axel parked behind the garage, out of the way of the snowmobiles and the massive snowplows. On his walk back to the assembly, he spotted a second county pickup with its tailgate down. It carried a second jumbo, insulated coffee jug and pallet-sized white boxes bearing the logo of a local bakery.

Arlyn silently walked stride-for-stride with Axel up to the pickup to get coffee.

Thorsten was to drive Tyler's snowmobile up to the lake, and from there Tyler would leave the snowcat and drive his own rig with Thorsten as passenger. Tyler White had corralled a friend, Josh Card, to pilot his second machine. Arlyn would go with Josh.

Thorsten stayed near Tyler's big machine and made no effort to engage Axel or introduce the new FBI man. *Fine, they're supposed to go with Marsh anyway.*

Thorsten's FBI associate from Billings was a big, pasty-faced young man. Axel noted that he had already teamed up with Paul Ridge's friend, Lennie Walters. The two of them appeared intent on consuming more than their share of the local bakery's acclaimed cinnamon-apple rolls.

Axel checked into the office to make sure Ollie had things under control and to see if Carrie Baxter was willing to provide any more information about Wellington's whereabouts. Ollie said that she had been quiet all night. Axel went back to the cells himself. *Just maybe, she's got a new tidbit – something that she had remembered or withheld up to now.* Through the bars she said that she had already told him everything she knew about Wellington. And she said her lawyer told her to stop talking. Axel told her there was no news on Spike in the Billings hospital. He was still in intensive care under heavy sedation. *Anne will check on him later. That man can't die.* Carrie replied that Spike and her father had worked together back in the late '80s and he was going to drive into Billings to check on Spike tomorrow.

Axel shook his head to make sure he heard that right. He immediately wanted to tell her that her dad had better not be messing with Spike's possible testimony, but after a second thought he said, "Hope Spike comes out of this OK." Axel turned, and walked to the door of the cellblock. There he turned back to Carrie and said, "Take care."

Axel gathered up his helmet and retrieved two deer rifles out of the gun locker to strap onto the county's machines. He checked the Montana Highway Patrol monitor behind Ange's desk: clear day, high in the upper twenties. Roads clean. No law enforcement incidents other than traffic accidents.

As he left the office Jennie Potts approached him and reported that she had flagged down Tyler White in the slow-moving snowcat at South Street, and the coffee, food, water, and CED communications equipment had been transferred and were on their way to Crystal Lake. As she started to turn away she said, "Sheriff, on the way back here I saw something unusual. Two Highway Patrol vehicles parked in front of Rosie's. As I drove by her place, three troopers walked in."

"Really, just now? It's not even seven o'clock. What are they doing here? Did you recognize any of them?"

"No, they were all bundled up in their quilted winter suits. And campaign hats. Two regular height and one, seemed to be an older fella', about half a foot shorter."

"Well there's nothing on the monitor about any activity in Rankin County. And they're not going out with us. Guess we'll just have to let them do their thing. Never know what those folks are up to."

Axel knew most of the senior personnel of the Montana Highway Patrol on sight, and figured that that the short, older man had to be Ham Frazier, the Assistant Commissioner, who was based in Helena, over two hundred miles away. If Ham was coming to town he usually called Axel ahead of time, and the veterans of *Crestfallen* would share lunch or, on a rare occasion, have dinner with Anne. This had to be a spur of the moment visit; something's come up in the last few days. And this was before seven, which meant that Ham had to have left home before five. *Very curious.*

There were no signs or sounds of Marsh's group. The arrangement with Marsh was that if Marsh couldn't get his group to the County Building parking lot by a quarter to seven, the two groups would meet at Crystal Lake and sort out the riders and routes. Axel had a fleeting thought that Marsh, because he had scored such a huge publicity win Monday night, might not want to bother going out this morning. But on second thought, Axel figured Marsh couldn't stay away from an opportunity to publicly show him up, whatever the score.

Just then he heard a low rumble reverberating off the buildings on Broadway. A moment later Marsh's snowmobile troop paraded in front of the County Building, headed south on Broadway. Axel, in the lot behind the building, stopped to watch them pass. He couldn't tell who was who, but there were five machines, two of which had two riders – seven guys. They didn't even turn their heads. *So, it's to the lake we go.*

Thorsten, who had also watched Marsh's parade, looked to Axel for a response.

Axel turned to him and said, "Guess we'll sort things out at the lake."

"Right."

Axel scanned the lot and spotted Tyler's friend Josh Card, who was straddling his big snowmobile. Arlyn was already on the back. Axel waved his hand in the air and approached Josh. He told Josh, "I don't want Marsh talking to Tyler. Leastwise, not before I do. Can you get up there before Marsh and keep that from happening?"

Josh, whom Axel now recognized as the best hitter in Grant's summer softball league, responded, "Damn right. I'll keep Tyler in the snowcat or drag him back in. We're gone." Axel stepped back. With that Josh turned towards Arlyn to make sure he was ready. The hooded and goggled Arlyn nodded his head and Josh punched the accelerator. Only then did Axel realize the machine didn't have a muffler. The front-runners momentarily came off the ground as the machine and its passengers rocketed down the alley. Axel watched as they fishtailed through a turn onto a residential street that ran parallel to Broadway. Axel considered that he had now, almost irrevocably, put his brother, the injured bar-fighter, into an unpredictable, perilous situation.

He turned back to the group and saw Thorsten mounted on Tyler's massive snowmobile. Its leather saddle was easily six inches higher than standard. Its clear plastic windscreen peaked at a foot and half above the body. The wide front-runners were five feet apart, wider than any stock machine. Thorsten beamed with delight as though he sat astride a wild stallion. Axel chortled to himself, thinking that whatever happened today the FBI accountant from Minneapolis would have stories to tell back in the office.

Chapter 34.

Wellington raised his head and looked to the cabin's solitary window, a narrow slit that from a certain angle allowed a view of the mine head. From the picnic table, it revealed a pale blue sky. The sun was already up over Mt. Elliott. The sky was pale blue. Wellington felt a spurt of exhilaration, but then, as he pushed himself up from the table, his pain returned. He collapsed and burrowed his head deep into the pillow. *Goddamn, that was worse than yesterday.* It was a different pain. It was in his head and felt as though he'd been pummeled with brass knuckles. His shoulder hunched inward and his left eye was pinched closed. As the initial tidal wave passed, he raised his head just high enough to survey the bare shed with a critical eye. *What the fuck? It's not going to get better on its own. Not here anyway.*

He had kept the fire going in the pockmarked iron stove. He figured that his indoor pile of split pine was enough for today and another night, but not tomorrow. That meant going outside and around the backside of the shed – not a journey he wanted to take.

While all his provisions were just where he had stored them, operating hunched over with one hand made the work of settling in slow and painful. He had managed to open a can of corned beef and heated it in a pan. In a second pan he had melted snow for water.

He hadn't yet made-up the metal frame bed or even unrolled his sleeping bag, but he was able to put two pillows on the rough-hewn picnic table, sit down, positioned a blanket over his shoulders and rest his head on one pillow and his wounded wrist on the other. And last night he slept.

This morning his wrist was the size of his lower arm and the skin was stretched to the point that it was shiny with a deep reddish-purple hue of fresh blood sausage. *Could the skin actually split open?* The bruising seemed to have an internal growth aspect – like the lead edge of a lava flow running down a volcanic mountain.

He could still move his fingers. He could touch his thumb and index finger together, but he couldn't hold a splinter of wood any heavier than a pencil or twist his wrist without a jolt of pain.

He got up from the table and drank some warm water from the saucepan on the stove. Then he sat down again, and again rested his head and his swollen wrist on the pillows, and, as sunlight crept into the shed, he fell back asleep.

Chapter 35.

At Crystal Lake Marsh's troop had parked at the far west end of the snow-covered parking lot. The five snowmobiles were spread out, each one pointing a different direction, as though they were ready to launch an all-points dragnet. When Axel entered the lot from the east, Marsh was standing knee-deep in snow with his hands on his hips examining each of the arriving snowmobiles and their bundled-up riders. He acknowledged Axel with a brief wave of his hand. Axel nodded and turned towards him.

From twenty yards away Marsh shouted over the noise of the machines, "So, you came out after all. I figured you might have had enough excitement the other night." He didn't wait for a response, but gestured towards Arlyn standing near the snowcat with Josh, and continued, "See ya brought your own criminal-terrorist with you. What the hell was that gibberish from Webber? A Form 8., talk about bullshit? A perversion of justice is what I'd call it. You Coopers must think your shit doesn't stink. Arlyn Cooper *will* stand trial though, you mark my words."

Axel had not heard Marsh's pronouncements but flipped up his visor, cast his gaze over at Arlyn and then turned back to closely examine Marsh. "Say, what?" he asked quizzically.

"Arlyn, the Arab, in his turban. Your brother should be in jail. Manslaughter, at least."

Axel forced himself not to turn again towards Arlyn – certainly Arlyn's head bandages were unusual. After assuring himself there were no witnesses, Axel said, "Hey, Arlyn didn't kill Norris.

I don't know who you've been talking to, but they got their head up their ass. Your vigilante Dickerson can't tell the truth or even a plausible lie." Axel could feel his anger rising. He looked Marsh in the eye and said, "You know, we can call this whole thing off. I brought out your FBI assault team. So you can show 'em around. It's not too late. Hell, we'll go back to town, and the FBI can find their own rides."

"No, no, no, young man. No need to be hostile. We got an early start, shouldn't we make this worthwhile? See this through? Hell, I wouldn't miss this for the Super Bowl." And then he sneered, "Just don't fuck it up, Sheriff Cooper."

Axel shook his head. "You just can't stop being the egg-shucking mule that you are, can you?" Not waiting for a reply he revved his engine and looped around Marsh back towards the snowcat. Over his shoulder he shouted, "Ten minutes, and we're heading out. Good to go."

Marsh muttered something in reply, but Axel couldn't make it out and didn't care what it was.

At the snowcat Axel dismounted and turned back to see Marsh trudging through the snow towards Thorsten, who was still straddling Tyler's machine. Marsh secured Thorsten's attention and pointed to one of his nearby officers and tapped Thorsten on the chest, as though conveying that the two were to ride together. Thorsten shook his head, patted the machine under him, and pointed back to the snowcat, where Tyler was in the driver's seat. Axel could only figure Thorsten wanted to go with Tyler, rather than with the policeman assigned by Marsh.

As Axel arrived at the snow cat, the city policeman who set up the CED amplifier was clambering down the short ladder. Once he had cleared out, Axel pulled himself into the cab and sealed the door behind him. Tyler, Arlyn and Josh were discussing possible routes Wellington could have taken. Tyler brought out a Forest Service trail map and spread it on the metal deck.

Soon they were all suggesting alternative routes to get from Crystal Lake to the higher elevations of the south and west sides of Mt. Elliott and Pinecrest Peak. The three mountain veterans threw the puzzle back and forth. Axel listened and watched as they modeled the terrain with their hands, pointed to spots on the map and proposed alternative routes, turning points, and destinations. Axel was particularly interested in Tyler's perspective.

There were three routes out of Crystal Lake's natural bowl. The first route, the Crystal-Ginger River Trail, called 'The C-Great' by the locals, was a re-purposed timber road. This primary artery carried a lot of traffic, even in winter. Initially it followed one of the creeks that emptied into Crystal Lake and then it skirted the western face of Mt. Elliott. About a mile from the lake there was an unmarked fork off to the left. The fork was not a Forest Service trail, but it was wide and clear as it ascended Mt. Elliott's western foothills. Two miles up this fork it split at a spot Tyler labeled 'Sergeant's Corner'. It wasn't on the map. The left leg carved a steep, wide arc around to the south side of Mt. Elliott. It ultimately converged with a game trail that zigzagged up to a plateau that overlooked The Flyover.

Tyler reported that the right leg dropped across a steeply pitched slope into a small pine forest. After bottoming out, its character changed to a narrow shelf that rose steadily up to a large flat outcropping that ultimately overlooked the Ginger River. On the far side of the shelf was an old mining company road that ran south down to the river. The road was wide and boulder-free, but it ran straight down towards The C-Great and the Park. Josh recalled that when last he was out that way, there was an abandoned shed on the shelf. Axel wondered why Tyler had not mentioned that earlier. Out of the corner of his eye Axel noted that Tyler's head was bobbing in agreement. *So, Tyler likes this route.*

After the fork, the C-Great continued to follow the creek to a marshy plateau and then dropped over a razor-backed ridge down to the Ginger River.

The second major route out of Crystal Lake was called the Delores Trail. It started in the far corner of the lake and then climbed three hundred feet in zigs and zags up Pinecrest to overlook The C-Great. It was a Forest Service trail, but it was narrow and poorly maintained. As it jagged west it crested a ridge and then it descended into a small, deep lake, Lake Delores, on the north face. The official trail ended there, but Arlyn knew of several seasonal trout creeks each with several game trails. He told the group that he thought the steep trails that coiled around the mountain would be virtually impassable. Arlyn leaned forward to show the spot on the old map. A sheer cliff overlooked The Flyover.

The trio readily dismissed Delores, as they couldn't imagine that Wellington could handle the small trail with sharp turns and, even if Wellington stayed below the tree line, any position on the north face would be easily visible from The Flyover.

The third major route was a game trail that started across the lake and went east through the forest and then up through several steep switchbacks around Pinecrest Peak below the sheer cliffs. Then it darted down to the Ginger River near its convergence with the Vermillion River. Again, the group readily dismissed this steep and highly exposed option – no place to hide.

Axel reckoned that even Wellington, the city boy, would be smart enough to avoid The Flyover and the unprotected slopes. The Mt. Elliott options off The C-Great seemed to be the better choices, but he also felt that there was more to the story and that it might come out once they were out on the trail.

Arlyn was good at knowing where Wellington wouldn't be, but Tyler might know exactly where he was. Axel could not help but conclude that if anyone found Wellington today, it would be Tyler.

Axel closed the meeting and the men shuffled around to zip up their bulky suits in the low ceilinged cab.

Axel opened the snow cat's door and worked his way slowly down the ladder. He had taken only three steps on the ground before he was accosted by Marsh, who was followed by Ben Jones, the head of the County Search & Rescue Squad.

Marsh started in with an edgy twang, "God damn it Cooper, are we doing this today or what?"

"We're good, just figuring out who's going where and how to avoid a wild goose chase."

"And?"

Just then Ben Jones joined the two bickering lawmen. "Sheriff," Ben said as he bobbed his helmeted head.

"Good to see you, Ben. Thanks for coming out."

"Well, this is not our usual beat, but maybe we can help."

Axel coughed and surveyed the array of bundled humanity and noisy machines. "Damned straight. Appreciate it. Figure we've got to spread the sleds out as much as we can. Wellington would certainly avoid anything that overlooks The Flyover, but on the other hand, I can't see him going in for bushwhacking far off a trail. So, it seems we should stick to the Forest Service trails and the wider game trails. We'll go down the main trails and see what we find. Send a few guys down the branches and forks and whatever else we come across. He's got to be somewhere between the Vermillion, the Ginger and the Park. Can't imagine that he'd start from here if he was going to the west side of the Ginger River." Axel stopped abruptly. He had said enough. Marsh knew nothing about Wellington's springtime plan to escape in Tyler White's old truck now garaged in Princeton. And today, Axel wasn't about to let Chief Marsh in on that part of the story.

To Axel's relief Jones interjected, "Sure, if he's looking to hide out in the West Harlans he'd save a lot of time going in through the Talker Creek Trail, west of town."

Axel continued, "I figure we divide up the routes outta here with two or three sleds each and then split off as the trails go. We can mix 'em up or assign the trails."

Axel knew which way he was going, regardless of Marsh's choices. Performing for Marsh and Jones, Axel said warmly, "I tell ya, Chief, you take the routes you want and we'll take what's left." Jones and Marsh looked at each other as though searching for an answer. Before they could speak, Axel focused on Marsh and said, "You good with the FBI?"

Marsh quickly replied, "Oh yeah. They're both riders. Passengers. You know their drivers?"

"Not really. One's Tyler White, mechanic who maintains the county equipment and drives a snowcat for the ski hill. He's got Clark Thorsten from Minneapolis. And I think the Billings FBI man is with a friend of one of my deputies – name's Lennie Walters – strikes me as the kinda guy anybody'd want for a day like today."

Jones coughed and spoke up, "Yeah, Lennie's a good pick."

Marsh said, "I want Thorsten to go with my gang. I brought him down here and I need to make sure he gets back OK. If this guy White's his driver, that's fine."

Axel was afraid that this might happen. He wanted White. And he wanted Thorsten too. *How am I going to work this out?*

The pack of snowmobilers was getting restless. It seemed to Axel that everyone was waiting for orders – scanning around, shuffling their feet to keep warm and nursing paper cups of coffee.

Finally, Axel got impatient, turned to Marsh and said, "Well, I'm for going out the main drain here," he pointed to The C-Great, "and then up one of the first coupla good side trails we get. Off to the left. Up the hill. I'm alone. That leaves one of my sleds for the rest of The C-Great and two to check out Delores."

Marsh was quick to reply, "I'll take some sleds out this way too." He pointed to the main trail. "Send one of my guys off on one of those early branches. Hold one back for later. I'll stay with the main trail. Less, of course, something comes up." Then he turned to Jones and said, "Can you take two sleds across the lake and cover Delores and the rest of Pinecrest?" He pointed to the gap in the trees across the small lake.

Jones looked across the lake and then swung back to Marsh and said, "Yeah, can't imagine anybody'd go that way, but, this guy's not anybody, eh? That's a hell of a snow drift on that south wall."

Axel could barely stop himself from grinning. Marsh had assigned Jones a very difficult route with little chance of finding Wellington, while giving himself the easiest route possible. It ran straight to the Ginger River and certainly was the route least likely to uncover anyone trying to hide. Marsh had no chance of finding Wellington.

Axel assigned Paul Ridge and Lennie Walters to go with Jones across the lake. "Stay below the tree line on that southern exposure. Call me when you get down to the Ginger. Could have another route for you."

"Got it, boss," Ridge replied sharply.

Marsh stepped away from Axel, turned and took his troop with him. Over his shoulder Marsh shouted, "You know, you're taking one of my FBI guys. But, he's yours now. Keep in touch, right? Through the CED?"

Axel answered, "Yes, sir. Roger that."

Marsh turned and walked away.

In the five minutes since he left the snowcat Axel had changed his mind about Arlyn – *he shouldn't be out in this weather.* He walked up to Arlyn, who was sitting behind Josh. Axel nodded towards the snowcat and said, "Hey Arl, I gotta talk to you."

Arlyn grabbed onto Josh's shoulders for stability and pushed himself up while swinging a leg over the wide saddle. He followed Axel five yards away from the others. Axel stopped and turned back and said, "Arl, I can't do this to you. You already helped a bunch, and I don't want you out on the trail."

Arlyn held his hands up. "What the fuck, I'm here, I might as well go for a ride. You want my help, I'm here for ya, and you know that."

"I said, you *have* been a big help already and you heard those guys in there," he tipped his helmet towards the snowcat. "They know where they're going. Hell, all you're going to do out here is freeze your ass off, pop a few stitches and get our asses chewed by my loving wife. Hell, we're probably in trouble with her already. Surprised she's not out here trying to drag you back to town."

"So, you think Tyler knows?"

"He could. And if he does, I think he'll let us know. He's on thin ice. Some prosecutor could easily argue that he was Wellington's accomplice – that he and Wellington set up this whole escape. I think Tyler's going to save himself, anyway he can."

"But, he is going with Marsh?"

"Well, that's what they think. I'm going to give him the choice of a lifetime – either work with the Rankin County Sheriff for an hour or two, or have a close encounter with the federal government, one that could last a couple of years."

"Not much of a choice."

"That's the way I figure it. Arlyn, I want you to stay here or go back to town. You've done what I wanted. You helped figure out where Wellington is most likely to be and where he won't be."

"Yeah, but really..."

"Bro, listen, you're freezing already, still on antibiotics, can't wear a helmet or a face shield. Those goggles are probably cutting off circulation to your scalp. We got some very good scouts to ferret out Wellington. You stay here. At the snowcat. Call Anne. Hell, if you can, get back to town. Back to the house. No big deal. I made a mistake. Help me out here."

Arlyn pulled up his goggles. His eyes were red and watering and his face was chalky white. He looked into Axel's eyes and said, "Yeah, you're right. I'm not ready for this. If I went, I wouldn't complain, but it would take days to recover." He smiled and his face lit up. "Hell, we'd both be in trouble with Anne." He threw up his mittened hands in mock surrender and said, "Good luck, stay warm. Tell Josh I'm out." The brothers stepped towards each other in a quick, loose hug. Arlyn pushed away and walked towards the snowcat.

Axel shouted after him, "Arl, do us both a favor and call Anne. Tell her you're OK."

Arlyn didn't respond, so Axel shouted again, "OK?"

Without turning around, Arlyn said, "Yeah, fuck it. I might as well go back to town."

"Good idea."

Axel talked to Josh and reassigned the Billings FBI man from Lennie Walters to Josh and his big, modified machine.

Chapter 36.

There was a cluster of multi-colored snowmobiles near The C-Great trailhead. Marsh's silver model with red lightning bolts on the cowling was at the front. Marsh was talking with a policeman he'd assigned to the Delores Trail. Straddling the next machine was one of Marsh's coppers and then Tyler with Thorsten on the back. Axel was next, followed by Josh and his new FBI passenger. Jennie Potts brought up the rear.

Axel suddenly dismounted. He went back to Josh and grabbed a shoulder of his loose-fitting snowsuit, jerked it sideways and commanded, "Come with me." His pull threw the larger man off-balance. Josh kicked his passenger as he swung his leg over the saddle.

Axel pulled Josh away from the machine and flipped up his face shield. Josh was rattled. "What's up, Sheriff? Problem?"

"No, we just gotta work fast. I want Tyler to lead me up that first turn-off we talked about in the snowcat. Remember, up to Sergeant's Corner?"

"Yeah, sure."

"Well, I want you to swap places with him without Marsh knowing it. So you follow Marsh down the trail and Tyler leads me off of the first fork. Got it?" Axel didn't wait for an answer and continued, "Right now, go tell Tyler to take that first turn-off, no matter how rough it looks. I'll follow him and then you go straight, catch up to Marsh and stay with 'em. Got it?"

"Sure, simple enough."

"Go tell Tyler now. I can't have Marsh seeing me talking to him. He might think something's up. The FBI guys don't need to know about this either, right? Thorsten will figure it out, but your guy from Billings won't care. He seems to be just along for the ride, no?"

"Yeah, he doesn't have much of a clue about where he is and where he's going. He'll think we're working the original plan. You want me to tell Tyler now?"

"Yeah, absolutely. It's now or never."

"Right." Josh shuffled through the deep snow up to Tyler, and the two of them took off their helmets. They turned away from Tyler's noisy machine, put their heads together for a minute and then scooted back to their machines.

Axel was frustrated with himself. *I shoulda just told Marsh I'm taking Tyler, and be done with it.* Marsh didn't seem to care much about Thorsten, or who else went with him. Or even if they found Wellington. Axel figured Marsh was just going through the motions to impress the FBI.

Then, without warning, Marsh revved up his machine and took off. His policeman took off right behind. Tyler, with Thorsten aboard, lagged a hundred yards behind. Axel waited awhile and then started off at a slow pace. Josh and Jennie Potts followed him.

After a ten-minute dash through the fresh snow Marsh slowed and looked back at the caravan behind him. The first branch was off to the left. Marsh waved for the first of his followers to take the offshoot. He kept moving ahead down The C-Great. Tyler dropped back from Marsh's group and swung to the left to climb up on the wide game trail following the single policeman. Then Josh goosed his machine and swung wide past Axel in order to catch up to Marsh.

Axel slowed and watched the two veteran snowmobilers execute the choreography. He lost sight of Marsh around a tight corner. He took a hand off the steering bar to wave goodbye.

Axel turned left to follow Tyler with Thorsten aboard as they climbed up the game trail through a thin brush field. Potts followed him. The path was not maintained or used by recreational snowmobilers but was still wide enough for Tyler's large snowmobile. Axel was third in line so the trail was somewhat leveled off and groomed for him. As they climbed Axel could feel the air temperature drop. The snow was not as deep as at the lake, but in the windy open areas it flew horizontally in random bursts. As they left the upland forest to scale the exposed wall of Mt. Elliott, the wind became omnipresent and dropped the apparent temperature another five degrees. At three miles out they ran through a patch of wind-twisted pines and reached the T-junction that Arlyn and Tyler called Sergeant's Corner.

All four snowmobilers stopped to discuss which way to go. The wide left fork made a sweeping arc up towards the backside of Mt. Elliott and ended up on a high plateau – visible from The Flyover.

The right fork was narrower, brush-covered and not as prominent, especially under the windswept snow. Axel stood up, straddling his machine and tried to see just where this meager route went. *This is Tyler's route? Not too inviting.*

While Axel hung back, Tyler and the policeman got off their snowmobiles to talk face-to-face. They used their hands to model the pitches and peaks that the alternatives offered. Tyler turned to give Axel an encouraging nod. Axel flipped his hands up to acknowledge the report.

The policeman wanted to go to the left up the mountain. Thus, Tyler got his preferred route without an argument. The policeman pulled out his CED phone and called in.

As the policeman took off on his chosen route, Tyler walked back to Axel. Thorsten, apparently not wanting to miss a tactical pow-wow, threw his leg over the saddle and joined Tyler at Axel's machine. Potts followed. Axel had pulled out a small thermos and offered coffee to the others. They declined and pulled out their own bottles. Thorsten held up a small opaque bottle and said, "Not my first rodeo."

Tyler had little to say, other than to outline their route. Axel held the group up for five minutes to make sure the policeman was on his way.

Once back on their machine Tyler and Thorsten slowly crested the ridge and dipped into deep snow carving a descending path across the lower sidewall. Potts followed, with Axel in the rear.

Chapter 37.

As he sat upright Wellington realized his lips were dry and cracked. As though performing intricate surgery he pushed the tip of his tongue slowly along the inside seam of his lips – left to right, right to left. *Water, I need water.*

He slowly rose from the table. Using his right hand, he lifted his left wrist with the delicacy an ornithologist would exercise in handling a rare bird. He looked to the stove. The water in the saucepan on the stove had evaporated. With his left arm pressed against his stomach, he carefully shambled to the kitchen storage box, pulled out a second pot and headed towards the door.

After several steps Wellington, saucepan in hand, stopped to consider the best way to unlatch the door without hurting himself. That was the moment he first heard the noise. It came from outside – a buzz that periodically changed its pitch and volume, but never went away completely. *No, it's not in my head. It's not a part of my pain.* He dropped the pot. He tightened his jaw and stared at the latch as though it had a message for him. The undulating buzz continued. He went up to the door, lifted the latch. And pushed his shoulder against it. The wind caught the door and flung it wide open and slammed it against the outside wall.

The glare of the sun bouncing off the snow momentarily blinded him. He gasped and shuttered his eyes. He now had no doubts about the sound – the variable, high-pitched whine came from snowmobiles, more than one. And they were straining to climb a steep slope – his route, the one he thought no one would ever travel in winter. But here they were. And they were looking for him. There could be no other reason. *God, it's over before it started.*

Without a coat, he high-stepped through the snow towards the boulder, near the trail. He found the least painful way of walking with his wounded wrist was to push it tightly against his chest and dip his shoulder in order to create a protective niche.

He stopped and listened again. The buzzing persisted. *They're climbing the back ledge – climbing the wall.* He turned back to the shed.

He had left the shed's door open and gathered up his pack and the bear gun. *What could she have told the cops? – Nothing!* The one-piece snowsuit had been difficult to take off because of his injured wrist, but now to put it back on he wrapped his wrist in a towel and rammed it down the sleeve. *Good.* He zipped up his black outfit, taped the towel in place, and pulled on his right mitten with his teeth. He listened to the buzzing machines one last time before he slammed on his soundproof helmet. He could feel his heart pounding and, for a moment, it seemed like the buzzing stopped. At the door he wondered briefly if they were gone. *Maybe they had turned back.* Then he shook his head. *No, they're coming and I'm leaving.* He went out to the snowmobile and, with his good arm, swept away the drifted snow. The machine started immediately. He threw his leg over the saddle and let the machine idle a moment.

Chapter 38.

Tyler gently nudged his machine up the last rise, about two hundred yards short of the shed. He turned off the trail and stopped behind a massive boulder. A thin but steady film of smoke streamed out of the shed's chimney and was caught by the swirling wind. He signaled to Axel and Jennie Potts to pull up next to him. Once they were stopped, Thorsten slid off the back of Tyler's machine and drew out a pistol from under his long, down overcoat. Axel and Potts positioned themselves behind their machines and crouched down. Axel unstrapped the deer rifle. He removed the lens caps on the scope and focused on the side door of the shed. He couldn't see Wellington's snowmobile, but figured it could well be on the far side of the shed. The four silently watched and waited.

A swirl of wind caught the edge of the shed's heavy wooden door, threw it open, and slammed it against the outer wall with a bang. The untethered door stayed open for a long moment and then slapped closed again. There are fresh footprints from the shed halfway to the boulder and back. Overblown snowmobile tracks were readily apparent. They led back to the backside of the shed, high above The C – Great.

Tyler turned to Axel, jerked his helmeted head towards the miners' road and mouthed, "Let's go." Axel held up his hand, *no*. He handed Jennie Potts the rifle and drew his service pistol. Without a word he mounted his snowmobile and sped past the shed. About hundred yards down the miners' road he turned sharply to angle towards the backside of the shed – all while gripping his pistol in his bare hand.

Tyler looked at Potts and said, "Do you think he's still here?"

She never took her eyes off the shed. "We'll find out right quick."

Just as Axel reached the far corner of the shed, Wellington accelerated straight towards him, but Wellington swerved to his right at the last possible moment to avoid a head-on collision. Axel also swung to his right away from Wellington, but their machines' widespread front-runners clashed causing Axel's sled to careen into the back wall of the shed. He stopped, turned back and tracked Wellington's exit with his pistol. He aimed at Wellington's broad upper back. The moving target was fifty yards down the road and getting smaller by the second, but still within range. Axel knew that he could hit him. He could hit a moving three-foot diameter target at a hundred yards – at least that's what he was told at the latest Law Enforcement Academy – Live Fire Training Course. He took a deep breath and lowered his weapon and put it back in its holster.

As Wellington sped down the miners' road, Axel continued around the shed to meet up with Tyler, Thorsten, and Jennie. Axel moved to the front and they started off at a slow, measured pace. He told himself to remain calm. He knew that Tyler and Jennie both wanted go all-out to catch up with Wellington. But Axel thought to himself: *Wellington's on the run. We'll get him. It's only a matter of time. We've got time and he doesn't.*

At that moment Axel's CED phone buzzed and Axel signaled an immediate stop. It was a call from Paul Ridge. Axel quickly pulled the boxy unit out of an interior pocket.

Axel took off his helmet and, over the sound of the snowmobile, shouted into the boxy device, "Paul, he's on the run from Ruud's Lookout. Down the miners' road. Going towards the Park. Can't be but a coupla miles upriver from you. Give it all you got, but stay a good hundred yards behind him. Last thing we want is a shootout. Call me if you see him. We're calling the Park Police. Got it?"

"Yes, sir!" replied Ridge with more spirit than he had shown an hour ago.

"Good. Tell Marsh and Jones we've got him on the run. And then leave as fast as you can. Who knows what they're going to do."

"Got it."

The C-Great was a flatter, faster track than the road. Axel calculated that Ridge, while further away, was in a better position to catch up to Wellington. But then, maybe neither of them would – Wellington was moving fast. *Better contact the Park now.*

He called Ange at the County Building and asked her to notify the Park authorities that Wellington might be coming up to the Park on The C-Great. *Could be the first time a federal fugitive escaped into a federal facility.*

Axel swung his arm forward and his followers started after Wellington down the miners' road.

Chapter 39.

Wellington was running his engine at fifty-five hundred rpms and faster than he'd ever gone. Its high-pitched whine was the only sound he could hear. His well-wrapped left wrist was numb. The road ran at a modest downslope across a west face of Mt. Elliott with no sharp turns or steep drop-offs. He was pleased to see that his machine, heavy as it was, could glide smoothly over the crusted base layer under the new, powdery snow. It reminded him of Monday's run up to Crystal Lake – before the heavy stuff hit and he smashed his wrist. He was gaining confidence that he could outrun his pursuers. *Why not?* He felt his chances of escape were improving by the minute.

The left side of the road abutted a near-vertical wall of snow. The right side had a sharp drop-off that ran from the road to The C-Great and then down to the river itself. Through the sparse pines he could see the trail's smooth white blanket as it followed the Ginger River upstream towards the Park. *Maybe I could cut through the woods and get to the trail sooner?* He moved to the right side of the road. *No, too many turns through the trees.*

His survey cost him – a sudden deep rut threw him to the edge of the road. Pushing hard on the steering bar with his good right hand, Wellington pressed the thumb-action accelerator. *Too hard. Too fast.* He skidded across the road, fishtailing sideways downhill. He tried to counter by pulling the right handle towards him, adding a weak and painful push with his injured left hand, but he knew it was too little, too late. He was headed for the wall of snow.

Axel saw Wellington slide sideways across the road, right to left. He slowed and signaled the others to stay behind him.

First one runner of Wellington's machine, then the other dipped off the road and pulled Wellington's sled with them. The snowmobile slid down into a shallow roadside gulley and then into the wall.

The left runner's slash into the outer shell of the white wall seemed minor to Wellington – a shallow groove in the white plaster. But almost immediately, the entire wall started moving, ever so slightly. The gash undercut the foundation of the snowpack on this face of Mt. Elliott's western-slope. Before Wellington could steer away from the wall, the outer plates of compressed snow broke apart. They fell in a massive cascade, accompanied by the sound of a major waterfall.

Free-flying slabs pummeled Wellington as if they were elements of a well-coordinated bombardment. The bottom edge of the collapsing wall pushed him forward. It flipped the snowmobile and suspended Wellington above the machine as it plowed forward. Finally, the crest of the wave curled over him. The envelopment was complete, instantaneous and irreversible. As though to assure his demise, seconds later, the wind-swept cornice – the snow column's capital – having just lost its foundation, thundered in a free-fall onto the jumbled debris of the initial collapse. It propelled the mass across the road, down the slope, across the trail and into the river. It swept away mature pines and boulders the size of small cars, and carried them out to the river and beyond.

Once the snow stopped moving there was the relative silence of the thin river ice crackling like broken glass. A cloud, thick enough to block the view across the hundred-yard wide slide, rose above the avalanche's track.

The entire collapse lasted less than a minute.

Everyone, including the policeman back at the snowcat, heard the avalanche. Many felt the rumble. While Axel was the only one to have seen the white wave topple Wellington's sled and sweep him towards the river, no one questioned whether Wellington had lived through the avalanche.

Paul Ridge, Lennie Walters and their FBI passenger moving up the river trail had the best perspective of the entire collapse. Perhaps they were too close, as the avalanche's run-out sprayed them with a mist of wet snow and small chunks of ice. Ridge later calculated that if they were forty-five seconds further down the trail the avalanche would have swept them away.

Ben Jones, Marsh and their crews quickly joined Ridge on the trail. They dismounted and silently walked forward towards the debris field. Some went further than others. Some scanned the mountain intent on locating the edge of the break in its snow shell. Others wanted to find Wellington immediately. Others wanted to traverse the avalanche's entire path. Some watched the river water pool up behind the new natural dam, and still others stood stock-still and were amazed at the size of the boulders and the toppled trees.

Ben Jones assumed control of the recovery effort. He declared that no one should venture onto the runout – too unstable. He called the Forest Service and Yellowstone National Park to declare the area off-limits. Both units agreed to send personnel and equipment out to the site.

From his vantage point of the elevated road Axel saw Marsh with a CED phone to his ear, pack it inside his coat and then slowly turn away from the avalanche. Marsh rode The C-Great back towards the lake. Axel assumed he was returning to town, perhaps to be the first to give an eyewitness account. Axel was surprised that Marsh had abandoned his men and FBI associates. *He's done?*

Jennie Potts discovered a narrow game trail that ran at a shallow diagonal through the trees to connect the miners' road with The C-Great. Tyler with his wide machine would have to do a bit of bush-whacking, but the standard sized snowmobiles would do fine. Axel's group of three snowmobiles slowly carved their way down the embankment and reported to Ben Jones.

Ben set up teams of surveyors, had them tethered together and established a grid system. An hour later a Park Ranger and his partner Paul Ridge found a runner of a large snowmobile just short of the river. It was buried a foot under the surface. After some more digging, the crew discovered Wellington's body. The force of the avalanche had spun his spine a full rotation and twisted his left leg up behind his right shoulder.

Chapter 40.

A county snowplow was parked at the east end of the Crystal Lake lot. In front of the plow was a cluster of men. Coming in off The C-Great Axel immediately recognized one of them as Ham Frazier. *Ham, here? What's he doing here?*

Axel pulled up to the nearby snowcat and asked a policeman what was going on.

The young man replied, "You're Sheriff Cooper, right?"

"Yeah."

"I think they've been waiting for you. Better talk to Commissioner Frazier," and nodded his head towards the snowplow.

Ham and Axel had last seen each other only ten days ago. Regardless, Ham, a stout strong man, approached Axel and gave him a bear hug that almost toppled them both. Pulling away from their clumsy embrace, Axel asked, "What gives? You got yourself a snowplow? Wellington's gone, ya know."

"Yeah, I suppose he saved us all a lot of effort prosecuting him. What, he slammed into a wall of snow and it fell on him?"

"Yeah, cut the bottom out and the whole side of the mountain came down. He never had a chance."

"An FBI bulletin out an hour ago put him as a person-of-interest in the death of his business partner. Killed over the weekend. Apparently he was going to be the fed's chief witness in

Wellington's fraud trial. Forensics says he was hit in back of the neck with a dull-edged piece of heavy metal. Cut the cord. Steep angle to the blow. Tall guy hit him from behind. Wellington was what, six-four?"

"All I heard Monday was that he was a 'big, big guy'. Damn, Riley Wellington was one bad dude. Squashed everything and everybody in his way. He'd do anything to avoid going to court. You come out to bring the news?"

"Came to see you, Sheriff Axel Cooper. Well, not really. But, I've been waiting for you, though. Was in town all day. Sat in on a couple of interviews and made an arrest. Quickest case I've seen without a confession. Started yesterday."

"Here in Grant?"

"Well, you missed it. I just arrested the Grant Chief of Police, Leslie Marsh, for extortion and official misconduct."

"You serious?" Axel responded with absolute incredulity.

"Hell, Ax, don't play so naïve. You knew about this. Victor Pepper's story is rock solid and so are the affidavits we got this morning from two other bar owners in town. Marsh had them on the same plan. Collected about six, eight hundred a month."

"This was a MHP swat team approach? Slam–bam!"

"No reason to wait. I talked to Ramsey and Milliman last night. We got sworn affidavits early this morning, and I figured that we had enough to go on. It wouldn't hurt to close this down right quick – while we're in town today. *Justice delayed is justice denied* – that works for law enforcement too. Heard Marsh was out here, so we got ourselves a couple of plows to come out here and get him."

"So, where is he?"

Ham pulled up the cuff of his bulky jacket and looked at this watch.

"Left here about a half hour ago with Milliman and Bill Ramsey – in hand cuffs. In the other snowplow. I kinda like that – classy exit. He'll be in Billings at the Yellowstone County jail by late afternoon, I figure."

"You serious, you arrested Leslie Marsh?"

"Damned straight." Ham laughed and shook his head, "Boy, greed will get 'em every time. He was pushing the three of them for another hundred bucks a month. If he hadn't pushed, I wonder how long his little scam would have run."

"Three bars. I am surprised it was only three."

"Oh, Ax, don't play dumb with me. He just hit up the ones with midnight licenses. You heard Pepper's whole story. I am not publishing a newspaper, but I saw your name in Milliman's report. And you better believe that Mr. Pepper wasn't going to tell his story to anybody but you. Milliman had the sense to put a cover note on his report to that effect. You were there, but not officially. Pepper trusted you. That's what's this business is all about – trust. And Pepper told a very convincing story."

"Hey, I sat there. Milliman did the work."

"Don't give me that crap. You were essential. Pepper would not have talked if you weren't there. Now, I am going to go into town and make some calls. There are about fifty-five other counties in this state. You be at the office later? You might have to serve as the acting chief of police, as well as the county sheriff. Gotta talk to some folks."

"*Essential, acting chief of police?* Does any of that come with a raise?" Axel replied with a smile.

"No, but it'll probably come with an avalanche, come April," Ham joked, referring to the upcoming election.

"I've had enough avalanches lately."

"Suppose so. How close were you?"

"A coupla hundred yards. I saw him get flipped by the lead-edge. Felt the rumble and got pelted with snow-spray."

"Yeah, close enough." Ham held up his mittened fist and Axel gave him a fist pump as he turned to go.

Axel put his helmet back on and pulled down his face shield to hide his grin. *Marsh was under arrest – can't be running for sheriff. Gotta call Anne.*

As Ham waddled through the snow towards the orange county truck, Axel turned back to the snowcat looking for Arlyn. The CED policeman told him Arlyn had stayed with him in the cab and went to town with one of the first sleds to leave, over an hour ago. The policeman said, "Coulda been with Josh Card. Anyway, Arlyn called from town and said that he checked in at the clinic. One more thing Sheriff, your brother said that he heard that Spike Reynolds was out of the ICU in Billings and the docs were able to set his leg with some metal ingots and a handful of screws. That's what he said, 'metal ingots and a handful of screws'."

"That would be my brother. He views the human body as some kind of construction project – an Erector set with plumbing and electricity."

As the big diesel snowplow turned around to leave, Axel scanned the lot looking for his people and, as he found them he sent them back to town. He spotted Thorsten walking towards him. Behind him the Billings FBI man was talking into a CED phone. Suddenly the man yelled to Thorsten to come back – a call from Minneapolis.

Thorsten was annoyed by the interruption. He waved at Axel and said, "I want to talk to you before you go into town. But, I gotta take this call – the boss, ya know."

Thorsten's boss was calling in regard to a new financial case in the West – this one at the Yellowstone National Park.

Thorsten, standing in the snow as a pair of whining snowmobiles sped by, listened intently as his boss described a new assignment from the Department of the Interior involving an embezzlement case at the Park. A new superintendent had discovered that one of his senior managers had created a private company that invoiced the Park for summer trail maintenance – work that was actually done by Park employees and summer interns. The manager had prepared and approved his own invoices for over two years and had collected about eighty thousand dollars in fraudulent payments.

Thorsten saw that Axel was approaching him. And said to his boss, "Jerry, I got to go wrap up this Wellington thing with the county sheriff. Can we talk more about this Park thing later? I've been zooming around on a snowmobile in the middle of a damn Montana mountain range and freezing my ass off. Hell, the avalanche only missed me by a couple hundred yards. Not quite the desk audit I'm used to."

His boss replied, "I understand, but you need to hear this now. That's why I called. You might have to do something later today."

Thorsten said, "Can't I take this up with the superintendent in a coupla hours? Not much more I can do out here. But, I am sure as hell not driving a snowmobile over these mountains to interview this guy this afternoon."

"OK, OK, the super's name is George Kenner, been there about six months. He's got your name and I told him you were in Montana and would want to meet with him later this week. Go figure out what it takes to wrap up Wellington, but call Kenner today and set up your trip down there, right?"

"Got it."

Thorsten saw Tyler climbing back into the snowcat, presumably to drive it back to the ski mountain and noted that there were only a few snowmobiles left in the lot. He was ready to end the call when his boss continued, "There's another thing with Kenner. Might be something you're sitting on right now."

Thorsten flicked his head. "So what would that be?"

"Well, the way Kenner tells it, this same guy was trying to engineer the Park's purchase of some ranch land. Apparently Interior has a funded program to buy land from the public if wildlife stray off campus and endanger folks or their private property. Basically, their solution is to make the Park bigger by buying more land."

"Sounds like the government. Taking the easy way out."

"Hey, smartass, maybe you've been out in the field too long already. Regardless, Kenner seems to think his rogue manager is pushing the purchase of some rancher's land adjacent to the Park, off the northwest corner in Montana. Elk are wandering around on the ranch and the rancher's complaining that they'll contaminate his cattle."

"What, we have dangerous elk or something?"

"That's the argument. Brucellosis, whatever the hell that is. Lung infection of some kind. Elk can live with it, cattle can't. Kenner thinks the rancher is actually pushing elk out of the Park onto his property, trying to force the purchase of some of his land. And our embezzler is pushing the deal. Apparently we pay a hefty margin to get the land we want."

"Herding elk. That's news to me. And what? The ranger splits the margin with our Park guy?"

"I'd expect so, but it's gonna to be hard to prove."

"Yeah, no witnesses, no paper trail, but maybe we can play them against one another. If the rogue is really in deep shit with his embezzlement, I'll bet he's already got a story of how the rancher talked him into this deal. No?"

"Mister Thorsten, quick thinking. This why we pay you the big bucks and send you to such exotic venues."

"Had a hell of a day today. It's not every fugitive that we carry out on a sled. But I gotta wonder whose idea this land purchase was in the first place. The rancher's a Montana guy?"

'That's why I'm talking to you *now*. Rather than later."

"OK, I give."

"Rancher's a local Montana police chief, Leslie Marsh."

"Leslie Marsh! You're shitting me? I've been with Marsh for two days running down Wellington. Holy mackerel. He's one weird dude, but I can't believe he'd try something like this."

"Well, our boy is already talking about Marsh. And we've got some video of Marsh herding elk out of the Park. Aerial surveillance.

Drones, flying around looking for grizzlies, spotted him and they watched him from a coupla hundred yards off. Three minutes. The video looks pretty conclusive; he's pushing a herd of elk down the hill. Can't say exactly where they were going, but he's herding 'em out of the Park."

"Ya know this guy was running for county sheriff. April election."

"Well, we might have some other plans for him."

"Yeah, so does the State of Montana. Not an hour ago he was arrested by the Montana troopers. Extorting cash from late-night bars."

"You serious?"

"Yeah, the Assistant Commissioner of the Montana Highway Patrol came ten miles up the pass in a snowplow to make the arrest. Marsh was collecting cash from some bars to let them stay open past their state license. Small change, but it was an annuity with monthly installments."

"So, Leslie Marsh is not going anywhere for a while, right? Regardless, you'd better talk to Kenner – muy rapido, amigo."

"Yeah, that sounds like the next step."

"Enjoy the mountains."

"Hey, boss, before you go, I need to tell you I have been working with Axel Cooper – the Rankin County Sheriff. I think we've got him on a bum rap. Not a bad guy. Doug Burns and Crestfallen have taken a toll on the man. One he doesn't deserve."

"You tell me more about that tomorrow after your call to Superintendent Kenner."

"Hey, I'm serious."

"You go down to the Park and see what we got there and then we'll talk about the sheriff."

"Yeah, I'll do that. But, right now my point is that Cooper's not the devil we've made him out to be."

"Right. We'll talk about that."

"Roger that."

The call was over and Thorsten turned back towards the snowcat to see Axel facing him, standing only five feet away.

Axel had his helmet cradled in the crook of his arm. He looked intently at Thorsten and nodded his head. As tears came to his eyes, he smiled and repeated, "Roger that."

* * *

Printed in the United States
By Bookmasters